The Final Olympics

Laurel Solorzano

Published by Laurel Solorzano, 2023.

The Final Olympics

Book 1

ISBN: 978-1-7373974-8-9

Cover Design by: Christine Savoie

To everyone who has ever been called "average" in life.

Part 1- The Training

Chapter 1

Elimination. It's the kind of thing that makes for good stories on Halloween night or at a sleepover, but the closer each person gets to their eighteenth birthday, the more serious it becomes.

Eden couldn't get the upcoming Olympics off her mind as she sat outside her apartment waiting for Xander. Her eighteenth birthday was in two days, which meant that she would be competing this year. She had a month until the competition would begin, and she didn't feel ready.

"Eden from Sweden!" Xander chanted like he always did.

Eden rolled her eyes and didn't even respond. No matter how often she reminded him that Sweden had ceased to be a country thirty years ago, he still insisted on singing it annoyingly.

"Hey," Eden said, lifting her hand casually. Xander settled into the grass next to her and squinted at the sun.

"How can you sit in the sun when it's already hot?" he asked.

"Guess I'm better than you at something," she responded. Unfortunately, being able to withstand the rising heat was not one of the competitions at the Olympics.

Xander lay on the grass and propped himself up on one of his elbows, studying Eden. He could practically read her mind which made it impossible for her to hide things from him. "It's almost your birthday," he said.

Eden nodded, pressing her lips together as she accepted the fact.

"Hey, birthdays are fun," Xander spoke in an upbeat voice, and Eden tried to get into his excitement.

"Yeah, they can be if you have the right cake," she said.

"And will you? Was your mom able to find sugar at the grocery store?"

"I don't know," Eden responded. The truth was that she couldn't care less whether there would be cake or not at the party her parents insisted on throwing. She couldn't get out of her head today. Then, she would get angry at herself for being in her head and continue spiraling downward. She wanted to have fun and shake off her worries, but she couldn't even bring herself to smile.

"Hey, if not, maybe I can check at a different one. I think my dad has to go down to Nuuk tomorrow. I can ask him to look."

"Thanks," Eden commented. She felt Xander's eyes on her, and that made her feel warmer than the sunshine did. She fell back onto the grass next to him, listening as a bike bell nearby chimed. Her mind tried to focus on something other than the upcoming Olympics.

"What did you do today?" Xander asked.

Eden's eyes scanned the high, filmy clouds above her head. "I . . . worked on running. My time is getting better." It was true. Her time was getting better, but when she had logged it on the stats site, all of her hope at getting faster had evaporated. No matter how much faster she got, everyone else was getting faster too. She still wasn't in the top ten percent, not even close.

"That's good," Xander said. "Worked on strength training today for wrestling." He showed off one of his impressive arm muscles, and Eden rolled her eyes. He had finally managed to pull a smile out of her.

"I've been using some punching bags too." He held out his hand and showed her the black athletic tape that protected his knuckles.

Eden reached for one of his hands and slowly unwrapped the tape. His knuckles underneath were raw. "I don't think it's working for you," she told him. "These look like a fisherman's hands."

"Maybe all this wrestling is just preparing me to be a fisherman," Xander joked, examining his own knuckles before unwrapping his other hand.

"You would be a terrible fisherman," Eden told him.

"What? Why?" Xander feigned outrage, and his theatrics pulled Eden out of her bad mood.

"Because *you* are not patient."

Xander's green eyes twinkled. "I'm not patient, huh? How about you? I saw you checking your phone for the time as I walked up. I know I was a couple minutes late, but you were about to go all teacher on me."

Eden laughed. "Hey, I'm patient when I need to be."

"So you don't need to be patient with me?" he asked.

"Nope, you need to learn to be on time. You've been late for your whole life. Good thing the Olympics don't rely on your ability to be on time."

"Hey, I'm here, and you're enjoying my company. If you were able to enjoy it for three minutes less, then too bad for you."

Eden shoved him, and he fell off his elbow onto his back. They lay there for a few minutes, soaking in the sun. Eden loved the warmth on this late April afternoon. In a couple of months, it would be hot, really hot, but for now, Greenland wasn't too warm. Not like the rest of the world that had slowly succumbed to unquenchable fires. Well, all of the world except Alaska, Russia, and Greenland. Supposedly, Antarctica was liveable too as far as temperature but the land wasn't healthy enough for anything to grow.

"Come on," Xander said, hopping up suddenly. "Let's do something."

"Like what?" Eden asked, taking Xander's hand as he pulled her to her feet.

"Like walk around," Xander said. "At least we can get some exercise."

"I got my exercise. I ran today."

Xander laughed. "I bet if I was suggesting we do some weird choreography you came up with, then you would be all for it."

"Okay, first of all, my choreography isn't weird. It's beautiful. Secondly, *are* you suggesting that?"

"No, I'm not," Xander responded. "I'm suggesting we do *something*. We're young, at least for another month we are. We might as well enjoy ourselves."

Eden looked at him sideways. Was this the Xander she knew and loved? Because right now, he was acting like some stranger. "Are you saying you want to go to one of the parties?" she asked.

She was always trying to convince him that it would be fun to live it up. Just not in a living room with awkward relatives she didn't really know, hence why the party her mom was throwing for her birthday would not qualify as fun.

Xander glanced back at the apartments. "Wouldn't your parents grant you an early elimination?"

"Probably," Eden said.

Dinner would be in an hour, and her mom had gotten really serious about family meals recently. She said that they needed to spend time together, and every moment was precious. She was probably part of the reason that Eden had miniature panic attacks every once in a while.

"Okay . . . go to your special dinner, then meet me here when it gets dark." Xander decided.

"Xander, if you get me killed, then I'm going to make sure everyone knows whose fault it is." But part of Eden was celebrating inside. She had always wanted to go to the parties teens in Sisimiut threw, but she wasn't about to go alone. Xander had always said he didn't want to do anything stupid that would mess up his chances for the Olympics. Yet here he was, a month before the Olympics, saying that he was going to enjoy himself for once.

"You won't get killed. I'll tell your parents I dragged you out of your room."

"That might get *you* killed," Eden said, laughing.

"Two hours then?" Xander asked.

Eden agreed and decided she would help her mom with dinner. If she did that, then her mom would be more likely to let her go out afterward. Helping her would be perfect priming, even if it was a little easy to figure out her motivation.

Eden walked up the stairs to the second floor and past the other doorways until she reached her own, remembering the first time she had met Xander.

They had been in the same kindergarten class together, but Eden remembered thinking he was a crazy boy. He zoomed around the room before throwing himself onto the beanbag chairs in the corner. Then, he had done the same thing again and again. She had tried to stay out of his path as much as possible.

After a few days of school, though, she still hadn't made any friends as she huddled in the corner with one or two toys, and he had been kind enough to invite her to play. All of his games were ones she didn't really like, but she was so glad to finally have a friend that she could tell Mommy about that she had played first soccer then basketball then hide and seek over and over again.

Now, Eden was glad that she had given Xander a chance and that he had thought she looked lonely enough to approach. They were different, but they had become good friends.

Eden pushed through the unlocked front door and saw her mother busy in the kitchen.

"Did you have fun with Xander?" her mom asked.

"Yeah, we just talked a little bit," Eden responded, wandering into the kitchen where her mother was chopping raw vegetables. "What are we making?"

"*We*? Are you helping?"

Eden smiled at her mother's surprise. "Maybe, I mean, if you need help or something."

"Sure, you can do the onions and carrots. I'm making beef soup with some vegetables." Eden took the cutting board and began chopping the carrots. It was too soon to ask if she could go out that evening. She figured she needed to help for at least fifteen minutes first.

"You still haven't told me what you want to eat at your birthday party," her mother prompted.

Eden sighed. "Whatever you want to cook is fine. You know I'm not picky." What Eden wanted was a big, fried chicken, but chickens had become hard to get recently. The last thing she wanted was her mom to stress about it. Food was food. If beef was easier to find, then that's what they would eat.

"I went ahead and bought some rolls. I know you love those. I figured we could do a casserole. Maybe some rolls and whatever meat we can find."

"Sounds great, Mom," Eden responded with fake cheerfulness. She wasn't the one who wanted to have a party. It had been her parents' idea. Eden thought she was too old for a birthday party.

"Do you have any plans to celebrate your birthday with Xander? I know he's coming to the party, but I didn't know if you were thinking about doing anything else."

Inspiration struck Eden. "Actually, Mom, Xander invited me to do something with him tonight. It's going to be . . . kind of boring, well, I don't know. He said that some of the guys from school are . . . having a wrestling match. He wants to go watch it, and he invited me."

Eden knew that her mother would say no to parties, but a wrestling match? She wouldn't say no to that, right? Her mother looked at her. "That doesn't really sound like a birthday outing. It sounds boring."

"Well, he said we'll see if we can find some ice cream or something afterward."

"Now I understand," her mom said, smiling. She knew that Eden was obsessed with sweets, and the fact that they were hard to get made her want them even more.

"Sure, you can go. Be careful, sweetheart, and stay safe." Eden nodded, agreeing to whatever requests her mother had. It suddenly seemed really important that she go to at least one party before she turned eighteen. Being careful hadn't gotten her anywhere.

Chapter 2

Xander grabbed his bike out of the front hall and bounced it down the stairs to the bottom floor. Eden had been too serious lately, and if going to a party would cheer her up, then Xander would happily agree. He straddled the bike, looked both ways for other bikers or a car and took off toward her complex. He had to ride uphill to reach her, but Xander enjoyed the feeling of sweat rolling down his back and soaking his shirt. His muscles pumped, and he felt the strength build as he exercised them.

Eden was already waiting outside her apartment complex, shifting back and forth in the twilight. "It's not dark yet!" Xander called up to her as he turned onto the sidewalk. "I'm early!"

"Technically, the internet says that sunset was seven minutes ago."

"Yeah, but there's still light from the sun, even if it's behind the trees."

He slowed down as Eden hopped onto his pegs with a practiced jump. Her hands gripped his shoulders. "We're going to a wrestling match, just so you know," she said, leaning down close to his ear.

Xander kept his face forward as he talked to her. "That's what you told your mom?"

"Yeah, she thought it sounded boring until I added that we might get ice cream. So, if we're not going to a wrestling match, then we at least have to get ice cream so I'm not a complete liar."

"You already lied twice, but I'll do my best to make you into an honest girl," Xander said. He whipped around the curve, not even pedaling as he picked up speed. Eden's fingers dug into his shoulders, and the wind carried away anything she might have said.

Xander had already checked with some of the other wrestlers, and he knew where a party would be that night. He quickly took the memorized turns, wondering what Eden would think when she got there. She had always said that she wanted to go to parties, but would she really like them once she arrived?

The party could be heard before it was seen. It was loud, really loud, and Xander couldn't believe that the neighbors weren't pounding down the Marxes' door.

"It's here," Xander said, leaning his bike against the tree where all the other bikes were.

"Well, I figured that out, thanks," Eden responded, sarcastic as usual.

"Ready to go in?" Xander asked, tilting his head toward the door. Eden took a deep breath and nodded, plunging ahead without waiting for him. Xander jogged to catch up. "Sure are eager to get in there, huh?"

Eden laughed. "Hey, my mom gave me a curfew of ten, so if I'm going to enjoy myself, I better start right now."

"What? You mean riding the bike with me wasn't enjoyable?" Xander joked.

Eden smiled as they reached the porch. The front door was open and several teens were hanging around the doorway. Eden would never push her way through, but Xander didn't mind. He used his elbows for the reason they were made and pushed his way inside, Eden following right behind.

Once they were in the house, she took in everything slowly.

Xander watched as she turned in a circle, and his eyes followed her gaze.

In the room to their right, the kitchen had a selection of bottled water, both flavored and unflavored. A bowl of chips was on the counter, and two boys were hanging around it like guard dogs.

Xander wasn't hungry anyway, so he looked into the living room. There were at least three couples making out like they had never had a chance to kiss anyone before. Xander fidgeted, twirling his thumbs in a circle as he looked at Eden to see what she thought of the party. She was the one who had wanted to go to one of these so desperately for at least a year. He enjoyed himself in the gym or on his bike, not with loud music and too many bodies squeezed into a small space.

"Xander!" one of his wrestling buddies said. Xander slapped hands with him and pulled him into a hug.

"Didn't expect you to be here," Connor said.

"I asked you for the address two hours ago." Xander rolled his eyes at his friend.

"That doesn't mean anything. You're always too uptight about having fun. I mean, dude, we might only have a month left to live. Might as well enjoy it."

"Eden's here," Xander said, moving off the subject of the upcoming Olympics. It was all everyone wanted to talk about, but Eden had clearly been upset about it earlier. He didn't want someone bringing it up now and spoiling the evening for her.

Eden gave a little wave, then studied the setup again.

"We're doing dares outside," Connor said, waving his arm to invite them. "Come on."

"In a minute," Xander said. Connor pushed his way through a couple of dancing teens before he disappeared.

"Okay, this is nothing like the movies," Eden said once Connor had disappeared.

"Well, most of the movies are from before everything changed," Xander reminded her. "It's not like people just have alcohol to throw away anymore."

"Thanks. I was really hoping for a history lesson right now."

"I knew you were," Xander said as he observed the couples making out in the living room. "*That* hasn't changed much."

They stood in the hallway for a couple of minutes. Someone tried to go through the front door, and Xander stepped aside to let them. As he watched everyone else having fun, he zoned out. Dancing or making out just wasn't his style, though if Eden made the first move, he probably wouldn't say no.

"Let's go out to the backyard," Eden suggested, stepping around people as she found her way toward the back door. Xander followed, taking in all the details. He wasn't a partygoer because he preferred to be careful. One accident, and he could put himself out of the running for a medal. Losing his chance at the wrestling medal would mean losing his only opportunity to win adulthood. With most of the earth uninhabitable due to the overheating of the planet, there wasn't a lot of space for adults who couldn't contribute to society.

The house had a big porch, and there were tiny lights all around it hanging like fireflies in the night. The backyard was lit by the periodic spark of a cigarette or something else, and the whole place had a haze of smoke hanging over it. The music inside pumped through Xander's body.

"It's pretty back here," Eden said, looking at a bush with blooming, pink flowers on it. "I tried to get things to grow in our window box, but there's too much wind up at our place."

"Is that the whole reason you wanted to come to this party?" Xander asked. "So you could see some pretty flowers?"

"See?" Eden said, sniffing the flower dramatically. "Parties are fun."

"I can go around sniffing random things any day I want," Xander told her.

Eden started laughing so hard that she grasped her stomach. A couple of people looked at them, but Xander didn't care. He loved cheering up Eden. She finally got control of herself, and Xander pointed to a circle of people under more of the twinkling lights. "Let's go see what they're doing," he suggested.

"Probably not as fun as our sniffing," Eden told him in a low voice.

Xander smiled back at her, and they wandered over to the group of six or seven teens. One was attempting to drink something while being held upside down. Eden made a face, wrinkling her freckles up into a line.

"Looks gross," she said.

"Heyyyy, Xander came to have fun!" Connor shouted, dropping the leg he was holding. The person swayed back and forth, and Xander stepped forward to grab the person's leg so he wouldn't fall on his face. He lowered him slowly to the ground, and the guy stood up and swayed back and forth.

"Want a turn?" Connor asked.

Xander shook his head. If someone holding one of his legs let go, he could easily fall on his face or break an arm or a leg. He could choke on the drink and potentially die. He could also . . . Eden broke into his thoughts.

"I'll try," she said tentatively.

"When I said have a little fun," Xander told her, leaning forward. "This was not what I had in mind."

Eden stepped forward and braced herself on the ground. The two guys lifted each of her legs, then someone else began tilting a glass into her mouth. Xander clenched his teeth as he watched Eden attempt to drink while upside down. Her shirt fell down, exposing her stomach, and Xander clenched his fists into balls. This was wrong. This was all wrong. Eden was going to get hurt, and it would be his fault for bringing her here.

Eden had just taken her first sip when the world disappeared.

The backyard went completely dark, and the music cut off suddenly. The person holding the drink dropped it, and glass shattered across the bricks. Eden yelped.

Xander's eyes adjusted to the darkness, and he saw that Eden had fallen onto the shattered glass.

"Eden!" he said, crunching over the glass to reach her.

Eden groaned and sat up. Xander could see the faint moonlight reflected in the glass shards peppered into her skin. She reached up to touch her face, but he was worried that she would cause herself further injury.

"Don't," Xander told her in a firm voice. "I don't want you to hurt your hands. Stand up. Can you walk?" Eden nodded slowly, a couple of pieces of glass falling off her face and shirt onto the ground.

"Okay, stand up, and let's get into the light."

Xander glanced at the house, but the windows were all dark. Teens were pouring out of the house and into the backyard where there was at least a little moonlight illuminating the world.

His eyes flicked to the houses on either side, and they both had their lights on. It wasn't a citywide failure. The kid hosting the party had run through their monthly electricity ration. Xander grimaced. It was only April 8th. His parents were going to be furious.

"My freckles hurt," Eden said, reaching up to touch her face despite Xander's warning.

Xander cursed under his breath. Of course this had to happen to Eden. Xander hoped her eyes hadn't been injured. "Let's get you where I can see you," he said. He grabbed her hand so she wouldn't touch her face anymore and led her through the emerging teens. Once they were through the house and onto the front sidewalk, Xander led her to his bike where he had a tiny battery-powered light.

He turned it on and gently pushed her shoulder so that her face was in the light. Eden squinted, and Xander gnawed on his lower lip as he assessed the damage. It was probably better Eden couldn't see her face.

"I'm going to pick the pieces out, okay? It might hurt, but I don't want you to get them in your hands."

Xander looked around for something he could use, but he hadn't brought his backpack. He took off his shirt, turned it inside out, and used the front of it to gently begin picking out the slivers of glass. This was nearly impossible.

"Is there a lot?" Eden asked.

"Don't talk. Glass might fall into your mouth," Xander said.

Eden squirmed away from him for a minute. "I need to see what I look like," she said. "I need to see myself." She reached for her phone.

"Eden, let me get the glass out first." Xander pushed her hand away as a couple of pieces fell off her shirt. Then, he began meticulously picking the pieces off her face. He took her chin and slowly turned her face from side to side to see if he had missed any. Eden opened her brown, worried eyes, and Xander smiled at her.

"Your face is clean." There hadn't been as much as he first thought.

"There's one on my arm," Eden said.

Xander held her arm up to the light, holding her fingers and twisting her arm slowly until the glass caught the light. He picked it out, and a spot of blood filled the empty space. "It looks like it's okay," he told her. He looked at her shirt.

"Your shirt has glass all over it though."

Eden looked down at her shirt. "Watch out."

Xander took a step back, and Eden shook herself. More glass clattered to the ground, but there was still some that clung stubbornly to her.

"Do you mind, uh, helping me get the glass off?" Eden asked. "Or you can give me the shirt and I can do it myself."

"I don't mind," Xander said, crouching in front of her. He slowly and carefully picked out the pieces of glass and threw them on the ground, focusing on the material and not the fact that Eden was right there, her body warm in the slowly cooling night.

"I think I got it all," Xander finally announced, standing up. He turned and looked back at the party in the house.

Some of the guests had left as soon as the electricity had run out, but others were still in the backyard, shouting and singing and having a good time.

Xander took a few deep breaths and felt much more under control when he turned back to Eden.

"Do you want to go home now?" he asked, silently begging her not to want to go back to the party.

Eden shook her head. "You promised me ice cream," she said.

"Ice cream? I don't remember making that promise."

"Well, I told my mom that we would get some after the . . . wrestling match. That's as good as you promising me."

"So next time I want something from you, I just have to tell someone you promised it. Is that how this works?"

"It's a one time deal," she said, smiling. Xander tried not to wince at the bloody specks across her face, but she noticed his look. "It's bad, isn't it? What is my mom going to think?"

Xander tried to think of an explanation that would work. "You could just tell her that a glass broke."

"And I fell in it?"

"Yeah, that's what happened. You just don't have to tell her it was at a party. Or just tell her the truth. I mean, what's she going to do? Ground you?"

Eden's face turned serious as she understood what he was implying. They might not have very much longer to live, and parents were noticeably more lenient in the final months before the Olympics.

Eden swallowed slowly. "I guess it doesn't matter anyway," she said.

"I always keep my promises though," Xander said, swinging himself onto his bike. "Let's get some ice cream!" Xander warily examined his shirt, but he had been careful to drop each piece of glass he picked onto the ground. He thought it was safe, so he slipped it on again.

They didn't find any ice cream that night. The three stores they checked had been out of stock for over a week, and they didn't know when they would get more.

"Oh well," Eden said when Xander skidded his bike to a stop in front of her apartment building. "You tried to keep your promise. That's what counts."

"Yeah, especially since I didn't make that promise," he reminded her.

Xander studied Eden's face in the moonlight. He could still see the spots of red covering her face and arms and knew her mother wouldn't be happy about it. He felt responsible. If only he had convinced Eden not to take the dare.

"I guess I'll see you at my birthday party on Sunday," she said.

"See you then." Xander spun his pedals backward until one of them was in the perfect position moving forward again. He waved at Eden then began pumping his way back across the parking lot to the downward hill. His night wasn't over yet.

When Xander reached his apartment complex, he shouldered the bike and crept up the stairs to the third floor. He knew the stairs well and didn't want to waste any of his battery light climbing them, but he stumbled on the last one, crashing into the wall beside the doorway with a bang. He winced and waited. Nothing.

Xander shoved his key into the door and tried to push it open as quietly as he could. His bike thumped to the ground, and that was when he heard his mother clear her throat.

"Xander," she said from the darkness that shrouded the couch.

"Hey, Mom," Xander said, setting his bike in its usual place against the kitchen counter.

"Did you have a fun night?" she asked.

"Yeah, sorry I woke you up. Are you feeling okay?"

"Just coughing a lot," his mother responded.

Xander heard her rustle around on the couch. "Don't get up," Xander said. "Do you need something?"

"No, I'm fine. Get some sleep," his mother said.

"Thanks, you too." Xander heard his bike sliding against the bar indicating that he hadn't propped it up as well as he thought. He hurried over to grab it before it fell, which would wake up the neighbors above and below them.

When he grabbed the handle, the flashlight turned on, illuminating his shirt. Xander squinted his eyes for a minute as he fumbled for the button where his fingers had just been. As the light snapped off, he heard a different tone in his mother's voice.

"Xander?" she asked. "Why is there blood on your shirt? Come here."

Xander approached his mother cautiously. "It's nothing." His mind was inventing excuses as he went along. He wasn't sure what story Eden would tell her mother, and their two mothers were friends. They would find out. "A glass broke, and Eden and I kind of got some pieces in our hands."

"Huh," his mother responded. She reached out and gripped the bottom of his shirt, pulling him closer. Xander waited as his mother examined his shirt through the faint light from the window.

"You need to be more careful," she said. "I don't want . . ."

Her voice broke off, and Xander knew what she was thinking about. He pulled her into a hug, her familiar smell of lotion hitting him hard. Then, she started coughing, and Xander backed away to give her the space she needed.

"Night," Xander said. He went into his bedroom and lay down on his bed after taking off his shoes. His birthday present for Eden would have to wait until tomorrow. He couldn't think about anything else now.

Chapter 3

On the morning of her birthday, Eden emerged from her room slowly. The apartment already looked like she had expected. Her mother was making breakfast, and it smelled different from the typical oatmeal or eggs they normally had.

Eden sniffed the air, her eyes glimpsing the big '18' that had been pasted on the wall with colorful sheets of paper. When Eden approached it, trying to sneak so that her mother wouldn't see her from the kitchen, she recognized the papers. They were old school projects, ones that had been special enough to deserve being written on paper, not just on the tablet or computer.

"Good morning, Eden!" her mother cheered from the kitchen. "Happy birthday!"

Eden turned away from the colorful number to where her mother was working on breakfast. Eden tried to smile, but it was as though she wasn't really there. She was watching the scene from one of the far corners in the living room. This couldn't really be *her* eighteenth birthday, the last birthday she was assured before the Olympics.

Eden's fingers itched to check the ratings online, but she knew it would only discourage her even further. She shouldn't think about the upcoming competition, not today. Her mother was already embracing her, squishing Eden's hair into her face and neck so that Eden winced.

Her mother stood back and examined Eden carefully, her eyes trailing over her still visible wounds. "It doesn't look as bad today," she said. "I bet if you put on a little foundation, no one would even notice."

Eden touched her cheek self-consciously, jumping back into her body from the distant corner where she had been watching the whole scene. "It doesn't matter," she said, feeling the sudden urge to cry. "So, um, what are you cooking?"

"Pancakes," her mother whispered.

Eden's mouth watered at the word, and she remembered when it had been easy to get chocolate chips. Her mother had made pancakes every weekend. Now, Eden headed directly to the kitchen, not worrying about the big questions in life, just wanting some pancakes.

"Where's Dad?" Eden asked.

"Still sleeping," her mother responded. "Go wave one of these under his nose, and he'll wake up."

"No way!" Eden laughed as her mother flipped a pancake onto a plate. "He'll kill me!" Her words flew around the room like a boomerang, hitting her hard upon their return. Eden's eyes turned to her plate, and she sat at the table that marked the line between the living room and the kitchen. Her mother brought over another plate with a pancake.

"How about you and I eat breakfast and just let him sleep in a little?"

Eden nodded at her mother's suggestion. She dug into the pancake, and the chocolate chips melted in her mouth. She tried to eat slowly so she could fully enjoy each bite, but all too soon, she had eaten three pancakes.

"Do you want to save any for tomorrow?" her mother asked, and Eden knew it was her way of gently reminding Eden that she shouldn't stuff herself.

"Yeah, sure, just make sure Dad doesn't eat them all."

"I'll guard them as well as I can," her mother promised.

Eden padded through the living room into her bedroom. She had always looked forward to birthdays, though in recent years, she had forgone the parties. Still, her family and friends had always managed to make them special somehow.

Eden smiled as she remembered her tenth birthday party. She was *big*, double digits, so Xander had made her a big 'Happy Birthday' sign in the parking lot using his bicycle and skid marks. She had felt famous that day. Then, her parents had sung happy birthday to her while she hopped along the letters Xander had made. She couldn't remember what present she had gotten, but she remembered snuggling up on the couch and watching a movie. She got to stay up way past her bedtime. That had been a special birthday.

She didn't think it was possible to make her eighteenth birthday special.

Eden looked in her mirror and picked at a scab that had formed just under her nose. There were at least six scabs on her face, interspersed with her freckles. They almost blended in. Eden told herself to stop picking at them, but her fingers didn't listen. Soon, a spot of blood was forming on her cheek.

Eden swiped at it, and another bubble of blood came up underneath. She turned away from the mirror. Looking at herself was doing nothing but making her more nostalgic for the days when she had enjoyed birthdays. The computer called her attention from the corner of the room, and Eden decided to check her rankings.

It wasn't a smart idea, not on her birthday, but she had to know. Maybe something had changed overnight. Eden had updated her information on Friday and hadn't looked again.

Eden pulled up the website and clicked her age. The list of competitions spread across the screen. Some of them were physical- such as the wrestling, running, and endurance tests. Those all had clear rankings. The mental tests were harder to judge, so Eden had to hope she stood a chance in one of those.

She clicked on wrestling first. She had no intention of competing in the wrestling competition, but she wanted to see where she was. The screen loaded slowly, revealing one tiny line at a time. Eden glanced away, and when she glanced back, she saw something that made her heart drop. Xander was eighth!

Each year, ten percent of the eighteen-year-olds, divided equally by gender, would win a medal in each competition. Because there were seven competitions, thirty percent of the eighteen-year-old population would be eliminated. Being in eighth place was in the top 1%, so Xander was basically guaranteed a medal.

Eden wanted to cheer, but she bit it back and went back to the list of competitions. She had worked on her running for a while, and she thought she had really improved. However, as she went through the list of names scanning them for her own, her heart dropped as she continued to scroll downward. There she was, in 298th place. There was no way she could work her way up to the top ten percent. She clicked on her name and saw the time she had uploaded on Friday- 8 minutes, 10 seconds.

Eden shook her head as she went back to the list of names, scrolled to the top, and clicked on the runner who had taken first place for the moment. The time beside her name was 3 minutes, 10 seconds.

"How is that even possible?" Eden said. She was *not* going to cut her speed by two thirds, not in a month. She should probably give up the running idea.

"Eden!" her mom called, knocking as she opened the door. "You're not looking at the rankings again, are you?" she asked.

Eden pressed her lips together as she closed out of the program. She tried to arrange her features so that it looked like everything was alright, but her mother knew her.

"Stop looking!" she said. "The program doesn't mean anything."

"Mom, the top-" Eden stopped herself. Her mom was right. Eden had already been told both by Xander and her mom that a system where people uploaded the times themselves was faulty. The top runner could have put any number she wanted in those boxes just to psych everyone else out.

"Eden, today is your birthday, and you already have a guest."

"A guest?" Eden asked, frowning and looking behind her mother. She had been so wrapped up in checking the stats that she hadn't heard anyone knock on the front door. She smiled when she saw Xander. He was holding a hand behind his back.

"I'll let you two talk," her mother said, leaving the room. Xander stepped inside, his hand still behind his back.

"What do you have behind your back?" Eden asked, trying to peer around his strong shoulders.

Xander removed the box dramatically and wiggled it in front of her face. Eden smiled and reached for it, but Xander yanked the box back. "You have to wait until your party to open it," he said.

"What? Why?"

"Because that's when you open gifts," Xander said. "Duh." He must be trying to make Eden laugh, and it worked.

"What about the 'It's my birthday. You have to do what I want.' rule?"

"That's not a real rule."

"Says you. My mom totally agrees with that rule. Go ask her."

"I'm not going to ask her." Xander stuck his tongue out at Eden and sat on the floor, settling his back up against her bed. She looked down on him from her place in the desk chair.

"Fine, then you'll have to take my word for it." Eden motioned for him to hand her the box. He just shoved it under the bed, then leaned against where he had hidden it. Eden wasn't four. She was now eighteen, so she didn't dive toward the bed and try to grab it. She tried to distract herself instead.

"Why are you here early?" she asked.

"I don't have anything else to do," Xander shrugged. "Why? You don't want me here?"

"I'm doing the whole 'serious thinking about the future because it's my birthday' thing."

"Don't do that," Xander told her, the twinkle leaving his eyes. "The future isn't fun to think about."

Eden tried to be the best version of herself that she could be. As calmly as she could, she congratulated Xander on his standings. "I saw that you were eighth this morning in wrestling in your weight category. You're pretty much guaranteed to win a medal."

"Anything could happen in the next month," Xander said, his face serious. "I've not won until I've won. Besides, there are three weight categories, so it's only top three percent in my category, not ten."

"When I checked my standing, it basically showed I have no hope."

"Eden, we've talked about this. You can't give up hope until there really isn't any. You could be in the top ten percent for any competition."

"Except wrestling." Eden gave him a wry look.

"Okay, maybe not wrestling, but you have a good chance in the others. Look, let all the other teens go to their stupid parties and get hurt before the competitions begin. We're going to stay here, stay safe, and wait for the competition to begin."

"So your plan for me to survive is to let everyone else break their legs and fatally wound themselves?"

"That's not my whole plan," Xander said. He started to say something else, but this time, Eden heard the knock on the front door. Someone else had arrived more than an hour early. Her father answered the door, and Eden saw through her open doorway that her cousins from Nuuk had arrived.

She had two younger cousins who were fifteen and nine, and they both came rushing inside. "Happy birthday!" nine-year-old Mary said, flinging herself at Eden.

"Hey, thanks!" Eden hugged her little cousin. Luke was cooler, so he stood in the doorway, assessing the situation. He spotted Xander and went over to him, shaking his hand. The two had met before, but it had been a while.

Mary bent down and whispered in Eden's ear. "Is that your boyfriend? He's really cute!"

Eden's cheeks reddened, and she glanced at Xander. It didn't look like he had heard her little cousin's comment. "No, and I already know," Eden told Mary. Mary giggled and watched Xander. He giggled back at her, copying the hands over her mouth thing and whispering something to Mary's brother.

"What did you say?" Mary demanded.

Xander just copied her giggle again, and Mary started whining as she tried to convince him to spill his secrets. Eden watched, laughing as Xander just shook his head and pretended to zip his lips and throw away the key.

She turned to her brother to get the information instead. "Lukeeee!" Mary whined. "Tell me what he said!" When Luke wouldn't give her a satisfying answer, she attacked him, fists pummeling her brother, even though he was much older and bigger than she was.

"You shouldn't mess with a wrestler," Luke told his little sister, once he had her hands pinned behind her back.

Mary didn't learn the first time and jumped at Luke again again. Eden watched as Luke pinned her then let her up. Mary elbowed Xander trying to get him in on the fun. "Mary, that's enough," Eden said, remembering Xander's warning about not getting hurt before the Olympics.

"Do you want to know what we got you?" Mary asked in a low voice.

Eden shrugged. "You can tell me if you want," Eden said.

Mary grabbed her hand and pulled her into the living room where a bright, reusable plastic bag was sitting under the big eighteen on the wall. "It's in there, and I know you will really like it."

Eden glanced at her mother and aunt. "Am I supposed to open it right now?"

"You can go ahead if you like," her mother said. "Not everyone will bring presents, so maybe you should open it now."

Eden leaned over the bag and saw right away what her cousins had gotten for her. There were art supplies in there. Paper and colored pencils, sharpened to a point. They were so beautiful that Eden wasn't sure she would be able to use them.

She took the box out and extracted the blue pencil, her favorite color. She twirled the pencil around and felt the sharp tip against her finger. Mary started spinning behind Eden and bumped into her, causing Eden's finger to break the sharp point. The blue pencil now ended with a jagged tip. Eden clenched her jaw. It was stupid, but as her eyes found the tiny piece of blue lead on the floor, she wanted to cry.

Why did she think she could do this? Who cared if the pencil broke? In a month, she would be eliminated, whatever that meant, and not be able to use it anyway. Those who were eliminated never returned to their houses to say goodbye.

Eden swallowed her emotions and replaced the pencils in the bag. "Thank you," she said, trying to clear her throat of the congestion. She wanted to just be alone for a minute, but Xander and Luke were still in her room.

The apartment wasn't big, and the only place she could escape to was the bathroom. Eden hurried in there and took a couple of deep breaths. She could do this. She could get through her birthday. She was not going to have an emotional breakdown in front of everyone.

"Eden!" Mary called through the door. "Some girl is here."

Eden took a deep breath, pasted a smile on her face, and exited the bathroom. Two other people had arrived, friends from school, and Eden tried to forget about everything else except enjoying this moment.

Xander came up behind her and whispered in her ear. "I'm going to be expecting a new picture from you once you break out those pencils."

"How did you know what I got?" Eden asked him.

"Mary told us as soon as you opened it." Xander smiled. "Seems like she's not one to keep secrets."

"Nope, not really," Eden agreed. "Fine, I'll draw you a picture on one condition."

"What?"

Eden saw her friend approaching, so she spoke fast. "Tell me what's in your present."

"You really aren't a patient person, are you?" he asked.

"I think you already have your answer. Hi, Celena." Eden waved.

"Happy birthday," Celena said, her eyes scanning the sign that Eden's mother had made. "That's a big one."

Eden nodded. She used to have a lot to say to Celena, but that was before they had entered the final year of school, the one that focused on training for the Olympics. Since then, they had kind of grown apart. Eden wished her mother hadn't invited this girl.

"So, what have you been up to lately?" Eden asked.

"Not much," Celena shrugged. "Just training. You know, the Olympics are coming up in thirty-five days."

Eden swallowed hard. At least, she tried to swallow, but it was like her throat was constricting so much that it didn't work anymore.

"I'm not sure how you can just have a party like this and pretend like the end isn't coming."

All of the voices around them seemed really loud all of a sudden. It was like Eden couldn't remember how to form words or how to function. She forced herself to breathe in and out. Her breaths were shaky, but she managed them. But she still couldn't remember how to speak, and Celena's face seemed so condescending.

"I . . . it's . . ." Eden couldn't get her words out, and the room suddenly felt hot, too hot. She had to get out of there. Eden tripped over her own feet as she ran to the door. She was almost out . . . of . . . there.

The morning air was already warm, and Eden felt a sheen of sweat on her forehead as she thumped down the stairs to the first floor. She saw another friend and family approaching from the right, so she turned left. She couldn't face anyone right then. Celena was right. This was ridiculous. She was going to die. She only had a month left. She wouldn't survive the Olympics.

Eden stumbled over her feet again, until she fell on her knees in the tiny patch of grass that passed for a lawn. She stayed there, folding into herself as the fear washed over her. She only had a month left. She only had a month left. She was not going to survive.

Suddenly, a hand was on her shoulder. She didn't want to talk. She couldn't talk. She couldn't . . . do anything. It didn't matter anymore.

"Eden," Xander's voice said, and Eden felt a tiny prick of gratefulness that it was him and not her mother. She had to be strong in front of her parents. She was their only child. "I'm here for you," he said.

Eden slowly unfolded herself until she was sitting up, her shoulders hunched forward. She took a few deep breaths. She had to at least try. She couldn't give up right now.

Xander lay on his back and gazed up at the sun. Eden tried to copy his nonchalant pose. It helped her feel a little less stressed but not much.

Then, she turned her head and looked directly into his green eyes. "Do you think I'm going to be eliminated? Be honest."

Xander's face tightened. "I can't predict the future."

"No one can." Eden took a deep, shuddering breath. "Just tell me what you think."

She searched Xander's face for some clue about what he thought, but his face was the picture of sympathy. That sympathy, the littlest downturn of the corners of his eyes, and the sadness pricking at the corners of his mouth was all she needed to see. She nodded slowly, then turned to face the ocean, watching the waves crash against the rocky coast below.

Everything seemed to hit her at once. This was probably her last birthday, and she had just ruined it. She would only have a few more weeks to enjoy this life, if she could even enjoy something that was about to be ripped from her grasp. Last of all, Xander would never understand her because he was almost certain to win his right to adulthood.

She crouched, making herself as small as possible, and buried her face in her knees. She didn't care how stupid she looked. Who cared about people seeing her cry when she was going to be eliminated in a few weeks anyway?

The tiny sobs turned into big, heaving ones. They took over her body as she stopped hiding her fears.

"Eden, Edie," Xander said, crouching next to her. He put his hand on her shoulder and pulled her into his chest. He smelled just like he always did, salty with sweat, and it made her feel for just one minute like the rest of the world's problems might not be so bad after all.

"Eden, I can help you," Xander said, pushing her gently away from him so that he could see her red, streaked face.

Eden heard the tone in his voice, his problem-solving tone, and she shook her head. There was nothing he or anyone else could do now. She was a lost cause.

"I'm going to help you train, okay? You pick the area you want to focus on, whatever it is; I'll help you get there. You can improve your ranking."

Eden shook her head again. She didn't think that training could help her, especially right now. She had been training the whole year in preparation for the Olympics, but what was training really? It only widened the gap between the best and the untalented, of which she was one.

"Eden, look at me," Xander said. He was taking that serious tone. "You're . . . my best friend, and I don't want you to be eliminated."

Eden pressed her lips together and hung her head. She and Xander hadn't ever been anything more than friends, but wouldn't that change if they both won medals?

Xander continued talking about the great training plan he was putting together. "All you have to do is focus on one thing. You've been scattered all year with different focuses, but you pick the talent you think you can really succeed at and go for that one."

"But what if I only have one shot, and I blow it?" Eden asked. "We're going to be competing against people from all three countries, and many of those are naturally talented."

"I think it's better if you have one really good shot than three or four mediocre ones."

His words hung in the air, the consequences of not winning a medal heavy on both of them. Eden nodded. She didn't think training with him or anyone would help, but she was willing to try.

"Okay, I'll do it," she finally agreed.

Xander patted her on the back hard, and Eden choked on the few remaining tears she had. Xander started laughing, then she started laughing before she choked again and her laughing turned into coughing. Xander aimed his hand at her back again, and she rolled away, enjoying a few more minutes of being normal.

Chapter 4

Xander stretched on the open track beside the school. After going to school five days a week for so many years, he was glad to have a year just to focus on his training. It was seven in the morning, and Eden was supposed to meet him. It was easier to run when it wasn't hot yet, but she still hadn't arrived.

How could the girl who was always clocking him be late?

Xander reached down and touched the ground, feeling the nudging burn in his calves. He thought that running was one of her best chances. She had a thin body that would cut through the wind, and she wasn't built right for a lot of the other physical competitions.

Xander began jogging in place, moving his neck around to crack it as he did.

"Morning," Eden called, hurrying up to him.

Xander smiled when she saw her in her favorite blue tank top and black jogging shorts. "Eden from Sweden! You ready?"

Eden shrugged. "I guess so. I ate breakfast. That's the best start, right?"

"I hope you didn't eat too much," Xander said. He was about to lecture her on the dangers of eating a lot before exercising, but Eden held up her hand.

"Thank you, doctor, but I didn't eat too much. I do know a couple of things."

"Alright, alright. Let's stretch, then I'll work with you on running." Xander excitedly led her through a few basic stretches to warm up her muscles. She had never let him teach her anything before.

Whenever Xander had tried to bring up the Olympics, she had been determined to talk about something else and keep the competition out of their relationship. Now, maybe he could get her ready for the Olympics. She could win a medal. He knew it was possible. With only three countries left with liveable conditions, adulthood had to be earned. Eden had definitely earned it. Of that, Xander was certain. Now, he just had to make the judges of the Olympics agree with him.

"I think my muscles are warm now," Eden said, pressing her bicep to her face. "Let's get to the running part."

"Okay, so in the Olympics, the track is a one mile loop. You're running a short distance, not a long distance."

Eden's eyebrows rose. "Maybe that's short for you. Going one mile is far for me."

Xander acknowledged her concern, but continued to give her tips. "You don't want to burst out of the gate at your fastest speed, because you're going to lose that speed and feel tired more quickly. We need to figure out a speed you can sustain for the full mile."

Eden nodded, and Xander checked her gaze to see if it was glazing over. Two boys trotted out of the school and onto the field, setting off on a basic pace around the track. Eden's eyes followed them.

"So, I shouldn't run the fastest I can?"

"You need to find a good pace for you that you can maintain the whole mile, so seven minutes give or take, rather than starting out of the gate going super fast and having to slow down later in the race. I hope that makes sense. If you have a burst of energy at the end, you can always use it to get past the finish line."

"The fastest person has a speed of just over three minutes," Eden told him. "If I'm running a mile in seven or eight, which is still faster than my current time, then I'm going to lose."

Xander shook his head. "Don't look at the stats. I'm going to delete the app from your phone, from your computer, whatever I have to do. Do you hear me? I don't even think three minutes is possible."

Eden shook her head, rolling her eyes in that way she always did when she seemed to be trying not to smile. "I think it's important for me to know what I'm competing against."

"You're not competing against that unless this person is the new fastest human. The world record is four minutes something, so no one is going faster than that. If they were, then . . . they wouldn't be in the Olympics. Anyone can upload the numbers they want on there. It's just a head game."

Eden pressed her lips together. "Fine. Help me run."

Xander nodded. That was something he could do. "Alright, how about you take a run around the track? I'm going to time you, then I'll see what improvements you can make." With the track being a mile long, she would be out of sight for several minutes.

Eden eyed him. "Is this just so you don't have to do anything this early in the morning?"

"Hey, I'm always up for early mornings," Xander told her. "Alright, get in position."

Eden crouched, one foot in front of the other.

"Okay, that's not a good position." Xander adjusted her back foot. "Try it like this. Really push off that back foot to start running."

Eden nodded, wiggled her feet just a little, then looked back at him.

"Three, two, one, go!" Xander shouted. Eden took off, and Xander watched as she ran, her arms pumping at her sides. She seemed uncertain, looking around as she ran. Xander wasn't sure who or what she was looking for, but that was definitely a big no-no. He glanced down at the clock as Eden disappeared down the far side of the track. She was at three minutes already.

She came down the other side, and Xander watched as she breathed hard. She looked at him, nodded, and kept running. As Eden circled the other end and approached the finish line, she slowed before she reached it. Xander didn't press the 'stop' button until she crossed the line- 7:44.

Xander approached her. She was breathing hard, and she grabbed the bottle of water she had set on the side of the track. Xander yanked it out of her hands.

"Hey!" she protested between gasps for air.

"You shouldn't gulp down water right after running, especially when you're about to run again. Take small, slow sips."

Eden eyed the water greedily, but Xander watched as she followed his instructions. "What was my time?" she asked. "Was it under seven minutes?"

Xander shook his head. "I don't want you to worry about the time. We're going to see how much we can decrease it today."

"So it was bad, right? You would tell me if it was good. Was it more than eight minutes? Nine minutes?"

"It doesn't matter," Xander emphasized. "Next, you need to only look at what is in front of you. Pretend that nothing else is going on. It's you and the track. You can lose precious seconds being distracted mentally by someone watching. Last, keep your full speed until you cross the line. Pretend like it's not there and just keep up your speed until you've passed it. Got it?"

Eden nodded, but she still looked distracted.

Xander patted her shoulder. "Are you ready to try again?"

Eden's eyebrows shot up. "Uh, how many times are you going to make me run a mile? I usually just go one or two times."

The other two runners started jogging in place near Eden and Xander, so Xander lowered his voice and spoke directly to Eden. "I think you can run five miles today. We're going to bring your time down, and if we do this every day until the Olympics, you'll feel a lot more confident."

It seemed easy to Xander, the basic bones of a training plan like they had learned last year in school, but Eden looked worried.

"Do you really think running it over and over again will make me faster? I mean, I've trained before, this isn't the first time, but . . ."

"Eden, stop thinking," Xander said. "Just do."

Eden frowned at him, but threw her water bottle on the ground and got into position. Xander reset the timer, checked her position, then counted down. Eden took off fast, too fast. She put all her speed into the first part of the mile, and as she disappeared around the far bend, Xander didn't think she would be able to sustain the speed for the full mile. At least she wasn't looking around.

"Why are you wasting your time with her?" one of the eighteen-year-olds said. This guy was tall and lean, the perfect build for running track.

"What?" His question didn't make sense.

"She's going to be eliminated. You might as well find a girl who's going to win a medal."

Xander shook his head and glanced at the spot where he expected Eden to reappear. He had learned to ignore all tactics from opponents trying to get in his head. He wasn't easily swayed, but the other guy kept his comments coming.

"I mean, she's kind of ugly too," he said. "Freckles? Really? There are a lot of girls in math who are pretty. You're guaranteed to win, so-"

"Shut up!" Xander barked without looking at the guy. He mentally berated himself for letting the guy get to him, but there was too much pressure on his shoulders. He saw Eden reappear around the corner, pumping her arms hard, her head flung back like she was asking for strength from the sky. Xander nodded as she crossed the finish line. He shot the loudmouth a dirty look before he approached her.

"T-time?" Eden stammered out, bent over on her knees.

"You were close to seven minutes that time," he said, "seven minutes, twenty-eight seconds."

Eden nodded, still gasping for air.

"Keep your muscles moving a little bit after you run so they don't lock up, even if you just walk in place."

Eden smiled wryly and started doing a weird robot walk as she moved. Xander was glad her run time had put her in a better mood, but now he was on edge.

Everyone acted like he had a medal in the bag. Sure, he was listed as seventh or eighth at the moment, but that ranking changed every day. He told himself and Eden not to check it, but Eden liked to update him periodically. He knew he could break an arm and lose his chance, and the fear of that happening haunted him.

"I need . . . a break," Eden said, slinking over to her water bottle and hugging it before she took a few slow sips. She seemed to notice the two guys watching them, and Xander wondered why they were there. Anyone could use the track during training hours, but they didn't seem to be training. They were just watching.

After Eden had refreshed herself with her water, she bent close to Xander, her back to the guys. "Are they watching us?" Eden asked.

Xander shrugged. "Maybe, but it doesn't matter."

Eden smiled a little. "Yeah, they won't learn anything from me. That's for sure. Can we wait, like, fifteen minutes before I go again? I'm so tired."

"Yeah," Xander agreed, his eyes darting to the guys, then away again. "Sure, a break is fine. Just don't remain stationary."

"How about we walk down to that tree and back?" Eden pointed.

Xander nodded, stuffing his phone in the little pouch he used when he was running. "Okay," he agreed. They started walking at a steady pace and not talking. Xander's mind kept going back to how everyone assumed he was going to win a medal and how he himself wasn't so sure.

"I brought some leftover cake from my party if you want some," Eden told him.

Xander smiled, knowing that the sugar wasn't good for his body but not wanting to make Eden eat it alone. "When you're done running for the day," Xander said.

As they kept walking, Eden glanced back. "They *are* watching us," she insisted.

"So what? Don't worry about what they're doing."

"Calm down," Eden said, looking at him strangely.

Xander felt the anxiety building up within him, but it wasn't fair. He couldn't let it out on Eden. Unlike her, he wouldn't explode into tears. He would explode into anger and start punching something, but he didn't want Eden to see him when he was angry. He balled his hands into fists. They had almost reached the tree Eden had picked.

"I think my muscles have calmed down now," Eden told him with a smile.

Xander nodded and pivoted when he was even with the tree. Eden turned and did some strange leap thing and started walking backward in front of him. "Xander, what happened? You're weirder than normal."

Xander shook his head. "Let's just keep training," he said. "We need to get you faster."

"I'm trying," Eden frowned at him. "Do you think I *want* to be slow?"

"No, I didn't say that." Everything was coming out wrong, and the level of stress within Xander was rising. "I'm just saying. We came here to focus on that. Let's do it." Xander took a few deep breaths as they headed back the way they had come. Eden studied the other two for a quick moment. They were now openly watching Xander and Eden, not even pretending to exercise.

Eden leaned close to Xander, her breath tickling his ear. "Why are they watching us?"

"They're checking out the competition," Xander responded.

"I'm not competing against boys," she muttered.

"Maybe they have girlfriends, and they want to know if you'll be a challenge."

"I don't like them watching me."

"Try to ignore it."

Eden took her position, getting ready to run. Xander could see that the two were really making Eden nervous. She swallowed a couple of times before nodding to Xander that she was ready. He counted down and pressed the timer to begin the count. Eden ran forward, and Xander forced his eyes to follow her and ignore the other two.

"Xander, man," one of the guys started. He clenched his jaw and kept staring at the track where Eden had gone even though he couldn't see her anymore. "You really need to think this through. She's not going to make it."

He continued saying something else, but Xander blocked out his words by staring at the timer and counting with the seconds. Eden came around the far bend, running toward them like one of those extinct polar bears was after her.

She crossed the finish line, shaving a few seconds off her time. Huffing and puffing, she approached him. "How . . . was . . . my . . . time?" she asked.

"You got seven minutes, fifteen seconds," Xander said, smiling at her. "One more run, and you'll be under seven minutes."

"Don't lie to her," the guy shouted across the track. "She was nine minutes and two seconds." He shook his head, and he and his friend finally headed back to the school's indoor training facility.

"What?" Eden asked, looking at Xander.

"No, he's lying," Xander said. He tried to turn his phone and show her the time, but his thumb slid across the reset button, and it disappeared.

Eden's eyebrows narrowed as she sucked at the oxygen. "Just tell me the truth. I need to know now if I'm going to be eliminated."

"I'm telling you the truth!" Xander said.

"Why would he lie to me?"

"I don't know, Eden. Don't you trust me?"

Eden didn't answer. She just stared at Xander's face. He shook his head and stuffed his phone into his pocket. "Then, train yourself," he said. He marched toward the training center, leaving Eden on the track by herself.

Chapter 5

Eden stared after Xander. Why was he getting upset? He was guaranteed a medal. She was the one who had to deal with the possibility of being eliminated. The rumors swirled through her head of what happened when someone was eliminated. All she wanted to do was run into the training center and bury her face in Xander's shoulder. She wanted him to tell her everything would be alright.

But he wasn't there, so Eden did the only thing that made her feel better. She went into a private training room off the side of the gym and started playing the song she had been using called "Not Again."

The running had to be enough of a warm-up, so Eden went straight into the piece she was choreographing. The music sank into her bones as she leaped, then twisted, then turned, finally ending on the floor, her back to the pretend audience.

Eden closed her eyes, two seconds of silence flooding her ears with worries before the next song started. Eden stood, restarted her song, and went through the routine again, watching herself in the mirror and critiquing how she should improve. It was definitely better than it had been, but she was not fully straightening her back leg on that leap. It had to be perfect.

Eden ran through the routine at least five more times before she was panting for water. She thought of Xander's drinking advice as she took slow sips and peered out the window in the door. Even though she couldn't see the screen, she knew it indicated that the room was occupied for another thirty minutes, so she could do whatever she wanted while the room was hers.

Eden sat down in front of the mirror and stared at herself. The speckles of red still made her look like she had chicken pox, but she looked past her cheeks into her eyes.

"You have to enjoy April," she told herself seriously. "Enjoy yourself. Dance as much as you can, and . . ." Her voice broke, so she finished the sentence in her head, *record the video for your parents.*

Eden took a couple of deep breaths, her eyes searching her own face for reassurance. She switched to the other song she had selected. This one was a little slower, and she hadn't finished choreographing it. She only had a couple more weeks to finish the choreography.

Eden closed her eyes, took a deep breath, and fell into the fluid motions that went with the lyrics. 'Thank you for all you've done. You gave me love when I had none.' She dipped forward, gracefully extending her leg behind her.

She heard a click from the doorway which startled her out of the correct position. She almost fell on her face, but she caught herself with her hands as she turned around. Someone had come into the room, but Eden calmed down when she realized it was Xander.

"Hey," he said.

"Oh, it's you," Eden said. She didn't ever let someone see her dancing. It was kind of embarrassing, and no one else really understood the beauty of the art and how much she loved it.

"You sound disappointed." Xander came over and sat next to her on the foam mat. "Look, I'm . . . I'm sorry about walking off. I want to help you, but-"

"It's okay. I don't need help, Xander. I've got it."

"No, but I want to help you. I said I would, and I'm going to."

"What if I don't want your help?" Eden asked. She didn't need a coach who got mad at her for nothing. That only made her more stressed out. "I just want to enjoy the time I have left," she said, "instead of wasting every second training."

"I don't want this to be the only time you have left," Xander told her. "I want to do what I can to make sure you win a medal. Maybe running wasn't where we should focus our time. Maybe we should focus on one of the mental tests, like math or something."

"*You* could help me with math?" Eden asked. Xander had always done badly in math classes, so it was good he knew how to wrestle.

"Well, maybe I wouldn't teach you how to do it or anything, just quiz you with questions and see if you got the answers right."

Eden hung her head, pulling her bottom lip into her mouth as she thought. "I just . . . I- I don't want to think about the Olympics for a day or for a week or something. I just want to be happy."

Something sneaky popped into Eden's head. Something she had been thinking about for a long time, at least a year. The closer they got to the Olympics, the more she thought about it.

"I want you to be happy too," Xander was saying.

Eden took a big breath. She started to talk, "I was thinking. I don't know. This is weird, but . . . never mind."

"What?" Xander asked. "What's weird?"

Eden met his dark green eyes and shook her head, shrugging and smiling at the same time. She was so dumb. She shouldn't bring it up.

"What?" He asked, curious now. "If you don't tell me, I'll put you in a headlock, and you know I can do it."

Eden shook her head, and Xander made good on his promise, grabbing her by the neck so that her face was squished next to his not-so-nice-smelling armpit. "Tell me!" he demanded playfully.

Eden laughed as she fought against him, but he wouldn't budge. "Fine!" she shouted. He released her, and Eden rubbed her neck. She waited, and the silence stretched out in front of them.

"Well?" Xander asked.

"You didn't say *when* I had to tell you," Eden teased back.

"Hey! Do you need me to put you in another headlock?"

"No!" Eden said, holding her hands up in front of her.

Xander smiled at her, and Eden took a deep breath. She was just going to say it. The worst he could do was say no. *Just say it,* Eden encouraged herself mentally. Another deep breath. Another letting it out. She was waiting too long. She had to say it now, or she never would.

"Well, I know we talked about it, like, six months ago and everything. And we were both, like, yeah, we kind of like each other, but we should focus on training and the competition, and then see what happens afterward. But yeah. . . I mean, if I'm eliminated, there is no afterward. So I was just think-ing, that maybe . . . well, I don't know. I don't want to be eliminated and never have kissed anybody. I know it's silly, but yeah, like, I don't know." Eden finally looked up at Xander, and he smiled at her.

She couldn't tell if he was laughing at her or what, so she started babbling again. "I mean, like, you don't have to do it. But you wanted to know what I was thinking, so now you know. But yeah, I only have maybe a month left, and I just thought. . .well, yeah."

Xander started laughing, and Eden stuck her tongue in her cheek, trying to figure out what was so funny.

"You said all that to say you want to kiss me?" Xander finally asked when his laughter subsided.

Eden shrugged, feeling pretty dumb now. "No, it's whatever, I mean. I know we both kind of like each other, but you're right, we should just focus on the Olympics, and then, well . . ."

"I don't think one kiss would make a difference on whether we get medals or not. So. . .why not?"

"Why not?" Eden repeated. And now that she had asked and Xander had kind of agreed, everything felt even more awkward. Nobody was supposed to talk about kisses before getting them. It was just supposed to be something that happened.

"So . . . like, right now?" Eden asked, biting her lower lip and wincing with how awkward she was.

"Yeah, why not?" Xander asked. He chuckled and started leaning forward. Eden slammed her eyes shut. She had already gotten so many things wrong today. She had to at least get the eyes shut part right.

She smelled Xander's salty mix of sweat and deodorant as he leaned forward and touched his lips to hers, pressing harder into her lips. Eden felt butterflies rise in her stomach, her body playing music all of its own as she tasted Xander.

He pulled back, and Eden smiled. Kissing wasn't so hard after all. Xander studied her for a second before looking away, facing the wall that didn't have a mirror.

"So," he said. "Do you want to train some more?"

"No, I kind of just want to lay here and do nothing," Eden responded. She relaxed back on the mat, staring at Xander until he looked back at her.

She couldn't believe he had just kissed her, even though she had kind of pressured him into it. She couldn't wipe the smile from her face.

"Nothing is good sometimes too," he responded, leaning back on his hands before turning his face away from her again.

When Eden arrived home, her mother was already in the kitchen cooking dinner. Eden hoped to slide right through the living room to her bedroom, but her mother's hearing was better than a dog's.

"Eden! You're home!" she said excitedly.

Eden cocked an eyebrow at her. Her mother wasn't usually this excited about anything, and Eden's birthday had just passed. What other surprises could her mother have in store?

"I talked to your father this morning," she said.

Eden approached the table and gripped the back of her chair for support as she waited for whatever her mother might spring on her.

"We've decided to hire a tutor."

Eden felt like the breath had been knocked out of her. Tutors were expensive. Some even came with money-back guarantees if your child was eliminated, but Eden didn't think that clause would apply to her since she was just starting tutoring a month before the Olympics.

"I don't know if. . ." Eden started to protest. She didn't want to ask how much it cost, but she knew it wasn't cheap.

"We've already paid for your first session. She's going to work with you on the mental tests. She's only twenty, so she was in your same place two years ago."

Eden nodded slowly. She wanted to ask why her parents were even trying. They should just give up, but then, Eden saw her mother's face, the quivering showing that she was struggling not to cry.

"Uh, when's she coming?" Eden asked, hoping that she could keep her mother from crying.

"Your first session will be tomorrow. She's coming at 4:00. Please be back from the training center by then."

"Yeah, I'll be here," Eden said. Eden's stomach filled with guilt as she went into the bathroom to shower away the sweat from her running practice and dancing. Here she was, basically throwing away her opportunity to win so she could enjoy her last month. Meanwhile, her parents were scraping together money to pay for a private tutor. Eden should try harder, try her best.

Still, as much as she resolved to focus on the competition again, Eden was confident that if she checked her ratings, she would fall apart. As she rubbed the shampoo into her long, brown hair, she thought about Xander kissing her. It hadn't taken much convincing to get him to do it. If they both *did* get medals, would he want to live happily ever after? Eden wasn't sure she would ever find out.

Chapter 6

Xander had a specific routine for when he arrived home from the training center. He put away all of his wrestling gear and washed anything that needed to be washed. He hung it up to dry in his room, then showered. He liked his routine, because it helped him stay grounded, especially when he had so little control over things.

When he got home today, though, his mother was lying on the couch. She hadn't moved all day.

"Mom, you okay?" Xander asked.

His mother started to answer, but she coughed instead. Xander winced. He had learned long ago that no amount of back patting could help her coughing. He just had to wait until she stopped.

"I'm sorry," she said. "I was going to cook some dinner for you and your father, but . . . I took a nap. And when I woke up, I felt more tired than I was before."

"Don't worry about it," Xander said. "I can cook something. Do we have any rice?"

"I think so."

Xander set his gym bag on the counter and went around the bar to check the cabinet. There was a half-full bag of rice which Xander took off the shelf.

His body was exhausted, so he shuffled around the kitchen without talking as he got the rice started and looked around for some sort of meat. The only meat was frozen. Xander shut the freezer and went into the fridge again. No meat. They would have to get protein from lentils that night. He grabbed an onion and took it to the cutting board.

Xander's thoughts turned to the time he had spent with Eden earlier- the kiss they had shared. It had been awkward, sure, but it wasn't bad either. Still, he had to remind himself that neither one of them was guaranteed adulthood. It was better not to get off track right now. His mother said something, but Xander couldn't hear her over the chopping of the knife against the wooden cutting board.

"Yeah, Mom?" he asked, going around the bar again.

"How was your training today?" his mom asked.

"Good," Xander said, glancing at his bag. He should go ahead and wash his things. The rice and lentils were cooking, and they didn't need babysitting. He took his wrestling shorts into the bathroom and rinsed them in the sink before scrubbing them with soap.

Once Xander had showered and taken the food off the stove, his mom got up from the couch. "Your father should be home in a couple of minutes," she said, settling into her chair at the table. "I'm not hungry. Just give me a little."

"Mom," Xander told her. "You're supposed to eat a lot. Remember what the doctor said last time?"

"I know, Xander," his mom responded, not amused with his reminder.

"Are you going to go to the doctor again and see if it's progressed?" Xander sneaked around the outlawed 'c' word.

"No, I can't go to the doctor again, Xander. I don't want to talk about it. I'll be better tomorrow. Sometimes, I just have tired days."

Xander knew better than to argue with his mom. His dad came through the door whistling a cheery tune, and Xander hugged his dad before remembering that the stove was still on.

The rice had browned nicely on the bottom, and Xander began scooping the food into three different bowls. He hoped his dad wouldn't say anything about the quality of the dinner. His mom already felt bad enough.

Everyone chewed in silence, Xander glancing at one or the other of his parents between bites. They were both quiet that evening, and Xander kept thinking about the day he had spent with Eden.

"Xander, how did your training go?" his father finally asked when he was halfway done with his plate.

"It went well," Xander responded.

"Good, have you checked your rankings?" his father asked.

"I don't like to check that," Xander reminded his father. "They can be rigged, and..."

His father glared at him. "Check your ranking when you're done eating," he said.

Xander hated that stupid website and wished it had never been invented, but he would do what his father said. Once he shoved the last spoonful of mostly tasteless rice into his mouth, Xander marched to his room and opened his laptop to the website. Once he clicked on the ranking, he remembered that Eden had updated him recently. Had she said he was seventh or eighth? It was something like that.

Xander's fingers mechanically clicked the right buttons, and he pulled up the wrestling category for his weight. He checked seventh and eighth, but he wasn't in either one. He scrolled down and saw himself in the nineteenth spot. Had he really dropped so many spots in one day?

Xander stared at the number again, trying to make sure he saw it correctly. Because of the number of eighteen-year-olds, he would still win a medal in nineteenth, but not if he continued that same downward trend.

"Where are you?" his father asked from the doorway.

"Nineteenth."

His father grunted and left the room. Xander took a deep breath. He had to work harder and train more if he was going to keep his place. Suddenly, Xander didn't feel tired. He couldn't spend the next four hours pacing around his room and waiting to fall asleep. He would go for a bike ride.

Xander left his room, not trying to be sneaky, but not announcing his departure either. His mother was lying on the couch.

"Where are you going? It's almost dark."

"It's only seven o'clock," Xander reminded her. Dark meant nothing when it came to living in Greenland.

"Be safe," his mother warned him.

"I will." Xander shoved his bike through the front door, annoyed that his mother thought he was going out trying to get hurt or something. Didn't she think he was smarter than that?

No, he was going to casually ride by Eden's place and see if she was out. If she was, then they could talk. If she wasn't, then he would bike until his muscles burned, maybe see if Connor was doing something other than going to a big party tonight.

He started up the steep hill, his muscles rejoicing at being used. The last rays of sunlight ducked behind the trees on his left as he broke into a sweat.

When he reached Eden's apartment complex, she wasn't sitting in the grassy area, so he circled the building a time or two, hoping she would come out. He wasn't sure what he would say if she did, but he knew that he wanted to spend more time with her. He could have just texted her, but he wasn't sure what to say exactly.

He smiled when he thought of how cute she had been asking him for a kiss, but the meaning behind it couldn't be forgotten. She was sure that she was going to be eliminated. Xander couldn't think about that, but he couldn't forget it either.

Just when Xander was giving up and deciding what route he would take back down the hill, Eden emerged from the stairway in the middle of the apartment building.

"Hey," she said, waving to him but staying by the stairs as he whipped by her on his bike. He skidded around the end of the parking lot and came back to her at a slower pace.

"Hey," he responded, stopping right in front of her.

"My parents are hiring a tutor for me," she said.

Xander's eyebrows rose. Tutors weren't that unusual, but it was a little late for that. "What subject?"

"Mental, but I don't know what specifically. I guess she'll see what I know and pick the one I'm not hopeless at."

Xander read the fear in her voice. "That's good. Someone working with you one-on-one will really help."

Eden nodded but kept her eyes trained on his bike. She opened her mouth to say something, then closed it again. Xander slid his hands across the handlebars, the grips picking at his calluses. She started to say something again, but didn't.

"What?" Xander said, poking her in the side. "Are you going to ask me for another kiss? You don't have to ask me every time, you know."

"That's *not* what I was going to say, but good to, um. . . know."

"Just say it. You've never been shy around me before." Xander ran a hand through his hair, and the ends stuck up straight from his workout.

"Well, talking about your upcoming elimination is kind of a conversation killer, but it's all I can think about."

"Then, talk about it."

"But you'll just try to encourage me to train some more. You'll tell me I can do it, and I want to believe that. But . . . I don't think it's true."

"So what do you want me to say?" Xander asked. He didn't understand. Did she want him to pretend that it was okay that she might be eliminated? Because it wasn't okay.

"I just want you to . . . understand. I don't know what happens when I'm eliminated."

Xander's heart sped up. Everyone had heard the rumors, but none of the judges had ever confirmed what being eliminated really meant. "Say what you need to say. I won't judge you or tell you that you're going to win a medal if that's what you want. Just say it."

"There's so many rumors about what elimination really means. Do you think I'm going to be killed? Do you think they'll just shoot me and bury my body somewhere?"

Eden gripped his handlebar tightly as Xander rolled his bike forward and backward. Her words hit him in the back of the head, but he kept his mouth closed. The truth was that he had no idea what elimination really meant. He couldn't reassure her if he didn't know himself.

"These girls last year said that they thought when people were eliminated, they were just taken to the overheated parts of the planet and left to die. I don't even know which one's worse. I mean, I'd rather die right away than suffer, I think. But I don't know."

"You-" Xander stopped himself, remembering that she didn't want him to fix her problem.

She studied his face. "Someone else said that they use you as an experiment. You know. . ."

"I've heard," Xander nodded. "But I don't think they really use you as a test subject. They have animals for that."

Eden bit her lower lip, and Xander could see that she was going to cry. She had never been the type to cry all that much, but facing potential death was enough to make anyone cry.

"Xander," she said. Xander got off his bike and wrapped his arms around her. Someone came down the stairs, and Xander moved both of them out of the way as Eden sobbed on his shoulder.

"I don't want to die or suffer or anything like that. I can't," she said.

Xander patted her on the back, wondering if he was allowed to comfort her now or if he was still supposed to keep his mouth shut. He swallowed hard and listened to Eden's fears.

"Some of the most annoying humans in the country will win medals, and those of us who are nice and try and . . . we won't."

"Are you calling me annoying?" Xander asked.

"Not you." Eden sniffed and wiped at her eyes as she looked up at him.

Xander remembered what he had told her about not having to ask if she wanted another kiss, but he didn't think this was the time. "Okay, good to know you haven't just been faking our friendship all this time."

A raindrop fell on Xander's head, and he looked up at the night sky. He pulled Eden to him again, squeezing her so that she would understand he was there for her even as she faced the scariest thing in her life.

Another few raindrops splattered on his head, and Eden seemed to notice them. "You should probably go home before it starts really raining," she said. "I don't want you to slip on that hill."

"Okay," Xander agreed. "You know my phone number. Text me."

"So I can keep whining to you?" Eden half-joked, her face still the picture of grief.

"Yeah, exactly. Your whining keeps me from thinking about my own problems."

"Like what?" Eden asked.

"My mom," Xander responded. How could she forget?

"Oh, yeah." Eden squeezed Xander's arm and stepped back under the shelter of the stairs. Xander climbed on his bike and started down the hill, keeping his speed to a minimum so he wouldn't slip. The last thing he needed was a broken leg right now.

Chapter 7

Eden glanced at the time on her phone again. She had learned to decipher the time through the myriad of cracks, and she knew that there were only two more minutes until her tutor would arrive.

Eden straightened her books on the table so that they lined up perfectly with the edge. She glanced at her computer but refused to check the ratings. It wouldn't help her right now. She needed to focus on studying. Eden opened up her math book and re-read the section on probability. She could do a simple math equation if it was laid out in front of her. Her problem was figuring out what equation to do when it wasn't specifically stated.

Tap, tap.

Eden straightened and approached the door. When she opened it, an adult who looked like she could be the same age as Eden waved at her.

"Hi! You must be Eden."

"That's me," Eden said, motioning for the adult to come inside. "Uh, what's your name?" Her mom had said it that morning, but it had flown in one ear and out the other.

"Claire," the adult responded, settling down at the table across from where Eden had been sitting. Eden sat in her seat self-consciously.

"So, Mom said we have two hours," Eden told Claire, then realized how dumb that sounded. Claire would know. She was the one being paid.

"I think the best way to start would be to do a quick evaluation of the mental tests and see where you're strongest. We'll focus on that area."

"Okay." Eden nodded. "I can tell you that science is probably my strongest one, but it's still not . . . very strong."

"That's okay. That's what I'm here for," Claire assured her. She pulled out her own stack of books. "I've got questions on my tablet here that are specifically for the Olympics. None of these questions will be on the actual tests, but they give you a good idea of what you need to know."

Claire flipped casually through different screens on her tablet as Eden's stomach turned pirouettes inside her. "Let's do a few math questions," Claire said. "Let's start with finding the area of this shape. What's the area of it?"

Eden evaluated the convoluted shape. It had so many bits and pieces that it would be hard to figure out. "Well, I know the main part has an area of 56," she said. "Well, no, I guess not, because of that small square. So, it would be nine, not eight." Eden clamped her mouth shut so Claire wouldn't have to hear all of her uneducated rumbling.

"Keep thinking. Speed is helpful, but not essential. Think about it. If you know the correct process, I can teach you some ways to speed it up."

Eden nodded and turned her head to look at the shape from a different direction.

"Can I . . . use my screen to take notes?" she asked.

"Yes," Claire said. "Go ahead. Show your work."

Eden slid her calculator closer to herself and punched in number after number, noting the ones she wanted to remember on the screen next to the problem. "I think, uh, 202?" She peered uncertainly at Claire.

"No, but that's okay. You gave it a good shot. I'll come back and explain it in a minute. Let's go through a couple more."

Eden did the same painful calculations over and over as Claire watched. After fifteen minutes, she had only gotten one math problem right.

"I think math is probably not the subject we should pursue. Let's go on to science. You said you were strong there. Can you explain how to predict the genotypes a child could potentially have based on its parents?"

Eden nodded, finally confident about something. She rambled on about the Punnett square, and Claire congratulated her. Then, she tapped a few things on her screen. "Okay, let's see what you can do here. You need to pick the three ingredients necessary to make gunpowder."

Eden's eyes widened. Had she heard Claire correctly? Claire nodded at her encouragingly, so Eden looked at the options on the screen. Suddenly, the letters of the periodic table mixed together in her mind, and she couldn't even figure out what her options were. She clicked on three and waited. The screen buzzed at her.

"I guess that wasn't it?"

"You were one ingredient away from gasoline, but not close to gunpowder."

"Well, I never really did that stuff in science class. We mostly worked on learning how the body works and . . . stuff like that."

"Okay, one last evaluation, then we'll be ready to choose your focus."

Eden nodded, her hands twisting and untwisting in her lap.

"Let's do a few logic puzzles. This is the hardest area to improve. So, if you're naturally talented, then we'll keep practicing. But if you're not, then I say drop the logic competition altogether so you can spend as much time studying for science as possible."

Eden swallowed and listened carefully as Claire laid the question out before her.

"It occurs once in a minute, twice in a moment, but never in an hour."

Eden's mind kicked into high gear. A second occurred in every hour, more than one. That couldn't be it. Maybe breathing? What else did she do once a minute? Blinking? Eden's heart beat more often.

"Can you, uh, repeat it?" she asked.

Claire repeated the riddle.

"Uh, I guess . . ." Eden shook her head, knowing she was wrong even as she gave the answer. "Breathing?"

"No, I breathe more than once a minute. Don't you?"

"Well, I don't know."

"The letter m," Claire answered.

Eden thought about the riddle again and nodded. "Oh, I wasn't thinking about it like that." She was terrible at guessing things, but when her life depended on it, she would keep trying her best.

"Let's try another one. Remember that you want to think outside the box. Is it legal for a man to marry his widow's sister? Why or why not?"

Eden took a deep breath. Outside the box. His widow's sister. That would make the sister his sister? No, that wasn't right. His sister-in-law. He could marry his sister-in-law. Unless she was already married.

"It's not legal," Eden responded, trying to sound confident.

"Why not?" Claire prompted.

"Because his sister-in-law is already married?"

Claire shook her head, and Eden's hopes plummeted. She dug her nails into the side of the table as Claire explained. "His widow's sister. If she is a widow, that means that the man is dead. He can't marry her because he is dead."

"Oh," Eden started chewing on her bottom lip as Claire flipped through some different slides on her screen.

"Let's try this one. What number is missing in the pattern? 16, 06, 68, 88, mmmm, 98."

Eden thought it was strange that Claire said zero six, instead of just six. "Can I see the numbers?" she asked. "I do better seeing."

"Sure." Claire tapped her screen, then turned it so that it was facing Eden. Eden studied the numbers in front of her. They were all even numbers, so whatever she chose should be even. But other than that, she couldn't see a pattern. She squinted at the numbers. She thought it should end with six or eight, but she wasn't sure which or why.

Holding her breath, she finally made a guess. "78."

"Yes!" Claire's eyes went wide. "How did you know? What was your clue?"

"Well, they were all even, and here, it seems like just counting by tens with an eight on the end. It seemed like it would fit."

"So you didn't figure out the pattern," Claire looked disappointed. "If you turn the number upside down, you're counting by ones. Look, 86, 87, 88, 89, 90, 91."

"Oh," Eden stared at the screen that was now upside down. She felt stupid.

"I think you're right," Claire said, "we should focus on science. That's your strongest area."

It might be her strongest, but that still didn't mean she was good at it. "Okay, how should I study?" Eden glanced at the time and saw that thirty-two minutes of their two hours had been spent determining her strongest area.

"You know that scientists are in high demand," Claire told her, holding eye contact until Eden squirmed. "Science is one of the last competitions, so you won't be competing against as many others. People will have won other medals along the way and dropped out before that competition. Do you know your current ranking?"

"This morning, I was one eighty-two," Eden admitted.

"That's not unredeemable. You have to consider that some of the people above you in science might take the math test, for example, win a medal, and drop out of the Olympics."

Eden nodded slowly. She had never thought about it like that before. Maybe she really did have a chance!

"You need to memorize these elements and how they can be combined. Fifty percent of the questions on my science test focused on that."

"What competition did you win a medal in?" Eden asked.

"Logic," Claire admitted. "But I took all the other tests and participated in all of the competitions so I could become a tutor and have experience in each one of them. Let's focus on you. I'm going to call out one of the abbreviations. I want you to tell me what it stands for and how it can be used."

Eden swallowed. "Okay, I can try."

"We'll start easy. H."

"Hydrogen."

"Yes, now how can it be used?"

Eden searched her mind for the answer. The only thing that kept popping into her head was "hydrogen peroxide" even though she had no idea what that meant. She blurted it out anyway.

Claire blinked. "Yes, it is, actually. There are many other uses for it as well. What else contains hydrogen?" Claire glanced at her screen, then back at Eden.

"H_2O?" Eden asked.

Claire nodded. "Yes, but what else?"

Eden grimaced as she tried to think of something else that contained hydrogen. She shook her head. "I can't think of anything else."

"Hydrogen is one of the most common gasses or chemical elements on the earth. It's used in a lot of things." Claire read the list of things, and Eden's mouth dropped open.

"Do I have to memorize all of those?" she asked.

"You should," Claire said. "You never know what they're going to ask. With hydrogen being the most common chemical element, you should definitely know its uses."

Eden took a deep breath. "Can you repeat them for me?"

Claire read the list slowly, and Eden muttered each word after her.

"Repeat them back to me," Claire said, and Eden listed hydrogen peroxide, fertilizer, and ammonia. Claire continued to stare at Eden, waiting for her to say another one, but Eden shook her head.

"It's like they disappear from my brain as soon as I hear them.

"What do you typically do to study material?"

"I just study it and try to remember."

"You need to take an active part in remembering," Claire suggested. "Don't just stare at the screen and hope the information will jump into your brain. Write it."

"We don't have any paper," Eden said, glancing at the stack of used papers that had been used to make a giant eighteen on her birthday. "Unless there is still space on those."

"It doesn't have to be with pencil and paper. It can be on a screen. Open your notes app. Now, click the 'draw' tool. I want you to write each of these as I read them to you."

Eden wrote them down. Her writing was messy and hard to read. Why she couldn't just type the names she wasn't sure. This seemed like a lot of work for nothing. She still didn't remember anything.

"Okay, close the app and look at me."

Eden followed the directions, still fidgeting with the stylus.

"How can we use hydrogen?"

"Rocket fuel, hydrogen peroxide, ammonia . . . fertilizer."

"No, the ammonia goes into the fertilizer, so that's the same thing."

"Okay, well, we can also use it for . . . hydrogen acid."

"Hydrochloric acid, yes. What else?"

Eden squeezed her eyes shut and tried to remember what she had written, but it was gone. It was like her brain couldn't remember it no matter how hard she tried. "I don't know," she admitted quietly.

"That's okay. We have a start. Let's focus on what each of the letters in the periodic table represents. Next session, we can talk about how they are used.

In fact, you can study that before our next session, and we can review it together."

"Okay," Eden agreed, even though it wasn't okay at all. Claire began throwing letters at her, and Eden was only able to identify 25% of the elements. She had to write every one that she got wrong, and she didn't want to admit to Claire that she had guessed on a few of the ones she had gotten right.

Eden's mom walked in the door and waved to her with a smile as she passed wordlessly into the kitchen and began to prepare dinner. Eden tried to keep her voice down so that her mom wouldn't hear how many she was getting wrong.

"Well, that about wraps up our two hours," Claire said, putting her screen in her bag alongside the book she had brought. She smiled sweetly at Eden, then lowered her voice to a whisper. "Eden, I think you're a sweet girl, but I have to be honest with you. The only way you're going to win a medal is if you cheat."

Eden's stomach dropped. Cheat? She had never cheated on anything in her life. It was against the rules. "I . . . can't," she responded, blinking several times to hold back the fear that was gripping her. She couldn't cheat.

"We have a couple of minutes left. I can show you a few cheats," Claire explained.

Eden just stared at her, so Claire began talking quickly, explaining several different methods to help her answer questions as well as sabotage her opponents. Eden absorbed the information.

"It's your decision, Eden, but I want you to have the option. I'll be rooting for you." Claire stood up and entered the kitchen to chat with Eden's mom for a moment. Meanwhile, Eden felt frozen to her chair. She couldn't cheat. It wasn't right or fair to the other contestants. But Claire, someone who had experience and knew the Olympics, said that she would be eliminated if she didn't. Eden's real choice was if she was willing to accept elimination or not.

"Bye, Eden!" Claire called as she passed back through the living room to the front door. Just as she brushed past Eden, she slipped a tiny bag of white powder onto the table. Instinct told Eden to hide it, so she slipped it into her pocket to investigate more closely when she was alone. The door shutting behind Claire was like the hammer pounding into Eden's final hope.

"Well," her mother asked from the kitchen. "How did it go?"

Eden hurried into her bedroom to avoid answering.

Her mother shouted after her. "You know, I wouldn't have won without my tutor. You do everything she says. Do you hear me?"

Chapter 8

No thanks. I don't want to train today.

Xander slammed his phone back onto his bed as he finished getting dressed. Eden was stubborn. She didn't want to be eliminated, but she didn't want to train either. If there was a rule that said she had to train every day, she would be there bright and early. But on her own . . .

Xander shook his head. He texted her back. *You sure? Training promises sweat, sore muscles, and snacks. I know you like all three of those.*

Eden replied quickly with a few laughing emojis, but nothing else. It was clear that she wasn't in the mood. Xander hoped against hope that somehow she would manage to pull it out. Maybe the tutor yesterday had given her the best tip ever and now she was so confident about winning a medal in a mental competition that she didn't even need to work on running anymore.

Xander opened his texts and saw that Connor had invited him to practice wrestling together. Xander texted him back. *Be at the center in ten minutes.* Then, he stuffed his phone into the little pouch he wore while biking and rushed out of his room.

His mother was propped up on the couch, a laptop on her lap as she tried to work. Xander winced as she had a particularly bad coughing spell when she tried to tell him goodbye. Xander waited it out, feeling each cough in his very soul. She finally stopped, a hand over her throat, and waved to him.

"I hope you can get a lot done today," Xander told his mother. His mother nodded. They didn't talk about what would happen if she didn't. His mother had excelled in the math competition. She had never worried about winning a medal, and she was now part of the team that researched and analyzed potential solutions for the global warming problem. Xander didn't understand the ins and outs of her employment, but he knew that she was good at it, unless she was feeling too sick to work.

Xander hopped on his bike, the difficulties of his life clouding his ability to focus. He glided down the hill, not needing any focus to make the correct turns to get to the training center. A car beeped its horn at him, and Xander jumped, his handlebars turning right as he tried to get out of the car's way.

Xander's bike slid on the wet pavement, and the car swerved to avoid him. The bike coasted out from under him, going left while he went right. The pavement came up to meet him, and he lay on the ground gasping for breath. In and out, he reminded himself. In and out.

Finally, his lungs remembered how to work. He evaluated his body mentally and knew that his knee had been injured. He didn't want to look, to know just how badly he was injured.

The driver had gotten out of the car and was walking over to him. He picked up his bike and rolled it over to where Xander lay, almost on the side of the road. "You okay, man?"

"Yeah, fine," Xander responded.

"Here's your bike. You should stop and check the road before you cross."

"Yeah, thanks," Xander said. "Just, uh, set my bike down there. I'll get up in a minute."

"Do you need to go to the hospital?" the man asked.

"No, no, I'm fine. Just got the air knocked out of me. Need a minute."

"Okay, well, bye then."

The man got in his car and rushed on to his job. Xander shook his head as he sat on the side of the road and stared at the wet pavement. Here he was, five minutes later, and no other car had come. It was just his luck that a car would come right when he was crossing.

Xander finally got up the nerve to look at his right knee. It was bloody, but that didn't bother him. The stinging feeling was more worrisome. If he was seriously hurt, then that would knock him out of wrestling. Without wrestling, he would have nothing.

Xander stripped his shirt off and pressed it on his knee, carefully dabbing away the blood until he could see how badly it was hurt. There was a gash down the side of his knee, and the skin had been ripped away from a space about an inch square. Not bad. Not as bad as he had first assumed.

Xander pressed his shirt into the wound, grimacing at the pain as he waited for the bleeding to stop. He couldn't let anyone see his knee. If it got around that he had a weak spot, everyone would aim for it. Xander would have to change into athletic pants instead of his usual shorts for wrestling. He had some in his locker at the training center.

Xander stood and tested out the leg. It still worked just fine. He breathed a sigh of relief and got on his bicycle again, taking his time at each intersection to see if anyone was coming.

When he arrived at the training center, his phone started ringing. Xander checked it and saw that it was Connor. He answered it. "Hello?"

"Where are you?"

"Just coming in," he responded.

"Been a long ten minutes," Connor replied, ending the call.

Xander locked his bike to the rack outside the center and started to jog toward the locker room, but as soon as he brought his knee up, he felt the pain shoot through his leg. Xander grunted and slowed to a walk. His leg didn't seem to hurt him when he walked.

Xander spun the combination on his locker and found the sweatpants he had stored in there. He didn't usually wrestle when wearing long pants, but he was going to do it today. Xander was just pulling them on over his shorts when he realized that his knee had started bleeding again.

"Great," he muttered, dabbing at it with the shirt. He shook his head. He would go one round with Connor, then pretend his mom needed him or something. He pulled up his pants and was just throwing his shirt into the locker when Connor entered.

"Whoa! You get in a fight or something? What's all that blood from?"

Xander pretended like he didn't hear him. He slapped hands with his friend. "Hey, sorry, my mom started talking to me just as I was leaving. You know how that is."

"We've got less than four weeks left," Connor said, bouncing on the balls of his feet and throwing a punch at Xander.

Xander dodged it.

"Dude, not in here. It's too crowded." Xander stretched out his arms and followed Connor out to one of the open mats. "Let me warm up."

Connor dropped to the floor and cranked out a few push ups while he waited. Xander took his time stretching, evaluating his knee as he did. It didn't seem to hurt that much. It was like an itch, annoying. He would have to ignore it.

He bounced back and forth on his feet. He felt ready.

"Let's go," he said to Connor.

Connor completed two more push ups before hopping to his feet and heading to one of the three open mats in the gym. "Sure you're ready, number 19?"

"Connor, you know I . . ."

"I know," Connor responded with a smile. "I just like to check for you. Don't worry. I'm still sixty-one, so . . . you know, if you don't help me get better, then it's really your fault if I don't win a medal."

"You have science as a fall back," Xander told him. "You've been in the top twenty for science for at least a couple months."

"First, top twenty is not a medal. Second, I want to win for wrestling," Connor responded. "I don't want to be assigned some job working on building rockets or something."

"Let's go," Xander urged him again, calling out the start.

Connor lunged at him, and Xander ducked, swerving around Connor, biding his time. Connor was strong, but he put too much effort into each one of his attempts. Xander just had to wait him out. Xander stepped back again as Connor tried to grab him around his stomach.

He ducked a potential blow, falling into his routine of ducking, parrying, and lunging. Finally, Connor got him around the middle and took Xander to the ground in one swift motion, but Xander used the smack to his advantage, rolling on top of Connor and securing his head so that he was almost cutting off his breathing. Connor hit the ground two more times before Xander let up.

He stood, the pain of his knee coming back to him like a bad memory. He wanted to examine the laceration and see if it was even worse, but he didn't want Connor to suspect he was hurt. Connor shook his head and started muttering about how Xander always took him down.

"You go straight for the throat. You're like a wolf."

Xander smiled at the compliment. "Guess you better keep training."

"Can you show me how you do that?" Connor asked.

Xander took a deep breath before responding. He didn't want to give all his tricks away. He had to look out for himself, but Connor was his friend. He didn't want Connor to be eliminated either. Why couldn't the Alaskans and the Russians be the ones who were eliminated? Then everyone in Greenland who he cared about would be safe.

"Okay," Xander said. He walked his friend through the move slowly. "It doesn't always work. If they get a hand up like this, then the move is ineffective. But most people won't be able to figure out that's what you're doing quickly enough."

"Cool, let's practice it a few times."

"Let me go get some water," Xander said, heading toward the drinking fountain. He wanted a chance to see how his knee was doing too. The dull ache wouldn't go away, and when he had faked to the right, he had needed to hide his wince.

He would just step into one of the private training rooms beside the drinking fountain and check it out quickly. Xander stepped inside without glancing at the sign and started taking off his pants when he realized that the room was occupied.

He pulled them up in embarrassment before he realized it was Eden.

"What . . . are you doing?" she asked.

"What are you doing here?" he said at the same time.

They both looked at each other. Music was playing softly in the background, and Eden quickly turned off the song. "I'm . . . uh, relaxing," she said.

Xander scanned her face and saw a line of sweat along her hairline. She was lying to him, not relaxing. Why wasn't she being honest?

"You're sweating a lot to be relaxing."

"It's hot in here," she responded. "Besides, me sweating in a room by myself isn't nearly as weird as you entering said room and taking your pants off."

"I didn't. It wasn't like that." Xander half-laughed to cover up his embarrassment. "I'm wearing shorts. I promise." Even if Eden was acting weirdly, he knew that he could trust her. He slowly slid his pants down and turned his leg so that she could see his knee.

When she saw it, her mouth dropped open. "Whoa! What did Connor do to you?"

"Nothing, I got in a bike accident this morning. I skinned it on the road."

"Does it hurt?"

"Yeah, a little bit." Xander probed at the pink skin that was near the wound. "I think it's slowed down a little." He smudged his finger into the blood, but it didn't look like it was bleeding as heavily.

"You should be more careful," she told him, like he had *tried* to almost get hit by a car.

He rolled his eyes. "Don't tell anyone. I don't know how long it will take to heal."

"Can you put your pants back on now?" she asked.

"Don't make it weird."

"Too late."

Xander covered his knee again and studied Eden across the room. Her breathing had returned to normal, but she was clearly exercising in here. He raised an eyebrow at her, and she knew what he was asking without him having to say a word.

"So, tutoring happened yesterday," she announced.

Xander nodded. "And?"

Eden motioned for him to move closer, glancing at the door. Xander frowned but went to her. She lowered her voice to a whisper. "She basically told me my best shot was science. She and I studied science for an hour, but I didn't get any better. Then she said . . . that the only way I could win a medal was by cheating."

Xander leaned back as the word hit his ears. Cheating? It wasn't like people hadn't tried before, but it was always big news when something like that was discovered. Xander wondered how many people had cheated and not been caught.

"What are you going to do?" Xander asked her.

Eden's eyes darted around the room. "I mean . . . I can't break the rules. It's not fair to everyone else, but. . ."

"But . . ." Xander encouraged her to continue speaking.

"But I don't want to be eliminated. I want the chance to become an adult, and if that means I have to cheat, then maybe . . . I don't know."

"You have time to think it over," Xander told her, his stomach flipping. He wouldn't risk cheating himself. He was confident that he could win a medal, at least he felt that way most days.

"What do you think I should do?"

"I can't tell you," Xander said, lifting his hands in protest.

"Why not? You know I can't, but if I don't, then . . . I don't have a choice. Either way, I lose."

Xander placed a hand on her shoulder, and it felt sticky under his touch. "You have to make your own decision. It's your life, but . . . I'll be here for you whatever you decide. And if you're going to cheat, do it well."

Eden half-laughed before her eyes filled with sudden tears. She swiped at them. "Sorry! Sorry! I don't know what's wrong with me. It's like I cry about everything now." She rolled her eyes at herself, and Xander pulled her into a hug, secretly hoping that she would cheat and win a medal. He needed her, especially with his mom's health the way it was. He was being selfish, but he didn't want to win a medal without her.

Part 2- The Competition

Chapter 9

Three Weeks and Four Days Later

Eden sat at the table waiting for her mother to bring the food over. It was as though everything was moving in slow motion. Her mother's arm revolved over the pan, stirring Eden's favorite pasta dish.

Eden looked down at her hands, seeing them as if for the first time. There was still a scar from where she had fallen into the glass at the party, a tiny red mark standing out against her light skin. The shadowed creases in her palms contrasted with her light skin, three lines issuing from the inner part of her palm and spreading out as they fled away from her thumb. These were her hands, and the thought suddenly seemed amazing.

Eden rolled her neck back, hearing the cracks clearly as she stared at the back of her mother's head. Her mother had brown hair, just like Eden, but hers looked uncombed today. Eden's eyes noted the tangles.

Her mother turned around, holding the spoon in the air, and Eden watched as a drop of pasta sauce descended slowly, slowly. The red sauce splattered to the floor, and everything snapped back into focus.

"... I can make for you," her mother was saying.

"Thanks," Eden nodded, motioning to the dish of garlic bread her mother had already put in front of her. Her father walked through the door. Instead of taking off his things, changing into his slippers, and avoiding the world for half an hour, he instantly came over and hugged Eden, his arms almost collapsing her ribs.

"Hey," Eden managed to get out.

Her father kissed the top of her head and went into his room to get changed into his house clothes like he always did. Eden turned to make a comment to her mother, and she saw her mother wiping away tears before they could fall.

Eden stood and embraced her mother, really taking in her scent. She smelled like lotion, like she always did. Eden knew that her mom's lotion was one thing she wanted to take with her when she left tomorrow. "I'm sorry," Eden said, apologizing for losing. She hadn't lost yet, but she could tell where everything was going. This would probably be the last time she saw her parents.

Her mother wrapped her arms around her and just held Eden there. Eden wished she could do something to make her mother feel better, but there was nothing she could do. Eden took a deep breath as the noodles on the stove began to boil over, pushing her mother into action.

"Oops," she said tearfully. Eden swiped under her eyes. She didn't want to cry the whole evening. She would have time for that when she arrived on the island and the Olympics began. Right now, she just had to be here for her parents.

Her father reemerged from the bedroom and sat at his place at the table. Eden sat in hers, and her mother brought over the rest of the food.

"I hope you like it," her mother said, and her words held more meaning than they usually did.

"It's great, Mom, thanks," Eden responded, struggling with the last word. She served herself and dove into her plate of food, wanting the meal to finish so she could go into her room for the night. She knew she should go to sleep as early as possible, but she couldn't think of anything except surviving one more day.

"Eden," her mother said. "We love you so much. We want you to know that. You have been such a light in our lives, and we love seeing all of your creative endeavors."

"I haven't been eliminated yet, Mom," Eden said, trying to bring humor into the situation, but she choked on her own words. She knew as well as they did that she wouldn't be able to bring her phone or communicate with others at home in any way. Either she won a medal and came home to fanfare or she was eliminated and never came home at all.

"We just wanted you to know." Two tears rolled down each side of her mother's face, and Eden looked away so that her mother wouldn't see her eyes filling again as well. She focused on the food, eating it one bite at a time, even though she wasn't sure if she was hungry or not. Eden wondered how Xander's last meal with his family was going. Were they crying? Cheering him on? Was his mother even able to join them at the table?

"Do you want to play a card game?" Eden's mother asked as she began collecting the dirty plates.

"I . . . not tonight," Eden responded, knowing that if it wasn't that night, it would most likely never be again. But right then, she didn't want to be around others. She tried to soften her answer. "I don't feel up to it. Thanks, though."

"Of course," her mother responded, weeping almost silently as she began to wash the plates. *Almost,* but Eden still heard her catch her breath funny every few minutes. Eden tiptoed into her room, grabbing her phone from the nightstand.

It was time.

The night had come.

There would be no graduation from high school or the training center. There was no sense of accomplishment until someone had a medal in their hand, and if they didn't win a medal, then they really didn't have any accomplishments at all.

Eden began deleting the photos and videos on her phone one by one, tears running down her cheeks as she remembered jumping off the big rock into the ocean on a dare from Xander. The time she and her mother had pretended to host a drawing show while coloring pictures. Her father teaching her to play checkers. Delete. Delete. Delete.

She left only one video on her phone. The video she had recorded that day in the private training room at the center.

When she was eliminated, her parents would have to deal with all of her things. Eden wanted to make it easy for them to see what she had made for them.

Eden placed her phone down on the nightstand and stared at her computer across the room. She shouldn't check the stats again. It wouldn't do anything to put her in a better mood before she began her travel to Upertavik Island, but still. She shouldn't know how bad it was.

Instead of checking her computer, Eden approached the little packet Claire had left with her. It was a packet that was guaranteed to knock out some of her opponents. Eden would be searched before her flight to the island. She had asked Claire how to hide it, and the older girl had given her several ideas. The detector couldn't pick it up, so she just had to make sure it was hidden well.

Eden looked at her bag in the corner. They would search her bag thoroughly, but they wouldn't search her, not as thoroughly. Realizing that this was a decision she couldn't turn back from, Eden ripped open her coat, stuffed the bag inside, and began the tedious process of sewing it back up. It wasn't the most inventive way of doing things, but she didn't have a lot of options. She had to cheat if she was going to win a medal.

Eden, the rule-follower, was going to break the rules.

Chapter 10

Xander stood in line at the airport. His father stood silently beside him, but his mother had decided not to come. If she started coughing and someone caught on to how sick she really was, then she might not still be there when Xander came home.

Xander watched as person after person was scanned, their bags opened and thoroughly searched. What they were looking for, he had no idea.

He checked the line behind him. There was Eden, staring straight ahead like she had seen a ghost. Xander waved at her, but she didn't respond. She was probably too caught up in her own thoughts. That was okay. They could talk later.

"Name," the adult standing by the metal detector stated more than asked.

"Xander Coxon."

"Put your thumbprint here," the adult indicated, and Xander placed his thumb on the pad, waiting as a light scanned his thumbprint. The man took Xander's picture, then indicated that he and his father should move forward.

Xander zipped open his suitcase, and another adult began searching through it. He watched as the man fingered his photo, opened the back of it, then closed it again carelessly. They had no right to search his luggage, but Xander huffed and let them do what they felt like they needed to do.

"Your suitcase is good to go," the adult said, zipping Xander's suitcase closed and setting it on the floor. "Let's do a quick search of you."

The adult patted down Xander's pockets and tapped his cell phone. "No phones allowed. You know the rules. Give it to your dad or turn it in here."

Xander fished his phone out of his pocket and handed it to his dad. It seemed so normal to have his phone in his pocket that he had completely forgotten.

"You can continue forward now," the adult said.

Xander left the inspection area and stood there awkwardly with his father. Other eighteen-year-olds were standing with their parents as well, none of them quite ready to say goodbye yet.

"Xander," his father said. He looked to his bulkier father, waiting for whatever wisdom he might impart. "Win a medal."

Xander nodded. "That's the plan, Daddy-O."

His father narrowed his eyes. "Xander, don't-"

"I'm going to win," Xander said with confidence he didn't possess. His eyes followed Eden as she had her picture taken. It was clear from the color of her face that she had been crying.

"You better." His father clapped him on the shoulder, a sudden movement that surprised him, and Xander winced. His father left the tiny airport, and Xander continued to stand with his suitcase while he waited for Eden.

Once her suitcase was approved, Xander watched while trying to look like he wasn't as both of her parents said goodbye to her. She started crying again, and Xander looked away. She was going to be pegged as an easy one to beat, but Xander didn't think everyone should give up on her so soon. She could still win, especially if she cheated. It wasn't like he could ask her about that here, though.

Fifteen minutes later, her parents left her, and Eden sank to her haunches beside her suitcase, her head falling forward. She was clearly too wrapped up in her own world to even notice him.

"Hey," he said.

Her head snapped up, and when she saw it was him, she launched herself into his arms. He squeezed her gently as she continued to cry.

"Eden," he chastised softly. "Why are you crying? You're going to win a medal."

"But I might not," she whispered, wiping her nose on her hands. "I might have just said goodbye to my parents for the last time."

"You can't think about that," Xander said. "Come on! This will be fun. We'll get to stay in the hotel and see a new place. You've always wanted to do that."

"Not like this. I wanted to see a new place like the way they describe in history books, taking vacations and flying all over the world for fun."

"Okay, Eden, take a deep breath." Eden followed his instructions. "Now, I want you to tell yourself that you're going to win a medal."

"I'm going to win a medal," Eden whispered.

"I want you to say to yourself, 'Xander is here for me.'"

"Xander is my crazy best friend, and he's here for me," Eden said, the tiniest hint of a smile on her lips.

"See, you've got the hang of it."

Eden swiped at her face. "Now, I want you to say to yourself that you're crazy, and you don't know how Eden has put up with your weirdness this long."

Xander obliged her. "I'm crazy, and I don't know how you've put up with me for this long."

"You've got it," Eden teased.

"Come on. Let's get to the gate so we don't miss our plane. You *are* on the 8:00 a.m. plane, right?"

"Yup." Eden pulled out her ticket. "Seat 8B."

"Aw, I'm seat 15A."

Eden shrugged. "The flight's only going to be an hour and a half, right?"

"That's what they said," Xander responded. "Then, the plane will come back for another group."

Xander led Eden closer to the gate where they were already calling seat rows, boarding from the back of the plane to the front. Xander found his seat, shoving the suitcase in the bin above his head before sitting down on the fifteenth row. The plane only had eighteen rows, so he was close enough to smell the fakely clean bathroom odor float over him. Xander wrinkled his nose as a boy took the seat next to him.

"Hey," Xander said. He didn't recognize the boy. He must be from another town in Greenland. Planes were only flying out of Sisimiut, so people who lived in other places had to drive or bike to Xander's city first, since it was the biggest one in Greenland.

The boy didn't respond. He gripped the armrests of his seat like the plane was in mid-air and coming down fast.

"I'm Xander," he said to the boy, evaluating his body style. He didn't think this eighteen-year-old would be a competition for him in wrestling. He looked more like the nerdy type that would probably go for math or science.

"Colt," the boy finally responded.

"Nice to meet you." Xander offered his hand.

The boy didn't shake it. "Not really nice circumstances," he commented.

Yes, he was definitely one of the nerdy types, always looking for the negative in everything. "What's your expertise?" Xander asked.

"Math," Colt responded. Xander wanted to punch the air. Maybe if he didn't win a medal in wrestling, he could win one for lucky guesses. "Let me guess, you're wrestling."

Xander nodded. "Though I'll compete in something else if I need to."

"Anything to get a medal, huh?" Colt asked.

Xander agreed. They were silent for a moment as Xander gazed at those boarding. Row ten, then nine, then eight filled. Eden's eyes looked round and scared as she found her seat without locating Xander. She was not acting like herself.

"So . . ." Xander said. He wasn't used to not having his phone to entertain himself if he got bored. This was going to be a strange plane ride. "Where are you from?"

"Kangerlussuaq," Colt answered fluidly. Xander frowned. He knew by the sound of it that the city was in Greenland. It had to be, but he hadn't paid attention in geography class. Other than knowing that 95% of the world wasn't safe to live in now, he didn't remember much.

"You drove here?"

"A bus brought us to the airport."

Xander nodded, interested in learning more about how everything worked. He had seen the solar panels on the plane before entering it, and part of him wondered if the solar panels had collected enough sunlight to fly them all the way to Upernavik Island. What would happen if they ran out of power mid-flight?

"You have a big family?"

"I don't want to talk about them."

Xander stuck his tongue in his cheek as he tried to think of what else he could say to this unconversational boy. "If you win a medal, what type of job do you hope to get?"

"I hope to be a scientist, but I suppose I won't know if I'll be anything until after the Olympics."

Xander glanced at the boy out of the corner of his eyes and noticed that the boy didn't look very happy. He looked frustrated or upset, so Xander shut his mouth. He would leave the boy alone if that was what he wanted.

The tiny window's cover slid open easily. It was only the size of his hand, and he had to press his face up against the glass to see anything. He saw the airport and the hills of Sisimiut where he had lived his whole life. Instead of seeing the ocean, like when he rode his bike, he was looking back on his world, his whole world up until now.

Xander pressed his finger into the wound on his right knee. It had mostly healed up since the bicycle accident. The scab had covered the skin like a snake's scaly flesh, but he had peeled it off too soon. It was a little sensitive now. Still, he wasn't worried about it presenting a problem to him when he began fighting.

"Everyone should sit down and remain seated for the duration of the flight. There will be no seat changes. You may only get up if you need to use the lavatory at the rear of the plane. If you were to need it, there is a life jacket under your seat."

Xander reached under his seat, found the puffy life jacket, and left it alone. Watch them be on their way to compete in the Olympics and the plane crash. That would be one way to get rid of the extra population!

As the plane slowly backed up, Xander smashed his nose against the window to see as much as he could. This might be his only plane ride ever, though he sure hoped he was guaranteed a seat on the one back.

The plane slowly lifted, and Xander left his stomach behind. At first, he felt sick, but then, he liked the feeling of rising. The land outside seemed to sink more rapidly than he thought possible. His whole life, summed up in one tiny town, was soon smaller than the pad of his thumb. He could see the rest of Greenland as well as the sea stretched out before him. The world was huge!

A foggy cloud blocked his view, and Xander pulled away from the window. This was the start of the Olympics- his chance to win adulthood.

After a few minutes of watching the clouds stream by his window, Xander became bored and tried to strike up conversation with his seatmate again.

"You, uh, ready for this competition?"

"How can you really be ready for it?" Colt asked, and while he might have tried to respond flippantly, he had a point. How could anyone ever be ready for something they had never done before? Practice and advice were helpful, but did that really prepare anyone?

"I guess you can't," Xander responded a few minutes later, after Colt's comment had really sunk into his head.

"Do you know what happens to you if you're eliminated?"

Xander sighed. "I've heard all the rumors."

"All of them?" Colt asked.

"I think so, unless there's something new."

"In Kangerlussuaq, everyone says that they keep you in a laboratory and take your blood and organs little by little to do experiments on your DNA. You just starve to death or go crazy while they take you apart."

"No, they wouldn't do that," Xander responded immediately. "I've never heard that before."

"It comes from a reliable source- one of the scientists who used to live in our town but moved to Nuuk to be closer to the research center once he became an adult. He said that when he came home to visit his parents."

Xander weighed the option against the elimination stories he had heard before. "I guess it doesn't matter. If you're eliminated, you won't see your family or friends again."

"You only say that because you're guaranteed a medal."

"What?"

"I know your face. You're a wrestler. You've floated between places five and twenty for the past six months. The chance of you being eliminated is approximately 1.5%."

"Why 1.5%?"

"You could get injured before you fight. Even if you were distracted by something in the audience, that would only throw off your concentration by 32% for a maximum of four seconds. It might get you thrown to the ground, but you would probably be able to turn it in your favor."

Xander blinked at the numbers. He wondered if Colt was just making them up as he went along to pull Xander's leg or if he had really calculated some sort of probability that Xander would win.

"What about you?" Xander asked.

Colt shook his head. "I only stand a chance in math, and it's much harder to calculate the chances of who will win the mental tests."

"Hey, if it counts for anything, you seem like you know your stuff," Xander told him.

Colt nodded. "It doesn't, but thanks."

"What about, uh, Eden Pearce? What's her chance of winning?"

"I don't know her," Colt frowned in concentration. "I only calculated the odds of whoever has been in the top ten in the last six months. If she was lower, I didn't calculate it. I thought if I knew the probability of everyone, it might make me lose hope."

Xander nodded, his eyes searching for the back of Eden's head. He couldn't see her brunette hair through the other heads, but he hoped that she was doing okay. Xander glanced at Colt, then out the window again, Matt looming in front of him without warning. Matt had probably boarded the plane with as much hope as Xander had, but Matt's hopes hadn't panned out very well. Xander hoped his time on Upertavik Island didn't end the same way.

He couldn't be eliminated, not like Matt was. He had to come back for his dad, or his dad wouldn't have anyone. This Colt kid seemed to think his odds were pretty good, but Xander couldn't trust the odds. He would wait until the wrestling competition came to see where he really stood.

Chapter 11

Eden stepped off the airplane. The air felt . . . not hot. It wasn't cold, no, but she didn't sweat immediately, and that was a welcome change. She looked around the strip of land once she reached the bottom of the stairs.

"Keep moving," a girl behind her shouted.

Eden shuffled out of the way, glaring at the girl's back. She better not be rude to Eden or Eden might end up targeting her. As soon as Eden had the thought, she cringed. Who was she becoming?

Xander came up behind her and patted her shoulder. "Let's go," he suggested.

Eden nodded wordlessly and followed her friend across the strip of pavement to the tall building. It looked close, but it took them at least ten minutes to walk to it, a string of eighteen-year-olds across the landing strip.

Finally, they reached the front door and had to wait in line as they were checked in. "Who did you sit with?" Xander asked.

"Some girl from school," Eden responded. "She never liked me. It was really awkward." Eden's heart thumped rapidly for no reason. Part of her was excited to see something new, but another part of her was scared out of her mind.

They got up to the front of the line, and Eden was asked to scan her thumbprint again. "It might have changed since you got on the plane," Xander joked.

"Which competitions are you registering for?" the woman asked in a bored voice.

"All of them," Eden announced.

The woman looked at her pityingly. Did she know that Eden had no chance of winning?

"Well, not wrestling," Eden justified. No use getting hurt, then not being able to participate in anything else. The woman clicked a bunch of boxes and handed the portable screen to Eden.

"Please read and sign." Eden scanned her information, saw all of the checked boxes next to the competitions, and sighed. This was it. This was really it. She scrawled her name across the screen and handed it back.

"Room 205," the woman said, handing Eden a key. "A presentation will be held tonight at 6:00 p.m. in the gathering room which is to your right. Do not be late."

Eden nodded and stepped aside so that Xander could complete his check-in process.

Eden saw helpful signs posted everywhere, but she zoomed in on the gathering room. It was huge, bigger than the training room back at home. She wondered what it would feel like to do pirouettes round and round and round that room.

"Ready," Xander said from beside her elbow.

"What room are you in?"

"318," Xander told her, showing her his key.

"I really want to go see my room. Are you coming with me?"

"No boys allowed on the girls' floor," Xander said, raising his eyebrows at her. "Didn't you hear that rule?"

"No, did the adult say it? I honestly didn't hear her say anything."

"Selective hearing," Xander said, pointing at Eden.

"Hey, I was listening to her. I promise. Are you sure you're not making it up?"

Xander shook his head, and Eden decided to believe him. She didn't want to get in trouble, though she wondered what kind of trouble she could get into when she was already slated for elimination. Thirty percent of the rising eighteen-year-olds each year were eliminated, based on the number of total births, of course. With the top ten percent taken from every competition, that left thirty percent without a medal.

"So . . . I don't want to just sit in my room for seven hours until the talk thing. I'm hungry."

Xander pointed at the sign. "Dining hall is down that way. I'm in the 12:00 shift for eating. What about you?"

Eden flipped open the envelope where her key was. "Me too. Whew! I don't want to eat by myself. Hey, do you think-" She stopped abruptly when she saw that a camera was pointed in her direction.

She lowered her voice. "They're doing the filming thing."

"Well, yeah, we've watched the Olympics every year since we were kids. There have to be cameras in order for people to do that."

"Duh," Eden finished for him. Still, she felt conspicuous as she walked down the hallway, the camera blazing a hole through her back. They reached the stairs and climbed them in silence.

"I guess see you in an hour and a half for lunch?"

"You know I won't miss a meal," Xander said.

Eden slammed into the door that led to floor two, leaving Xander to find his own way to his room. The hall was quiet except for the sound of Eden's bag bumping over the carpet. She counted the room numbers in her head. Finding 205, Eden shoved the key into the lock and turned it. The click echoed up and down the hallway. She pushed open the door and stared at the room.

It smelled stale, like it hadn't been cleaned in a long time. Eden wrinkled her nose as she advanced into the small space. It was smaller than her bedroom at home and didn't have nearly as many things in it. There was a television blasting hotel updates to the empty mattress against the opposite wall. There wasn't a bathroom, so Eden would have to find that later.

Meanwhile, she stepped up to the TV to click it off, but before she could, she saw her own face flash across the screen. It was only a second, so fast that she doubted herself as soon as it disappeared.

There were other shots of the Greenland airport as well. Families embracing and saying goodbye and kids crying as they boarded the airplane. Eden sank to the edge of the bed and stared enthralled at the screen. She had watched the games every year, but here she was, actually participating in them. She was one of the faces that the seventeen-year-olds would watch from home, searching for clues about how to win a medal.

Eden reached for her phone. Her mom should-

She felt the emptiness as soon as her hand touched the pocket where her phone should be. She couldn't tell her mother. The only way her mother would have of knowing how she was doing would be by watching the Olympics on TV. Eden swallowed hard.

She didn't want to be by herself, but she had another eighty-four minutes to fill before meeting Xander.

Eden wandered to her window, if it could be called that. It was no wider than her arm and only showed her a sliver of the world. When she peered out, she saw more ocean than she did from her home. The island was surrounded by the bluest water she had ever seen. She could see land, maybe another island, in the distance. But if she turned her head just right, she could see the ground below. She saw a track, stretching out in an oval and disappearing under the shade of a few scraggly trees.

A track.

The track.

The one where her time would either win her a medal or not.

Eden couldn't see much else, so she stopped pressing her face against the window in different positions. Instead, she walked back to the TV and stared at it. She looked for a remote but couldn't find one.

She opened the two drawers in the cabinet underneath the TV. Nothing in there. How was she supposed to change channels? Unless she wasn't. She would just be forced to watch the news all day, every day.

Eden settled for unpacking her suitcase while keeping an eye on the TV for anything important. Finally, after checking the time in the corner of the TV for the eleventh time, it was almost twelve.

She grabbed her key and headed down the stairs for food. Just as she reached the door to the first floor, she heard two voices above her. She wasn't sure what prompted her to do it, but she wanted to hear what they were saying. She shoved herself into a corner under the stairs and listened as the girls talked.

" . . . easy. They don't even seem like real competition."

"Because they don't *train* in Greenland. Once all of us win this year, then we'll have enough adults on our continent to make a move on one of the others."

"Do you think the Russians will be easy to beat? I haven't seen any of them around here yet."

"They're probably too scared to even show up."

Both of them laughed before the metallic *bing* of the door scraping open cut them off. The door slammed shut again, and Eden stayed where she was, considering what she had heard. After Eden exited the stairway, she heard an electronic sound and looked up to find a camera in her face, surveying her directly. She startled backward, banging her head on the wall.

"Ow," she winced, clutching the back of her head in pain. She heard footsteps behind her and tried to keep her pained noises to herself.

"Eden?" Xander called, ducking his head around the doorway. "I'm pretty sure the dining hall is that way." He pointed down the hall.

"Yeah, I was just exploring."

"Down a hall that's off limits?"

Eden could tell that Xander knew there was more to it, but she didn't want to explain. Luckily, he didn't push it. She took in the sheen of sweat across his forehead, and as her stomach sank, she knew that he had been exercising in his room. Of course he had! He was very focused on the Olympics while she could only sit and watch TV.

Eden bit her bottom lip with frustration at herself as they entered the dining hall. Food was offered across a menagerie of trays, just the way it had been at school. The options here were much the same too. Healthy foods and not a spot of sugar in sight.

The least healthy thing she could find was macaroni and cheese, so she grabbed it along with green beans and crackers.

"Let's sit over there," Xander suggested.

Eden followed Xander to a table, her eyes scanning all of the eighteen-year-olds. Some of them were in loud groups, laughing and having a good time. Others were eating by themselves, looking worried.

Taking a few bites of her food, Eden's nerves were on edge for whatever might happen next. A large television on the far wall was playing the same footage Eden had seen earlier.

"Isn't it weird knowing that everyone in the world is going to be watching us on television?" Eden asked. "I mean . . . if I don't win a medal, I don't want everyone to see how embarrassing that is."

"You wouldn't be the only one," Xander muttered.

The television suddenly changed from clips playing to one of the familiar reporters- Sean. He had a concerned look on his face. "Breaking news. There has been a terrible tragedy in regards to one of the planes from Russia."

Everyone in the dining hall turned and faced the television. The talking died down almost immediately.

"The pilot got out a call for help just before the accident. Let's take a quick listen."

The newsanchor's voice disappeared, and an audio recording began playing. Through the static, Eden clearly heard a distressed voice. "...solar panels are malfunctioning. We're going down! I'm trying to land in water. Coordinates are 74°00'08.6"N 6°21'14.6"W.... emergency chute."

The TV cut back to Sean's face as he nodded solemnly. "Rescue efforts are being sent to those coordinates, and should arrive within an hour. We must congratulate the pilot, Edward Millan, for his brave effort in communicating and getting us the coordinates. We will update you once we have reached the coordinates and have more knowledge about who has survived."

The news cut back to the footage of families hugging their children in the airports and groups of eighteen-year-olds walking to the hotel. All Eden could think about was what she had just heard.

As the voices in the cafeteria rose, discussing Sean's announcement, Eden couldn't help but feel the tiniest bit of relief. She wondered if everyone on the flight had died and how many competitors that was. Were they competitors who would have knocked her out of the running competition?

She was jumping to conclusions, she knew, but her mind couldn't help hopping around, wondering what this meant for *her*. Eden made eye contact with Xander, and he shook his head dolefully.

"You think it was on purpose?" he asked, his voice low.

Eden blinked a few times. "On purpose? Who would kill someone on purpose?" Well, there was the whole elimination thing, but that was different. Elimination, she knew, was done so that the world didn't outgrow the small amount of resources it had before a viable solution was found.

But sabotaging a plane?

Eden remembered the strange powder she had hidden in her jacket. Well, it wasn't that much different from what she was aiming to do, was it?

Eden quickly searched for a difference to justify herself. She would only be aiming at a couple of people, and they wouldn't necessarily die.

They might, but . . . Eden's conscience started pricking her, and she flinched. She wished she could stop thinking about it, that things could just go back to the way they had been a few years ago when the Olympics seemed far away and it was something that they talked about to scare each other.

All of a sudden, Eden didn't feel hungry anymore, so she pushed away her plate of half-eaten food. She watched as Xander pushed shovelful after shovelful of food into his mouth. He didn't seem too affected by the news. Eden turned her eyes back to the television, waiting for some sort of update.

She sat there ninety more minutes until one came.

Sean, the same news anchor as before, appeared in the middle of some footage of a group from Alaska walking into the hotel. "This just in. We have confirmed that out of the thirty-two passengers, only twelve survived, two of them with severe injuries. All twelve will be given the chance to compete as normal in the Olympics. They will be arriving at Upertavik Island later this evening. The families of the deceased will be contacted personally soon."

On hearing the announcement, Eden took a deep breath. There it was. No more guessing. Twenty people had been killed. Xander's idea still floated through her mind, the idea that maybe it wasn't an accident.

Eden felt sick. She wasn't sure that she could go through with using the drug from Claire on someone. She would be responsible for their family's grief, responsible for their friends going home without one of their companions. She couldn't do it.

"You feel okay?" Xander asked.

Eden didn't realize she had been clutching her stomach, but she did feel sick. "I don't know," she responded. "I don't feel good about this."

"About what? The Olympics?"

"About everything, about my life," she responded. "I think I'm going to stay in my room for a little bit. I'll be back at six, okay?"

"Okay. Be safe." Xander studied her closely, and Eden felt like he could see into her mind. He had told her that the cheating was her decision. Now, she had made her decision. She couldn't do it.

Chapter 12

At six o'clock, the gathering room was filled to the maximum. Xander periodically scanned it then glanced at the doorway as he waited for Eden. She hadn't come down from her room yet, but he had seen the light go out of her eyes at lunch. Something was happening in her head, and Xander hoped the others weren't getting to her. She didn't hold up well under pressure.

"Everyone should have signed in by now," an official-looking someone said, taking the stage. Xander glanced at the back of the room. *That* must be what the big line had been. He had just skipped it. He sighed as he gave up his chair and got behind the few other people who hadn't signed in either.

The person on stage continued droning on, and Xander tried to listen carefully despite his racing thoughts.

"My name is Lory Chambers, and I'm in charge of making sure that everything runs smoothly. Tonight, we're going to talk about the rules and how everything will proceed in the next few days. Some of you may think that you know everything about how the Olympics work because you've watched them on TV. However, there is a lot that happens behind the scenes. I'll wait for the rest of you to take your seats."

Xander hurriedly typed in his name and pressed his thumb against the screen. He acknowledged the big, green check mark and glanced at the doorway one more time. Eden was just hurrying inside.

He pointed at the screen and waited for her to sign in, feeling like this Chambers lady's eyes were boring into them both meanwhile. He would ask Eden later why she hadn't arrived on time. She hated being late for anything, and it wasn't like her trip from the hotel room to the gathering room was a long one.

The only two chairs left together were in the middle of the gathering room, so they trekked down the aisle as quietly as possible. Lory Chambers scanned the audience again, which had started talking when she had stopped speaking.

"Silence, please," she said. Everyone quickly complied. "The first thing we will go over is how things will proceed here, in the hotel. The only places you have permission to go are your room, the dining hall, and the training space on the sixth floor. There is also a viewing room beside the lobby where you can watch movies or videos. You may *not* leave the building for any reason unless a competition is taking place and you wish to view it."

Eden raised her eyebrows at Xander, and he shrugged. Maybe someone had tried to run away from the competition before. It wasn't like there was anywhere to go, though.

"Does everyone understand the rules about where you may be?"

A few heads nodded, but one girl in the front row raised her hand. "Excuse me, what are the consequences for not obeying those rules?"

Lory shook her head, and Xander heard her make some sort of snorting noise into the microphone. "You shouldn't ask."

Xander felt something on his arm and looked down. Eden had placed her hand there, and she started squeezing. Her knuckles were turning white.

"Don't worry about it," Xander whispered to her. "You won't break the rules, so it doesn't matter."

Eden's grip relaxed only a little. Maybe the idea of elimination was feeling as real to her as it was to him. Xander paid close attention to what Lory said next.

"There are screens throughout the lobby area, the dining hall, and the training room so that you can see an upcoming schedule of events. The first event will be wrestling, and that will begin tomorrow at 9:00 a.m. If you registered for wrestling, please check the screens, so you know when your match will start.

"By 8:30 tomorrow, a clear path will be marked if you wish to make your way to the gym to view the wrestling matches. There will be two sets of matches. If you lose in the first round, you will be out of the competition. If you lose in the second round, you will also be out and have no chance of winning the medal. Those who win both rounds will be compared based on their performance to see who will win the medals.

"If you win a medal in wrestling, you will receive that medal in a ceremony here after all matches are complete. Even if you win a medal in the first event, you will be required to stay the duration of the Olympics until transportation is ready to take back all winners.

"As I'm sure you've noticed, there are cameras everywhere. These are for your safety as well as to keep everyone back home updated on the events here."

Xander nodded. Everything was straightforward enough. Wrestling being first meant that he would know tomorrow if he had won a medal or not. His stomach felt queasy, but those were just nerves. He had won hundreds of matches. He had to win when it counted tomorrow.

"Do you want to check the schedule?" Eden asked him, her nails still digging into his arm.

"Uh . . . let's give it a minute. Everyone's going to rush to check it."

Sure enough as soon as Lory dismissed them, waves of eighteen-year-olds rushed to the screens in the lobby and dining hall. Eden and Xander were the only ones who stayed in their seats.

"I'm kind of glad wrestling is first," Eden said. "I can watch the competition, since it's the only one I'm not competing in."

"Hey! What about cheering me on?" Xander teased her. "Don't you have some sort of cheer so I know someone's pulling for me?"

"I'm sure a *lot* of people are pulling for you."

"Yeah, but they won't be watching in the room. I can't hear cheers from the other side of the television." Xander was aware of one of the cameras slowly turning and scanning the room before stopping on them. He kept his eyes on Eden so she wouldn't see it.

"Fine. Xander, Xander, you can do it!" Eden half-cheered.

Xander shook his head. "That was weak."

Eden rolled her eyes but started smiling. "How's this?" She glanced around the mostly empty room and stood up, pumping her arms up and down. "Xander Coxon, strong as an oxen!"

Xander laughed at that one. "Okay, that was good. I'll give you points for that. Use it tomorrow!"

"You don't even hear anything when you're wrestling." Eden stuck out her tongue at him. "It's like the rest of the world doesn't exist."

Xander shrugged. "Hey, I do what I have to do to focus."

Eden started stretching, throwing herself down on her legs in ways that Xander could never do. The thought of performing a split made his legs ache. He sat in comfortable silence while his mind wondered what was on the screens in the lobby.

"Want to check the screens now?" he finally asked Eden.

"I'm just waiting for you," she said.

Xander stood up, bent over backward as his back cracked, and strode toward the other side of the gathering room. The lobby was still kind of crowded, but he only had to use his elbows twice to get through to a screen.

Xander started scrolling through the schedule, and he stopped on his name. He was in match 52, set to take place at 9:40. His opponent was listed as Jayce M. from Alaska. Xander nodded. He would have to win that round to advance to the next level. If he won his second match, he was almost guaranteed a medal as long as his form was good and his take down time was short. Xander nodded. He could win two matches.

Eden's hand was on his back as she tried to peer over his shoulder, bringing him back to reality. "What time?" she asked.

"9:40," he answered. "I guess it doesn't matter if you're a morning person or not here."

"9:40 is not early," Eden told him. "You met me on the track before that."

Xander's mind could barely focus on their conversation as he realized that in less than sixteen hours, his match would begin. "I'm going to . . . go to bed," Xander said.

Eden frowned at him. "You haven't eaten since lunch."

"I kind of had a lot then," Xander told her, and Eden smiled.

"I guess that's true, but it's . . . early. Why do you want to go to sleep?"

"I just want to go to my room," Xander told her. He didn't want to hurt Eden's feelings, but she wasn't the one with a medal on the line tomorrow. He needed to get his head in the right place.

"Well, sleep well, and I guess I'll see you in the morning."

"Okay, you too," Xander said. He hurried to the stairs and walked up them.

When he reached the third floor, though, he didn't stop. He kept climbing the stairs, up and up until he was at the sixth floor. That was as far as they went. He pushed through the door, strode across the hall, and entered the training facility. He wanted to keep moving. He didn't want to be cooped up in his room. He had to move.

Xander looked around the training facility which looked just like the one from back home. There were no new machines or fancy equipment. He walked the length of the room, looking for another door, somewhere to keep moving, but there was nothing.

Xander shook his head, feeling the pressure of tomorrow building up in his head. He walked down the stairs to the ground floor again, then turned around and jogged up to the top.

His breath came in short gasps, and Xander focused on pushing himself more and more. He didn't want to be able to think, so he pushed himself harder. His legs burned, but he continued to pick them up and put them on the next stair.

More. He had to do more.

Even as his legs protested and his lungs ached for air, Xander pushed himself harder and harder and harder, his mind working.

He stumbled on a stair and fell onto the landing just above it. He gasped for air for a minute, the sharp edge of the landing pressing into his stomach.

"You okay?" a voice asked.

Xander slowly rotated his head until he could see who was addressing him. It was that boy from the plane, though Xander couldn't remember his name.

"Yeah," Xander sputtered.

"Is it normal for you to lie on the stairs? By all indications, you appear to have fallen."

"Yeah," Xander responded again. "I did."

"Would you like a hand up?" The boy pushed his glasses up his nose and extended his hand.

Xander forced his arms to move again, and he grabbed the boy's hand. "Thanks," he said, the muscles in his legs physically shaking from all of the exercise he had done. They both stood there for a minute, and Xander searched for something else to say.

"Good luck," he told the boy, trying to figure out what landing he was on and which direction his room was in.

"Thanks. You too, Xander."

Xander nodded, ducking to see the number on the floor below him. Floor three. His floor. Xander nodded at the boy again, then made his way slowly to his room.

He sat on his bed, the television blaring the news at him, updating him on the safe arrival of the remaining occupants of the fallen plane. He massaged his legs slowly, one and then the other.

Between shots of the current Olympics, victorious moments from past Olympics were being played. Xander clenched his hands into fists as he stared at the screen, wanting to see him but not wanting to see him at the same time.

The first Olympics, from thirty-four years ago, flashed up on the screen with their crappy cameras and hard-to-see footage. A couple of moments from each year were played on the screen before flipping to the next year. Xander didn't see his parents in their Olympics even though he searched. Finally, the Olympics from three years ago popped up, and Xander leaned in closer.

The winners of the endurance challenge were announced, and all the faces of those who thought they were in the running were shown.

Xander fell to his knees in front of the screen and pressed his thumb against the TV to cover one of the faces. The shot changed, and Matt was gone.

Xander ran his fingers along the edge of the television, searching for the off button. He finally found it and clicked the room into silence. He lay down on the thin mattress and stared at the wall, willing sleep to come. It didn't. He just saw Matt's hopeful face change as his name wasn't called for a medal.

Xander didn't want that to be him.

Chapter 13

At 8:35 a.m., Eden followed the crowds of eighteen-year-olds out of the hotel and down an unpaved path to the gym where the wrestling matches would be held. She was anxious for the matches to begin but also scared at the same time.

8:42 a.m.

Eden and Xander entered the gym and silently found the tenth ring.

8:46 a.m.

They sat on some uncomfortably hard chairs and waited.

And waited.

And waited.

8:52 a.m.

"Do you think they're going to start on time?" Eden asked, glancing at the clock on the wall for the tenth time in six minutes.

"They better," Xander said. "They've got a lot of matches."

Eden checked his wrestling attire again. He was dressed in red shorts and a tight, white shirt that he would remove when the match started. He had a mouthguard dangling around his neck, and he continuously pressed one fist into his open hand.

"Are you nervous?" she asked.

"Yeah."

"Well, I'm cheering for you." But even as she recited her silly cheer from the night before, he didn't react the same way. He just stared straight ahead at the two wrestlers who would be matched up first.

Xander took a deep breath and let it out.

"You've got this," Eden said seriously, squeezing his arm.

He shook her off, and Eden frowned at him. Now wasn't the time to argue, but he didn't have to be rude.

8:56 a.m.

A referee wearing black and white stepped into the ring and walked around its edges, checking for something. Eden watched him closely. She remembered two years ago when there had been this big complaint about a referee being bribed to declare a certain winner. They had ended up letting both of the competitors win a medal, but Eden wondered what would happen if the ref just decided he didn't like Xander for whatever reason.

8:58 a.m.

The referee motioned for the first two competitors to step onto opposite sides of the wrestling mat.

"Hey, that's your friend!" Eden said, pointing at the boy from the party.

Xander nodded and leaned forward, his elbows on his knees. Eden glanced back and forth from the ring to Xander.

9:00 a.m.

The bell rang, and the fight began. There was no explanation of rules, and Eden's heart thumped as the first competition of the Olympics began. Another ref outside the ring monitored the fight as well, and he kept raising his hands and making signals that Eden didn't understand. Other matches were happening on mats across the gym, and the refs all shouted over each other.

"No!" Xander shouted, leaping to his feet.

"What?"

Xander sat back down, his foot tapping repeatedly as they watched the next segment of the fight. "That wasn't a takedown," Xander mumbled, his eyes trained on the fight.

Eden swallowed, wishing there was some explanation of how wrestling worked. Xander had told her a little bit about it back when he first became interested, but she hadn't paid very much attention.

"Takedown two!" Xander exclaimed, rising just a little before wincing sympathetically and sitting down again. He really was into this match.

The rest of the crowd was talking. Some were excited. Others were laughing like this was a fun game, while one person was already crying.

Eden squinted at the girl and recognized her from school. Why was she crying?

The ref called out something else, but his words were drowned out by the crowd shouting.

"What? What happened?" Eden asked.

"Connor," Xander responded, shaking his head.

Then, Eden understood. The other guy had taken Connor down too many times. Connor was out. He wouldn't get another chance to compete in the wrestling competition. He hadn't won a medal.

Eden trained her eyes on Connor as he stalked across the gym, ignoring the crying girl who trailed after him.

"Do you want to go . . . talk to him?" Eden suggested.

Xander stared at the next two opponents entering the ring, completely ignoring her. Eden evaluated the way Xander's fists flexed and unflexed, the way his leg jiggled, the way he couldn't keep his eyes in one place for too long.

The deep bags under his eyes told stories. Xander had slept very little last night.

Eden kept her mouth shut as they watched the next round. They didn't know either person in that round, at least Eden didn't recognize them. She watched the clock tick forward until the time of Xander's match.

9:24 a.m.

9:29 a.m.

9:32 a.m.

9:36 a.m.

Xander stood up and left Eden sitting alone on the row without even a goodbye. Eden stared after him, silently sending him good luck, good vibes, and silent prayers, begging whatever forces there might be to keep Xander safe and help him win this round.

9:39

Xander and his opponent stepped onto the mat. Xander took his shirt off and laid it outside the clearly marked lines that surrounded their fighting area, the place that would determine if he won a medal or not.

9:40

The ref blew his whistle, and the two eighteen-year-olds began circling each other. Eden leaned forward, forcing herself to breathe as she watched Xander fake forward then step back.

Xander's opponent lunged forward and grabbed Xander around his middle.

Slam!

They both went down to the mat, and Eden leaped to her feet.

"Come on, come on, come on," Eden begged.

Xander wriggled out of his opponent's hold, and Eden breathed a sigh of relief.

Xander- 1, Jayce- 0

"How did he get a point for-?" Eden started to ask, but she didn't care. As long as he was getting points, he was closer to winning. She didn't sit down again, but swayed back and forth on her feet as the match proceeded.

Xander lunged forward, but he went too hard.

Jayce dodged him and came up behind him, getting a hand around Xander's waist.

Xander twisted, spinning out of Jayce's grasp, and hooked an ankle around Jayce's knee.

Jayce fell to the mat, and Xander descended on top of him.

Xander refused to let Jayce out of the hold, and the ref counted down.

"Takedown!" The ref shouted. "Back to your corners."

Xander took a sip from the water bottle provided, his eyes roaming the ring.

Eden glanced at the score.

Xander- 3, Jayce- 0

"Okay, this is good," she said, providing a pep talk for herself. "He's got him. There's no way he can catch up now. Just a couple more takedowns, and he's good. He'll have won."

The ref blew the whistle, and the two went at each other again.

Xander played it safe, backing up and dodging Jayce's advances.

Jayce sprang at Xander, and Xander dodged, but not quickly enough. One of Jayce's fists hit him in the face as he grappled for Xander's shoulder.

Xander grunted as he continued to bounce back and forth on his feet. As he turned to avoid another lunge from Jayce, he looked like he was in pain.

Spots of red dripped onto his chest, and Eden flinched.

His nose might be broken. Or was it just a nosebleed? How much did it hurt? Then, Eden saw that Xander's knee was red too. A tiny stream of blood made its way down his leg.

Xander lowered his head and dove onto Jayce.

Bam!

Jayce hit the floor hard, but he didn't stop moving. He slithered out from underneath Xander until he was standing strong in the corner. Jayce's movements won him a point, but Xander didn't even glance at the scoreboard. His eyes were fixed on his opponent.

Xander directed his head into Jayce's stomach, and once again, Jayce fell backward. Xander wasn't quick enough though, and Jayce got back to his feet before Xander could pin him to the ground.

Eden glanced at the scoreboard and saw there were only thirty seconds left in the match. Xander could do it. He could actually do it.

Jayce came at Xander, and they both held each other's heads as they circled, trying to get a better grip. Xander pulled back, then lunged forward, knocking Jayce to the ground. He secured Jayce's hands and waited for the ref to make the call. Jayce didn't resist.

Eden's eyes flicked to the scoreboard.

Xander- 5

Jayce- 1

Jayce didn't get up right away even though the referee beeped insistently. Xander headed to his corner, a broad smile on his face, but when he saw Jayce still lying on the floor, he approached him and offered his hand.

Jayce groaned, rocking back and forth slowly and clutching his side.

Xander leaned down to say something to him, but Eden couldn't hear it. When Jayce still didn't get up, the ref came over to see what the problem was. Eden squeezed her own hands tightly until she heard one of her knuckles crack.

A medic was called forward and helped Jayce to his feet, leading him away. A bell rang, and Xander was announced as the winner.

Eden practically flew down the aisle to the seats right beside the court. "You did it!" she shouted.

Xander shook his head, carrying his shirt in one of his hands, which were both peppered with sprinkles of blood. "It's not done yet. I have to win another match, and my takedown times have to be faster than the others who won this round."

He continued marching toward the door of the gym.

"Where are you going?"

"Need some air," Xander said.

Eden fell in step next to him, glancing over her shoulder as a new match began on the mat where Xander had just won. Her heart thumped excitedly in her chest. She was sure that Xander would win the second match. After his excellent first round, he couldn't not win the second. That wasn't how things worked.

Xander didn't say anything as he led the way back to the hotel, taking hurried steps. Eden glanced at him every few steps, trying to read his face.

"Is . . . everything alright?" she finally asked.

Xander shook his head. "No, Jayce won't win a medal for wrestling."

"But *you* might," Eden pressed home the good news. "Xander, more than a quarter of the population will be eliminated. You know that."

Xander just grunted. They reached the hotel, and Xander took one of the water bottles by the front table. He drank quickly from it, his eyes flitting around the room, but never landing on Eden.

What was wrong with him?

"When's your second match?" she asked.

"12:20," Xander responded. "I'll go up against the winner from the first match in ring 2."

"Okay, you've got a few hours," Eden said, trying to make eye contact with Xander.

Xander winced before squatting down in the middle of the lobby, his water bottle between his legs and his head in his hands. Eden laid a firm hand on his back. "Do you need to rest or something? Is there something I can do for you?"

"I need to be alone," Xander said, biting off each of his words as he mopped at his nose with his stained shirt. Eden quickly retracted her hand and let his words slap her in the face. What had she done wrong? He had just won a match. He should be happy. Sure, not everyone would win, but that was the way it worked. It wasn't a surprise.

"Fine, okay, I'll just be . . . in the gym," Eden responded, backing away from Xander as he crouched in the lobby. She backed up two more steps until her spine rested against the warm glass of the door. She stared at Xander.

He suddenly seemed so small.

He didn't look like the strong warrior she had seen him as during their whole adolescence. He looked weak, and Eden didn't want to see him like that. She closed her eyes, trying to shut him out. But the image of him small and unable to deal with his emotions hit her hard.

Eden slammed through the lobby door and jogged down the path back to the gym, trying to run away from her feelings of unworthiness. If Xander felt bad about beating someone fair and square, how could she consider poisoning someone and not feel guilty? What was wrong with her? She truly didn't deserve to become an adult.

Chapter 14

Xander took a couple of deep breaths.

His next match was starting in five minutes. The medic had said that he was fine to fight, but he had wrapped Xander's knee so that it wouldn't get infected. Now, the bandage stood out against his tanned skin like a white flag of surrender.

The two wrestling on the mat before Xander looked like cartoon characters. He couldn't focus on them clearly.

Eden was on the far side of the mat where he would wrestle, and he could feel her eyes fixed on him. She was relying on him to win. If he didn't win this match, then he stood no chance of winning a medal. If he didn't win, then he would be eliminated. And if he won, but not well enough, he still might be eliminated.

He heard his name like it was coming through the end of a long tunnel. "Xander Coxon."

Pushed by an invisible hand, Xander stepped onto the mat, feeling the eyes of the crowd on him. He took the corner farther from Eden's seat and tried to put her out of his mind.

He had to focus on the match now. As he stared across the mat, he realized that he hadn't taken the time to notice his opponent's name. The scoreboard didn't reflect the new match yet, so Xander just shifted back and forth on his feet.

"Xander, Nelson, please shake hands."

"Nelson," Xander said, reaching his hand forward and nodding. Nelson grabbed Xander's hand and squeezed tightly, tightly enough that Xander knew he was doing it on purpose. Xander never flinched or broke eye contact with the boy. Nelson was bulkier than Xander, and it was clear that while

Xander's family might have trouble finding meat at the store, Nelson's certainly didn't. Xander wasn't sure how they were in the same weight class, but now wasn't the time to question the viability of the match.

"Good luck to you," Xander said amiably.

Nelson squeezed harder, and the ref seemed to notice the extended handshake. He motioned for them to break apart, and Xander took a few steps back so that the painted circle in the middle of the mat separated them. All the feelings of guilt from knocking Jayce out of the running disappeared.

Xander faced Nelson across the ring.

He felt sweat beading on the back of his neck.

Xander watched as Nelson noted the wrap on his knee.

Sweat trickled down his back in a long trail.

He stared at Nelson.

Tweet!

The whistle's sound drove Xander forward.

He circled Nelson, eyeing the bulkier boy.

Nelson dove for him, and Xander dodged as Nelson's hand grazed his ear.

Nelson grunted.

Xander felt each of his breaths as he sucked the oxygen in and let it out slowly, blocking out the sounds of the crowd cheering. This was it. He had to do it.

Nelson lunged again.

Xander dodged, and his knee protested.

On the third attempt, Xander rounded Nelson and came at him from behind. He pushed his full weight into the boy, but Nelson didn't fall over. Nelson reached back and grabbed Xander exactly where his bandage was, causing Xander to release his hold.

He slammed into the ground but bounced back up, not willing to stay vulnerable longer than necessary. The two settled into their positions again, circling each other. Nelson lunged. Xander tried to dodge, but as Nelson fell forward, he grabbed Xander's knee again.

Xander went with the fall and kicked out to free himself. He scrambled to his feet, but he wasn't fast enough.

Nelson slammed into him, taking away his breath. For a minute, Xander forgot where he was and what he was doing. Nelson grabbed him by the knee and dug his finger into the wound, the wound that had mostly healed but was still sensitive, the white bandage drawing attention to it.

Ahhh!

Xander heard the scream from far away. Suddenly, Nelson's weight was removed from him, and Xander shut his mouth, cutting off the scream. He had to get his head in the game.

He glanced at the scoreboard and saw that Nelson had scored a takedown. Xander took his time sipping on his water, taking deep breaths. His eyes locked on Eden's accidentally, and she pumped her fist in the air, their signal that he could do it.

He could. He could do it.

Xander turned around and nodded. He was ready to go for it again.

Nelson dove at him, his eyes on Xander's knee. He seemed determined to exploit Xander's weak spot, but Xander was ready this time.

Xander dodged.

Nelson dove.

Xander dodged.

Once again, Nelson came at him.

Xander lowered his head and took Nelson out around the knees. They both slammed into the ground, and Xander moved right away, wriggling into position and holding Nelson in place underneath him.

He counted the seconds in his head.

One.

Two.

Three.

What? Nelson managed to slither away from him.

Xander glanced at the scoreboard. Nelson had scored a point for his escape, but Xander hadn't gotten anything.

Nelson laughed, his breath rancid, as Xander took the initiative, diving toward him this time. ". . . can't win," Xander thought he heard.

Nelson tripped as he tried to come at Xander, and Xander plunged onto Nelson.

One.

Two.

Three.

Four.

Tweet.

Xander got up. He had won two points for a takedown. He was on the scoreboard, and not far behind Nelson.

When the referee signaled for them to go again, Xander felt renewed with energy. He went for Nelson's legs again, pinning his feet together so that all Nelson could do was roll on the ground as he tried to escape. He tried to kick his feet, but he looked like a mermaid flicking its tail.

Xander pulled Nelson's legs underneath him and scored another takedown. He was winning by one point. There was only a minute left in the round, and he wanted to score at least one more takedown.

As he was walking back to his corner to grab some water, something barrelled into him from behind. He was walking, then he was on the floor.

He curled into himself as a heavy fist fell into his ribs.

Tweet! Tweet! Tweeeeet!

The whistle was doing nothing to stop the attack. Finally, the ref got between the two of them, and the weight was removed from Xander. The ref pulled Nelson into the far corner and began conferring with the other ref.

Xander slowly pulled himself to his feet. His body was on fire, particularly his left side. What was wrong with Nelson?

The ref approached Xander as he stood in his corner, trying to appear like his body was just fine.

"You're the default winner due to the unsportsmanlike behavior of your opponent."

"Default winner? I was winning anyway. How will I square up next to the others?" Xander asked. "If I don't have the opportunity to have as many points..."

"We'll compare you with what you have," the ref explained. "You can't finish the fight with an opponent who has displayed unsportsmanship-like behavior. He's already displayed that he is not worthy of a medal."

Xander took a deep, shuddering breath.

"Okay," he said. He slowly gathered his things and stepped off the mat, trying to evaluate what this would mean for his overall score. What if other winners had more takedowns than he did? He just wanted to finish the match, no matter how Nelson behaved.

He heard her footsteps before he saw her. It was a victory, but not the kind he wanted.

"Are you okay, Xander? I can't believe he did that."

"Doesn't know how to lose." Xander didn't feel guilty like he had with Jayce. He felt angry, like Nelson's loss was justified.

"Where are we going? The medal ceremony for the guys' wrestling is in less than an hour."

"Need some ice," Xander said. His head cleared as he walked back to the hotel, Eden at his side. He had won two matches, even if he hadn't won them the way he had wanted. He was done wrestling for the day. There was nothing else he could do to change his ranking. All of his training had cumulated in those two matches, and he wasn't even able to finish the second one properly.

"Here," Eden said, handing him a bag with ice. Xander winced as he placed the ice against his ribs, examining the injuries on his body. He was used to getting hurt in practices, but this was another level of pain. He should probably visit the medic, but he had already seen him once today.

Xander noticed a camera focusing on him as he iced himself in the hotel lobby. He tried to look the least hurt possible so that his mom back home wouldn't be worried. He imagined her working on her laptop from home, glancing at the television for updates. Most competitions streamed live, but due to work, many people had to watch the update reels in the evening. Xander hoped his mother would be watching the awards ceremony instead so she didn't have to see his pain.

Once he was in the main hotel, he decided that a visit to a medic was the best idea. "Find us some seats for the awards ceremony," he instructed Eden. "I'll come find you once the medic has checked me out."

The medics were busy. There were five on duty right then, and they were all attending to different wounds from the wrestling competitions. Xander waited and waited and waited, and no one had a chance to look at him. He didn't want to miss the awards ceremony, so he decided that it wasn't important for a medic to see him. He would probably have a few bruises, but he would be fine.

He entered the gathering room and found Eden quickly.

"Only eight minutes until the announcements," Eden warned as soon as she saw him. "What did the medic say?"

Xander shook his head. "I didn't see any of them. They were all busy. I'll go later." But he didn't know if he really would.

"That doesn't look good," Eden said, pointing to his ribs. Xander twisted to see that a bruise was already forming.

"Thanks," Xander responded, infusing some sarcasm into his response. What was done was done. He would either win or he wouldn't. He pulled his dirty shirt on, wishing he had used the time to shower rather than wait around for a medic.

"All male wrestling participants must sit in the first five rows," a voice announced repeatedly.

"Good luck," Eden said as they separated.

"No luck now," Xander told her. "Now, it's down to the facts."

He settled in the middle of one of the rows. Pressing the ice on his ribs, he shifted uncomfortably in his seat. He needed some pain medication and a nice nap. But first, he would see if he was actually called on stage or not.

Some of those who had wrestled earlier were wearing nice, clean clothes. Xander wasn't. He trained his eyes on Lory as she climbed the steps to the stage. She smiled encouragingly at the cameras, then at the first five rows.

"Welcome to our first medal ceremony," she announced. A few people clapped, but Xander just leaned forward. Even though he knew all hope of luck was gone, he still willed her to say his name. "Our female wrestling is taking place right now, and we have a lot of competitions scheduled for this week and the beginning of next. We'll play a recap for you of the current wrestling matches once the medal ceremony is complete. Now. . ."

Lory Chambers shuffled some papers around until she found the one she wanted. Xander's breath came shallowly. He saw Connor sitting on the fifth row on the far side of the gathering room. Now, they would learn the truth.

"We have had a lot of good fights today, but as everyone knows, not everyone can win a medal. Only the top 10% of the eighteen-year-olds this year will win a medal. I will begin calling names. If you hear your name, please come up to this machine here," Lory indicated a machine beside the stairs, "click your name, and press your thumbprint onto the screen. Then, come up the steps to receive your medal."

Xander gnawed on his lower lip. He wanted her to cut to the names already. Enough with the instructions.

"I'm reading these in no particular order," Lory announced, and the room became even quieter, if that was possible. "Marvin James." Everyone watched as a young, black teen from Alaska stood up and made his way to the stage. Xander envied him as he pressed his thumb onto the pad, then ducked his head and waited for Lory to place the medal around his neck.

Marvin smiled and raised both of his fists in a victory dance.

Lory began reading the names more quickly.

Lance Jones.

Brock Fitts.

Percy Heider.

Xander Coxon. Xander didn't react at first, but then, it was like his legs controlled his body. He was in front of the machine, pressing his name and his thumb onto the screen.

He climbed the stairs slowly and felt the rough material of the medal's ribbon against the back of his neck. The medal felt heavy as it hung there.

He had won a medal. He was guaranteed adulthood.

A slow smile spread across Xander's face as he searched the crowd for Eden. He couldn't find her face, but he continued searching as he backed up with the other winners of the wrestling competition.

There she was on the seventh row, waving her hand at him and smiling.

Lory finally announced the last name. When everyone realized that she wasn't calling anymore, some competitors on the front row began complaining. There was an uproar, but as soon as Xander was given the chance to leave the stage, he leaped off the front of it and pushed past everyone until he reached Eden.

He wrapped his arms around her and squeezed her hard. "I'm going home," he breathed into her hair.

"I'm so proud of you," Eden told him, "but you're really stinky."

Xander laughed. The world seemed full of light and happiness. He grabbed the edge of his shirt to wipe the sweat off Eden's face that had clearly gotten there from being pressed against his arm, and she shied away from the shirt.

"What? My shirt's too scary for you?" Xander asked, not even feeling his injuries anymore.

"You're too scary. Seriously? Can't you take a shower? You know . . . so people don't fall dead around you?"

Xander laughed again. "I could, but that's not as fun."

He picked up the medal and examined it for the first time since receiving it. It had his name burned into the back. On the front was a picture of a wrestling ring. He took a deep breath and let it out. Suddenly, all he wanted to do was kiss Eden. She reached forward and touched his medal, running her finger over the design, then his name.

"I'm so proud of you," she said.

"Now, it's your turn," Xander told her. "The race is in two days. You're going to win."

Eden hugged Xander again, burying her face in his disgusting shirt. Finally, she looked up at him. "Can we talk . . .?" she asked. "Alone?"

Xander looked around the gathering room. It was filled with people. Everyone with a medal was celebrating and making their way to the dining hall for a sort of celebratory meal.

"I don't know if that's possible here," he said. His heart thumped. He had won a medal. He was guaranteed a future. Was that what she wanted to talk about? What they had promised each other if they both won?

"Come on," she said, motioning him out the front door of the hotel.

They found a comfortable corner on the path by some bushes, and Xander sat down. He was thankful for the lack of cameras. "Are you going to cheat tomorrow or. . . for the race?" he asked.

Logic and problem solving was tomorrow. Even though Eden stood a better chance at winning the running competition, any chance was a good one. Cheating would help put her closer to the top.

"I don't know," Eden muttered. "I'm scared, but. . ."

"Scared you'll get caught."

She sighed, keeping her mouth shut as a group of people hurried down the path, talking about the medal ceremony for wrestling.

Xander couldn't have cared less about what they were talking about. All he knew was that he wanted the girl sitting by his side right now to have a medal around her neck. He couldn't go home on an airplane and leave her to be eliminated.

"I'll help you if you need it," he told her. "Think about it and let me know if you need me to do something."

Chapter 15

Eden milled around the dining room waiting for her turn. The logic and problem solving test was a little different from the other mental tests. It had to be done one at a time. All Eden knew was that she would go to the basement -who had known there even was one in this hotel?- and be put in a room. That was as much as she knew about the test, and those who had already finished were not allowed to enter the dining hall to talk with those who hadn't yet gone.

Eden paced to the far wall where the television replayed the results of the wrestling competitions, then she turned and walked the other way. She wasn't the only one wearing a path on the floor.

It probably looked like some weird walking race as eighteen-year-olds paced back and forth. Eden looked up and scanned the remaining participants. She had no idea when her name would be called, and it wasn't like she could really review for this test. Either she was logical or she wasn't. The bad thing about this was that boys and girls competed against each other. Instead of ten percent of boys and ten percent of girls winning. It was just ten percent of boys and girls which meant that potentially more boys could win than girls.

"Stop thinking," Eden whispered to herself. "You're just psyching yourself out."

She made another turn.

One of the officials appeared in the doorway, and everyone in the dining hall turned to look at him, like robots with creepy synchronization.

The man shouted eight names. Eden's was not among them. She took a deep breath and kept pacing. Another fifteen or twenty minutes of waiting.

This was going to take *all* day. It was almost lunch time, and there were still at least fifty people waiting.

Eden's stomach rumbled, and she glanced at the empty buffet. Was being hungry while she did the test just one extra challenge?

A couple of the cooks emerged and started bringing out dishes, and Eden salivated. Normally, she would wait until she was given a specific signal or someone *told* her she could eat. Right now, she didn't care about the rules. She needed something to do to keep her busy.

When someone else started filling a plate from the buffet line, Eden followed suit, getting some pasta and sauce along with a serving of canned vegetables. She began consuming the food, trying to be as slow as possible to keep herself busy.

The official appeared in the doorway again, and it felt like it had been a shorter wait this time. When he spoke, Eden heard her name and jumped up. Finally! She couldn't stand the suspense of waiting for her first test of the Olympics. She had no idea how she would do, but then again, neither did any of the others.

She followed the official toward the stairs. On the wall beside the first step was a door. Eden hadn't noticed it before, but she watched as the official scanned his thumbprint then put in a code. Finally, he opened the door and showed them down a dark set of stairs.

"Please go through the door and down the stairs. Do not *touch* anything when you get to the bottom of the stairs." Eden passed by him as he held the door open. Once everyone was through, he shut the door firmly behind them. Eden heard a beeping that sounded like it was locking, but she was more focused on the fact that she was supposed to climb down the stairs in complete darkness.

Eden had been the last one to go through the door, so she didn't have to worry about anyone pushing her down the stairs, but all she had to do was stick out her hand, and boop! Seven competitors would be gone.

Eden gripped the handrail tightly as the official behind her turned on a light. A hallway in the basement stretched out in front of them with doors on either side. The basement was clearly not as large as the hotel above it.

"Keep moving please," the official almost shouted in Eden's ear. She kept moving, now able to faintly see the back of the person's shirt in front of her.

Finally, she was on flat ground again. The official stood on the last step, and everyone gathered around him.

"Outside each room, you will see a screen. You must sign in on the screen. Once you have signed in, the door will unlock. You may go inside when I shout 'go'. If you open your door beforehand, you will have thirty seconds taken from your time. Does everyone understand?"

Someone on Eden's left spoke up. "Um, sir, what are we supposed to *do* in the room?"

"You are supposed to escape," the official told the girl. "You will have fifteen minutes on the clock officially. Once you figure out how to escape, then your timer will stop running. Good luck!"

That was it? He didn't have any further instructions for them?

Some of her competitors began moving toward rooms, and she heard the familiar beeping of them typing their names and pressing their thumbprints into the pad. Eden took a deep breath and moved further down the badly lit hallway until she came to an unoccupied screen. She put in her details, and the screen lit up. She heard a click as the door unlocked.

"Is everyone ready?" the official shouted.

Eden jumped when another official suddenly appeared out of the shadows almost directly next to her. He smiled at her, but that didn't comfort her rapidly beating heart.

"Go!" the first official shouted. Eden remembered what she was there to do and opened the door. She paused in the doorway. The room was completely dark except for a clock on the wall that showed 14:57. That must be her time. She had already wasted three seconds. When she shut the door, she heard a whirring sound.

Was it. . . .?

She grabbed the handle and wiggled the door, but it was locked. She was really locked in the room. She took a few deep breaths. It was dark. Anything could be in there. She went toward the clock and bumped into some sort of table or desk on the way.

"Ow," she muttered, running her hand along it. There was something there. She slid the object closer to her. It was a box.

Eden rattled the box. Something was inside, but she couldn't see! The thought that this was all wrong wouldn't leave her. She ran her fingers along the edge of the box, but it wouldn't open.

She set the box on the table once more and manually searched for anything else that might be on the desk. That was all. A box that probably had the tool she needed, but she couldn't open it.

Eden stared forlornly at the clock. 13:42.

She had wasted over a minute touching the box.

She looked around, but her eyes were met with blackness on every side.

Hands in front of her, she took tiny steps around the room, trying to find something else.

She stumbled over something in the corner, reacting more than necessary due to the dark. Carefully, she bent down and touched the object. It was cold and shaped like a tiny cylinder. As Eden rubbed her fingers on one end, she realized it was a flashlight. She clicked it on and blinked at the sudden light. It wasn't much, but she suddenly felt more powerful.

She waved the tiny light around the room and immediately noticed a portrait in the center of each wall. Each portrait had four people in it.

Eden jogged over to the box and examined it now with the light. There was a spinning lock built into the box, and it needed four numbers.

10:28

How had so much time passed? Eden scanned the walls as thoroughly as she could, looking for a number written there. She didn't find anything. The only furniture in the room was the table. She had a flashlight, a box sitting on the table, and four photos that seemed useless.

She looked at them more closely. They were very weird photos, because no one was looking at the camera. They were all looking in different directions.

Eden grabbed the box, then she couldn't help it. She looked up at the clock again.

7:18

She suddenly wondered what would happen if she didn't get out of the room. Her thoughts began taking over her productivity. What if she couldn't get out at all? They would let her out, right? What percentage of people were able to figure out this puzzle?

Eden started spinning the lock and trying random combinations. At first, she tried years that were important to the world's history.

2108. The year global warming had started the first unquenchable fire.

2125. The year that people had moved to the only liveable land.

2131. The year that the Olympics had begun.

Nothing. The box wouldn't open.

"I'm supposed to use logic," Eden said. "Logic tells me that there are a finite number of potential combinations. Instead of trying them randomly, I should try them in order so that I know which ones I have knocked out. I'll start with 0001." She spun the lock obediently to the combination. She knew there had to be a lot of potential combinations, but she didn't know what else to do.

She had reached 0218 when she looked up at the clock again. She had only a minute left. She didn't have enough time to try all the combinations, but she still moved the wheel steadily, wiggling the box.

Then, as the timer reached ten seconds, all she could do was stare at it helplessly. She whipped her head toward the door as the lock whirred and popped open. She tried the door handle, and it worked. Along with six other participants, Eden stepped out into the hall. Only one had made it out before fifteen minutes, and she stood victoriously watching as everyone else dug their toes into the ground.

"Once we reach the top of the stairs, your standing will be displayed on the screen by the stairs, and only that screen. You are free to wander the hotel except for the dining hall. When everyone has finished taking the logic and problem solving test, you will once again be able to go into the dining hall."

Eden trudged up the stairs behind the official. She wanted to ask the girl who had gotten out how she did it, but she also didn't want to talk about how badly she had done.

Someone else in the group asked the question. "How did you get out?"

"It was pretty simple," the girl explained. "All you had to do was take one of the pictures off the wall and use the picture inside to pick the lock on the door."

"What? That's cheating!" Someone else protested. Eden agreed. She hadn't opened the box or solved anything. But she had gotten out in under fifteen minutes, which meant that she stood a chance of winning a medal.

"I *almost* got out!" one of the girls protested. "I got the box open, but I couldn't figure out what to do with what was inside."

"If you're going to talk about it, as you might," the official rolled his eyes, like he was bored with the whole thing, "then you can do so in the exercise room, not near the dining hall. Unless you *want* someone to have a clue that will help them receive a better ranking than you."

The group turned toward the stairs, and Eden trailed after them. She didn't plan on exercising, but she wanted to hear more about what was inside the box.

"Maybe I could have solved the clue in the box if I had been able to open it," someone else protested.

"That part was easy," a boy with glasses said. "All you had to do was use the pictures."

"The pictures?" Everyone looked at him.

"Well, yeah, how else could you open the box?"

"Lucky guess," one girl said.

"Really lucky," he confirmed. "There are 10,000 combinations for a four digit number. If you were able to guess it, let alone have time to sort through the contents, then you must have luck on your side."

"So? Are you going to tell us?" someone else asked.

They were rounding the landing for the fourth floor, but Eden kept trailing after them, listening for where she went wrong so she could berate herself about it later.

"Well, the girl in the middle was looking in the same direction in every picture except one."

No one made a sound.

"So, I examined that picture more closely. There were two numbers written clearly on the back of the picture. You might have thought that was it, but when I looked at the picture more closely, I saw two scratches on the frame that looked like they could have happened when someone dropped it. But when I looked at it the other way, I realized that it looked an awful lot like an eleven. I didn't know which number went first- the one on the back or the one on the frame- but it was easy to test two options."

"Wow," someone commented.

Eden blinked at the boy. She hadn't really expected to win, but she hadn't expected to do so badly either.

"What was inside the box?" she finally asked.

Another girl spoke up, the one who had luckily guessed the combination. "There was a piece of paper. It had a letter on it that didn't make any sense. I know it was a clue to open the door, but I couldn't figure it out."

Even the boy with glasses shrugged. "I didn't have enough time to figure it out. I got the box open with six minutes left, and I'm a thoughtful reader."

They had just reached the training room, and people in the group started to split off, until Eden was standing there by herself, digesting her failure. She hadn't needed to check the screen to know that she was out of the running.

"It's not my last chance," Eden told herself, looking around for Xander.

Chapter 16

Xander had never thought that being a winner would be boring, but it was. Here he was walking around a hotel where there was virtually nothing to do. He could exercise, and that was it. The logic and problem solving competitions weren't broadcast on television. They said that it would give clues to future generations about how to beat the test more easily. Xander knew that he would hear all the details from Eden, though. *If* she was ever allowed to take the test and roam the hotel again.

Xander stared at the TV, trying out different positions.

The floor. His butt grew numb.

Upside down on the bed. His toes started tingling from lack of blood flow.

Lying on the bed. He felt too hot.

Xander finally left his room and started poking around the hotel, something that he knew he probably wasn't supposed to do. Still, who cared?

He walked all the way down to the end of the hall on the third floor, his knee reminding him that the wound had been reopened yesterday. There were only more and more rooms. He did find a second staircase at the end of the hallway. As he entered the less-used staircase, he noted that there weren't cameras here either. They really only monitored the most-traveled areas.

Rarely was the footage shown on TV, but sometimes, if a competition was dragging or on a day like today with the logic test, they might show snatches of basic footage- the eighteen-year-olds talking or socializing.

Xander climbed to the fourth floor and walked all the way down the hall. Once again, nothing exciting. He noted that there wasn't a staircase on that side of the hotel.

"Better hope there's not a fire," Xander said to himself.

A girl came out of one of the rooms and stared at him accusingly. "You're not supposed to be on this floor."

"Oh, I . . . isn't this the third floor?"

"Good try. It's the fourth."

Xander smiled sheepishly, but there was no exit on that side so he had to follow the girl back to the stairs. She was going down, so he climbed to the fifth floor, another boys' floor, and walked the length of the hallway.

He already knew what was on the sixth floor, but he climbed up there anyway. He had nothing else to do. His medal swinging back and forth felt strange.

He entered the exercise room and surveyed it.

"Ooh! You won a medal in wrestling?" a girl on an exercise bike asked. Xander noted a medal also dangling from her neck.

"Yeah, you too?"

She grabbed the medal and waved it at him, all the while her legs continuing moving on the bike. "I mean, it's nice to have a medal and all that, but it's weird now, watching everyone else competing, and we've already won. It would be nice if we could compete too, just to keep busy."

"I'm sure if you wanted to go down to the basement for the logic test, no one would say no," Xander responded, his eyes scanning the room again. There was nothing interesting that he hadn't noted before. One of the machines was calling his attention, but he was too restless to sit and lift weights. Besides, this girl kept talking to him.

"I don't know. I mean, I'm curious about it. They don't show it on TV, and you have to wonder why."

"Because if they showed it on TV, then the people who haven't taken the test yet would know all the answers. It's like the math tests. It's kind of boring to watch someone filling out math problems."

"I guess that makes sense. Still, they should have a movie theater with something other than old Olympics to watch or something here to keep us busy." The girl smiled at him, but Xander continued to look straight ahead. "Soooo, now that you have a medal, what are you going to do with your life?"

Her question opened a whole new world for Xander. He had barely digested the fact that he had won a medal. He hadn't really thought about a job. There were the obvious jobs that went to the winners of each medal, but other jobs were up for grabs to anyone who wanted them.

"I'll have to keep thinking about it. Anyway, nice to talk to you. I'm going . . . some . . . downstairs."

"Why are you in a hurry? There's nothing to do."

"I want to keep moving. I have a friend competing today, but I can't talk to her while she's waiting."

"Oh . . . oh!" The girl seemed to understand his words in a different way. "That's okay. I mean, I get it if you've already got a . . . friend. Bye!" She waved, fluttering her fingers like some sort of fairy tale princess.

Xander kept moving, going down the hall outside the exercise room to the public access bathrooms on the floor. There was one door past the bathrooms, partially hidden behind an awkwardly placed couch.

Xander wasn't sure what could be behind it. It obviously wasn't meant for public access or there would be a sign.

Still, he looked over his shoulder.

Nothing said not to go inside.

Xander tried the door. It was locked. The screen next to the door lit up and instructed him to put in his credentials. He knew that if he put in his information, it would turn him away. They would probably also have a record of him trying to enter.

Xander shrugged and was just about to go back down the hallway to walk around the lobby some more when he heard a group of people entering the exercise room. They were talking about the logic test.

Xander wanted to learn whatever he could, so he ducked behind the couch.

". . . impossible!" one boy wailed.

"I can't believe that's all we had to do. I've been studying logic puzzles and riddles for months. They were *no* help at all. I mean, the least they could do was tell us we had to break out of some demon trap."

Two voices got closer. "It doesn't matter anyway," one of them muttered.

"Why not? That was my best chance to win a medal."

"Because, I'm going to win a medal. My time was excellent, and I'm guaranteed to be in the top ten percent."

"I'm happy for you," the other girl responded in a voice that was anything but happy. "What about me?"

"You'll get it. You didn't today, but you're strong in endurance. You'll get one in a couple of days."

The couch squeaked as they sat down. Now, Xander felt awkward. He couldn't just pop up and say, "Hi, how are you doing?" But at the same time, he wasn't trying to listen in on a private conversation.

"We're from Alaska, and you know what that means."

Xander actually had no idea what that meant, other than they didn't live close to him. He held his breath, hoping that the girl with the high-pitched voice would explain.

"I know," the other girl whined. "But did you see the results yesterday?"

"Well, it can't be only Alaskans who win. That would be impossible. But still, we're good. Neither Russia nor Greenland provide free, required training to all its teenagers. We're guaranteed to win the majority of the medals."

Xander frowned. Nothing they said was illegal or showed that the results had been tampered, but he couldn't help wondering. The logic and problem solving test was done in the basement without any cameras. Who knew what was actually happening when they were down there?

"Will it really make a difference, though? Alaska can't support the population if everyone from there wins a medal."

"Everyone won't. That's impossible. Sammi, you never understand anything. Why do I always have to explain it?"

"Because . . . it's complicated."

Xander felt a sudden chill come over him, the kind of feeling he got when someone was staring at him. He slowly turned his head to look behind him. The wall was a couple feet behind him, but no one was there. Of course no one was there. They would have to pass by the couch, and the girls would . . .

The girls weren't talking anymore.

Xander slowly looked up, and a square-faced girl was staring at him angrily.

"Snoop much?" she asked.

Xander smiled in embarrassment and slowly rose, shoving his hands in his pockets.

"Oh, you have a medal," the square-faced girl said, her eyebrows uncinching slightly. Xander leaned on the back of the couch as he tried to think of some excuse for why he was sitting on the floor behind the couch.

Then, he realized. He didn't need any sort of excuse. He could be behind the couch if he wanted.

"Yes, I do. From what it sounds like, you might have one by the end of the day too."

The girl smiled at him, her smile spreading across her face and reminding him of a dog seeing a bone. "I'm Georgie. What's your name?"

"Xander," he told her. His eyes flicked to the quieter blonde girl. She sat staring at him in wonder. He spoke to interrupt her stare. "So, you think Alaska is better than Greenland, huh?"

"You're a Greenlander?" Georgie asked, groaning.

"Yes, you have a problem with that?"

"Just that Alaskans are better."

"That's what I heard. I'm not sure I believe it. The best in wrestling was a Greenlander."

"First doesn't matter. It just matters if you get a medal."

She was speaking the truth. "Anyway," Xander edged around the couch. "See you later."

He didn't glance back as he headed toward the stairs, desperate to go somewhere, anywhere that would make it impossible for him to snoop on anyone. Maybe he could check the screen and see if Eden had gone yet.

Still, Georgie's words were caught in his mind. There wasn't usually much enmity between the different territories. It didn't matter where you came from or how you trained. What mattered in the end was winning a medal. So why were these girls so hung up on their country and thinking that a country as a whole was better than others?

"Xander," a voice said next to him. It was Eden. She was at the top of the stairs, clearly having just come from the exercise room.

"How . . . did it go?" Xander asked cautiously.

"It went, but I'm not winning a medal. I already know."

Xander shook his head. "I'm sorry."

"It's okay." Eden still seemed pretty upbeat, even though she had just lost. "It was really hard. The only thing that bothers me is that this one girl cheated."

"Cheated?" Xander cocked his head and waited for more details.

"Yes, so they shut us in this room, and we had to escape. But it was completely dark, and it was really hard. I didn't even get close, but this one girl used a picture from the wall to pick the lock open."

Xander's eyebrows rose. "They just let her do that?" he asked.

"I guess. I saw her name on the leaderboard, so I guess that kind of cheating is okay. Or maybe any kind of cheating. Maybe they don't care how you get the medal as long as it's around your neck."

"What did she look like?"

"She was kind of short, angry-looking even as she was gloating about how she cheated."

The square-faced girl had been short. It didn't matter if it was the same person or not. Xander had learned something important. Cheating didn't appear to be punished, and that was good for Eden.

"Can we go to my room?" Eden whispered.

Xander raised his eyebrows at her. She was usually such a rule-follower that he couldn't believe she was suggesting something against the rules. Still, if she wanted to talk in private, he wouldn't say no.

Xander followed her down the stairs to her room.

At the landing was another screen announcing all the names of those who had won medals in the first competition of the Olympics. The girls' wrestling winners had taken part in the most recent medal ceremony, so those were still the names scrolling past at the moment.

Eden glanced over her shoulder. There were a couple of girls further down the hallway, but they weren't looking in their direction. She hurried to the door of her room and fumbled with the lock, finally getting it open. Xander slipped inside behind her. Her room was small.

He knew it had to be the same size as his, but it felt smaller, a lot smaller, with the two of them in there. Her TV was silent, but Eden went to it and turned it on before sitting on her bed. She wasn't saying anything to Xander, so he just hovered in the doorway, staring at the TV.

"So . . . what are you thinking now that your first competition is over?" he asked.

Eden pointed to the screen where the news anchor was talking about the competition that would happen the next day- running. A list of those registered to compete popped up on the screen and started scrolling. Eden bent to her knees on the floor and squinted at the screen. "I'm number 226," she said.

Xander nodded, taking a step closer to the TV. "That's your name," he agreed as the name scrolled past them. The list ended shortly after that.

"I'm not going to win a medal. There's no way I'll be in the top ten percent. No way."

Xander sighed. Winning a medal hadn't taken away all of his worry. In fact, having it hanging around his neck right now felt like a burden, one he wasn't sure he could bear, when Eden didn't have one as well. He sat on the floor next to Eden.

"You still have other competitions," he said, trying to think of anything that would be encouraging.

"Yeah, there are others. But what if I mess them up too? Why do I have to be so normal?" Eden almost shouted the last part.

Xander placed a hand on her knee and lowered his voice. "Are you going to . . . cheat?"

Eden pressed her lips together, and Xander noticed her eyes dart to her jacket hanging from the headboard. She had something in there. What was it? Notes for a test?

"What's your plan?" he asked.

"I've got something from Claire. She, uh, gave me a little bit just before she left after our first and only session."

"Notes? For which test?"

Eden shook her head. "It's called . . . stretchyeight or something. I don't remember. Maybe not eight, nine. Stretchynine?"

Xander made a face. "I've never heard of anything like that before in all of our science classes."

"It wasn't in my book. I tried to look it up today," Eden said, pointing to a science book at the foot of her bed. "I don't think it's something they want us to know about. Claire didn't say what it did, but she said it would help knock out some of the competition."

"It's a poison?"

Eden stood and pulled at the loose stitches in her coat to retrieve a small plastic bag. "This is it," she said. "I asked Claire if it was deadly or anything, and she said no."

Xander took the cool plastic bag in his hands and examined the white powder. "I'm pretty sure whatever it is, you have the name wrong."

Eden smiled just a little. "Maybe. You know how I get with long words, especially weird ones. But . . . I'm thinking of mixing it with the oatmeal at breakfast tomorrow, right before the races begin. Maybe it would give me a chance at the race."

"You think this would knock out enough people for you to win?"

"I don't know, but don't eat the oatmeal at breakfast," Eden warned him. "The girls are competing first. The boys' races start at 11 a.m., so the girls should eat breakfast first. By the time the food is refilled for the second group of people, it will be gone."

Xander handed the bag back to Eden. "Do what you have to do," he told her. His mind weighed every angle of the problem, but he could agree with her on one point. She was almost guaranteed not to win the race with the current standings. With this drug, maybe she stood a chance.

"I mean, what kind of cheating is okay? That girl was bragging about it with the logic competition, and the official didn't care."

"I guess problem solving is different. She solved the problem of being locked in the room, even if she didn't do it the right way." Xander didn't want to sound like he was defending her, but he was kind of in awe of the way she had thought of such a creative solution.

"I mean, I could have picked the lock if I had known that was allowed."

"Could you?"

Eden shoved him with her hip. "Yes, I could, but thanks for the doubt."

Eden replaced the bag in the pocket of her jacket and sat next to him on the floor again. The TV was showing shots of the dwindling number of eighteen-year-olds who still needed to take the logic test.

"There are only five more days of competitions," Eden said as her head slid onto Xander's shoulder. "Five more chances for me."

Her words felt like a punch in Xander's gut, but he agreed. She only had so many chances. And if she didn't win a medal, then she would be eliminated.

Chapter 17

The next morning, Eden awoke with a start. She had set an alarm, but she still had six minutes left until it went off. She needed to get down to the dining hall before it filled with people.

Her heart was beating nearly through her chest, and she wondered what her mother would think if she knew what Eden was doing. She would never have thought of cheating if it weren't for Claire. Had her mother . . .? No, certainly her mother would never have hired her if she had known what Claire was doing.

But maybe . . .

Eden checked for the little plastic bag. She put it in her right pocket for easy access and slipped on the jacket. It wasn't really jacket weather, but she hoped that no one in the hotel would notice.

Eden's alarm went off, and she slapped her hand on it like she was killing a roach. She really hoped this would work. If it didn't, then she wouldn't stand a chance.

"No," Eden told herself. "That's not true. I still have science or I might get lucky. Other people might win medals in the first few competitions, and I could win a later test."

Before Eden knew what she was doing, the music of her song was playing through her head. She turned and leaped as well as she could in the small space, mapping out the choreography. She knew it by heart, and somehow, completing the routine made her feel more confident. Suddenly, someone thumped on the wall beside her.

Eden smiled. Maybe she was being a little loud for 6:00 in the morning.

She slipped a hand into her pocket, and keeping her hand on the bag, she crept down the stairs toward the dining hall. She couldn't believe she had told Xander the plan. It wasn't that she didn't trust him, but she didn't know what he would think of her if he knew that she won through cheating. Would he still respect her as a human?

"Enough thinking," Eden murmured to herself. "Just do it."

Once inside the dining hall, she surveyed the room. Twenty to thirty people were eating, and there was only one person currently getting food. It was the perfect opportunity.

Eden hurried forward and took a plate, skipping by some of the more interesting dishes to head right for the oatmeal. She grabbed the scoop and pulled it closer to her, trying to pry the plastic bag's opening apart with her other hand.

"Morning," a sleepy voice said beside her.

Eden dropped the scoop into the oatmeal, and it splattered all over her jacket. She wiped at the spots.

"Oh, uh, good morning," Eden said. It was a girl she had never seen before. Why was the girl saying something to her now? Did she look suspicious?

Eden took a scoop of oatmeal and headed toward a table close to the food line, watching the other girl gather the rest of her breakfast. A group of three girls came into the dining hall and approached the buffet as Eden took a few bites of her oatmeal.

She would have to go through the line again. She couldn't wait for the line to be clear, because it would only get busier.

Eden grabbed a clean plate and slid it down the line again to the bucket of oatmeal. She wondered if the powder she had would be enough for all of that oatmeal. Would it be too diluted to do anything?

She glanced around the room. A couple of people were looking at the food longingly, probably trying to decide if another serving would make them too full to run. Eden gritted her teeth and grabbed a serving of the sweet potato hash browns.

Suddenly, the television made one of those beeping noises that meant an important announcement was being made.

Eden stood gaping at the television for ten whole seconds before she realized this was the perfect opportunity to put in the powder. She slid her plate down the buffet to the oatmeal and reached for her pocket again. She successfully opened the plastic bag, but as she tried to slide it out of her pocket, someone bumped into her from behind.

"Oops, sorry," a boy said without even looking at her. He was walking backward while staring at the television screen.

Eden took a shaky breath as she realized that some of the powder had spilled into her pocket. She couldn't really see what was happening in her pocket without looking suspicious, so she firmly grabbed the oatmeal ladle again.

"Are you going to get some or not?" one of the girls asked.

"Oh, sorry," Eden said. "Can't decide."

"Well, I know what I want. Can you move so I can get it?"

Eden stepped back, took one more step, then made her way to the table again. She sat there and studied the line and the situation. She had to just do it. She couldn't wait for the perfect time.

Eden reached into her pocket and carefully sealed the plastic bag again. She turned it over and slid it up her right sleeve. She reached over and scratched her wrist. She would easily be able to open the bag like this and dump the powder in. It shouldn't take more than two seconds.

"Good morning!" a cheerful voice said.

Eden whipped her head up to see Xander watching her. "Uh, hey," she said. "I thought you wouldn't come until later."

"Did you do it?" Xander asked, his eyes darting toward the food.

"Not yet . . . someone might see me," Eden mouthed her words quietly, worried about the cameras all around the dining hall. "Can you . . distract them?" Whatever had been holding everyone's attention on the television was long finished. Now, people were talking again in rowdy groups, and the number of people in the dining hall was growing.

"Okay. Let's get in line. You go first," Xander said.

Eden got in line for the third time that morning. She grabbed a plate and let the girl in front of her get three dishes ahead before sliding over to the oatmeal. As soon as she was in front of the oatmeal, she leaned forward like she was going to grab the ladle. Xander took his tray of food out of line like he didn't want anything else and headed back to their table.

Eden counted the seconds in her head.

One.

Two.

Three.

She couldn't stand there much longer.

Then, Xander did it. She heard a clatter behind her, and a couple of people started laughing at whatever Xander had done. She didn't take the time to look around. She reached both of her hands forward, undid the top of the plastic bag, and dumped the contents into the oatmeal.

Eden pulled back her hand and gave the oatmeal a few good stirs.

All the laughter had subsided. She should move.

Eden grabbed her tray and hurried back to her table, realizing that she hadn't taken anything from her trip to the buffet that time.

Her heart was beating quickly, and she couldn't look Xander directly in the eyes. He was having a conversation with someone who felt sorry for him after his fall. Eden reached for a piece of fruit that she had grabbed on one of her previous trips to the buffet.

"Hey, that's my fruit!" Xander said, slapping at her hand.

Eden frowned at him. "No, it's not," she responded. Why was he messing with her?

"Yes, it is. Why do you always think you can take my food?"

Xander pulled the plate closer, and Eden rolled her eyes. "Fine, I'll just go get something else."

The random person got bored and left their table. Then, Xander leaned closer. "Maybe you should go wash your hands before you eat anything." He nudged her tray with his elbow, and Eden saw what he meant. There was some powder on her tray. She swallowed hard. What if she had accidentally ingested some?

Her eyes went back to the line where several people were opting for oatmeal. What had been done couldn't be changed. She hoped it would be enough to get her a medal.

Eden slowly rose and made her way to the bathroom at the far end of the dining hall. She washed her hands carefully in the sink, but it didn't seem enough. How could she be sure that she had gotten everything off?

Was that a toothpaste stain or the powder? Eden splashed a little water on her sleeve. Finally, she couldn't remain in the bathroom any longer, so she wandered back to the table where Xander was heartily consuming a little bit of every dish except the oatmeal.

"It's almost seven," he said. "Are you going to get dressed for your race?"

"Yes. I should get dressed, shouldn't I?" She glanced at the large bowl of oatmeal again. It was impossible to see how much was left.

A couple of people screamed on the far side of the dining hall, and Eden rose to her feet, staring in the direction of the commotion.

A girl collapsed to the floor, and other people quickly gathered around her, blocking Eden's view. Eden pushed her way through a couple dozen people, standing on her toes so that she could see better.

The girl was curled up on her side on the floor, twitching. One of her arms extended straight in front of her, while the other curled into her stomach.

She grunted, then groaned, her eyes flicking from side to side.

Eden's empty stomach threatened to vomit. The girl's feet tapped the floor, extending then retracting quickly.

"Oh my god! What's wrong with her?" someone asked.

"Get the medic! Someone go get a medic! She's dying!"

No one left the scene, least of all Eden who was pretty sure she was responsible for this. There was an empty bowl of oatmeal at the table where the girl had been sitting.

One of the girl's arms curled behind her before flicking out again, and her noises got louder, like she was struggling against an invisible hand choking her.

"Is anyone getting a medic?" the girl who had been sitting with the fallen girl asked.

"I- I will," Eden volunteered, rushing out of the dining hall as tears pricked at her eyes. The infirmary was to the right of the lobby, so she rushed through the lobby and to the door. She knocked on it then tried the handle. It was locked.

"Hello! Hello?" Eden called as she banged on the door. "There's a problem in the dining hall. I don't know what's wrong with-"

The door was flung open, and Eden could see that a patient was currently being treated. "What are the symptoms?" the medic asked, calmly gathering a small bag.

"She's just twitching on the floor. I don't think she can hear anyone."

"A seizure." The medic frowned at her. He turned back to his patient. "I'll address this and be right back." The medic walked unhurriedly to the dining hall. No matter how quickly Eden strode, she kept having to wait for the medic to catch up. Either he had no interest in saving the girl or it wasn't such a big deal after all.

When they reached the dining hall, the girl was lying still on the floor. Eden let the medic lead the approach, hanging back to watch from a distance.

The medic knelt by the girl and felt for a pulse at her neck. The group of people then blocked Eden's view. Her heart thumped in her chest as she went back to the table she had shared with Xander. He was just finishing his last bite of breakfast. He wiped his mouth and looked at her with concern.

"Everything okay?" he asked.

"The medic didn't think it was a big deal," Eden responded. "He didn't run or anything, so maybe. I mean, she could have an underlying condition that didn't have anything to do with-"

Xander shook his head in warning.

"I'm going to get ready for the race," Eden said, tears pricking at the back of her eyes again. "Can you . . . tell me what happens?"

"Yeah." Xander threw his napkin on the plate and leaned back. "I'll let you know. Go get ready."

Eden trudged up the stairs to her room, the door shutting with a firm click behind her. She saw the girl's twitching again. This was what she had wanted, right? She had wanted to knock out girls who were ahead of her so that she would have a chance at winning a medal. Eden just hadn't known that it would feel like her hand was around the girl's throat, strangling her.

Eden looked in the tiny mirror, searching past her freckles to the depth of her eyes. She wanted to understand herself, to see who she really was. Her brown eyes gave no answers, however.

The clock beside the bed ticked by. She only had forty-five minutes until the first race began, and she hadn't even stretched.

Eden pulled on her running shorts and tank top. She pinned her assigned number to her shirt and approached the tiny window, the little piece of glass that showed her a sliver of the outside world.

Xander had changed overnight. He had become an adult, and he had the medal to show for it. Now, it was her turn.

Determined to win, Eden marched downstairs and approached the front door. Another girl dressed in running clothes was leaning against the water fountain, clutching at her side.

"I don't understand," she said to her friend. "I feel like I've just been running. I have a cramp that won't let me walk more than five steps. I'm hydrated. I don't know what's happening." She was almost in tears.

Eden turned her face away and walked out the front door. She should have read about the powder first, found out what it really was and what it was capable of doing. Now, every time someone experienced something out of the ordinary, she was going to blame it on herself.

The path that morning didn't lead toward the gym but toward the racetrack that she had seen outside. Eden took several lunging steps to stretch her leg muscles.

When she reached the track, there were layers of people around it. She couldn't even see the screen that announced who would run when. She thought she was running in the first race, but she had to be sure nothing had changed.

"Excuse me," she said quietly, standing on her toes to see the screen better.

No one seemed to hear her.

"Excuse me," she repeated, tapping the girl in front of her.

"What's your problem?" The girl whirled around, anger scrawled across her face.

"I don't . . . have a problem," Eden told her. "I'm just trying to see the screen."

"There's, like, five hundred of them in the hotel. What? You have to see *this* screen *right now*?"

"I mean, I don't have to see this screen. I just . . ." Eden took a step back. This girl was itching for a fight, and Eden had never been in one before. She wasn't about to start her fighting days right now.

"That's what I thought," the girl said, making a face at Eden.

Eden skirted the crowd, getting closer to the track and further away from the grumpy girl. Eden understood the pressure that the girl was under, but everyone was feeling the same thing. There was no reason to take it out on some random stranger. Even as Eden stepped onto her high and mighty podium, she realized that she had no place to start criticizing how other people dealt with pressure.

Finally, she got a glimpse of her name at the top of the screen. Twenty girls would run at a time. Each girl was focusing on her own time, so just because she didn't get first in her race didn't mean she wouldn't win a medal.

Eden hurried over to the gate that blocked the crowd from getting on the track. A large official was standing there patrolling it.

"Hey, I'm in the first race," Eden told him. "Can I go ahead and . . ." She motioned to the track.

"Name and thumbprint." The man pointed at the tiny screen next to the gate. Eden typed her name in and pressed her thumb to the screen. The screen lit up, and the man popped open the gate.

"The race will start in fifteen minutes. You can warm up over there. Your lane is lane thirteen."

Eden nodded, just reaching the gate to push through when a hand grabbed her arm. It was Xander.

His grip was steely, and she felt scared by the way his eyes widened. "Good luck, Eden," he told her. "I'll hold on to your room key while you're running."

"They have lockers," Eden said, pointing to the grouping of little doors by the gate.

"I don't mind holding on to it," Xander insisted, squeezing her arm even harder. Eden tried to read his expression. Clearly, something was going on that he couldn't talk about.

"Okay," she finally agreed, sliding the key out of her pocket and into his hand.

"Thanks," he responded. "Need me to hold anything else?"

"No." Eden turned away from her closest friend and his strange behavior and found a spot where she could stretch. As she bent forward, touching her knee almost to her head, the thoughts pounded through her faster than her heartbeat.

Xander was acting strangely.

She was about to race.

She was responsible for that girl's seizure.

If she didn't win this race, then she only had one more real chance.

Where was Xander now?

Was she going to race next to that grumpy girl?

Eden finally came up for air and looked around the track before leaning toward her other knee. A few other girls were stretching, but the grumpy girl was nowhere in sight.

Then, Eden saw the girl who had been leaning on the water fountain before. She was stretching with a pained look. Eden wanted to ask if she was feeling okay, but she never spoke to strangers. She wasn't the bubbly type who made friends with everyone, so she didn't say anything at all.

"Runners for the first race can line up now," an important-looking woman announced. Everyone started following her to the lanes, and Eden found the number thirteen. She looked to her left, where one the runner was slightly behind her. On the right, the runner was slightly in front. This was going to make it hard to know who was running faster.

Eden shook her head, cracked her neck, and rolled her shoulders. This was her chance to win. The girl on her left looked like she had never run a race in her life, but Eden knew she would have to beat more than one person to win a medal.

The one minute timer popped up, and Eden settled slowly into her take-off position, her muscles alert.

She watched the timer countdown, her blood rushing in her ears. She had to run, only focus on where she was going, and not worry about everyone else. She had thirty seconds. In thirty seconds, her speed would show her if she was worthy.

Twenty seconds.

Ten seconds.

Go.

Eden pushed off the ground as hard as she could, pumping her arms and staring straight ahead. She saw the runner to her right pumping her arms in time with Eden.

Eden's lungs burned after only a few seconds of running.

Eden urged her legs to keep moving.

One step after the other.

The girl to Eden's right stumbled and fell. Eden started to slow her pace, an automatic reaction to seeing the girl fall, but she couldn't. She had to keep pushing herself, keep running.

Keep going.

Eden passed the fallen girl who appeared to be having a seizure just like the other person this morning. Then, she was gone. Eden couldn't see her anymore, just another runner further to her right and further forward.

They reached the first bend, and Eden leaned into it, keeping her feet within the white markings. She pushed herself harder and harder.

Her legs ate the bend, and she dashed forward once again. She didn't see anyone to her right anymore, but someone on her left was running even with her. Eden remembered Xander's advice.

Don't worry about anyone else.

Look straight forward.

So, Eden did. She ran and ran and ran, ignoring her body's signals to stop.

The thick, white line approached, and Eden didn't stop.

She pounded over the line and continued forward, urging her legs to stop. They didn't seem to understand that the race was over. Her time had been clocked. Now, she only had to wait for the results.

Eden stumbled over her own feet, but came to a halt before falling on her face. She leaned over and sucked in air, too afraid to see her results on the board. She didn't want to know. She was too scared.

As she crouched, teaching her lungs how to breathe properly again, one of the people in charge came over to her. "We need to clear the track for the next race," he explained.

Eden nodded. There were other people coming. Other people had to race. She stumbled over to the side of the track, moving through the gate with a few of the other runners.

The girl she had seen stumble was being carried off the track on a stretcher. Eden's stomach flipped over, and she searched for Xander's face in the crowd. She didn't see him, but there were too many people. She looked for the screen instead, to see how bad it was.

There were no names. Just numbers. Eden saw number 226 in first place and froze. She thought she was number 226, but there was no way. She couldn't be in first place! Eden's hands scrambled at the number on her shirt, trying to see it clearly. She was 226.

She jumped up and down as she stared at the screen, waiting for it to change and show her that it had only been tricking her the whole time. But no, her number was still in first place. As she stared at the screen, she watched the numbers transformed into names and origin countries.

Eden P. Greenland steadily showed beside a number one.

Eden looked around, wanting to celebrate. She and Xander both had medals! But no, not yet. There were still many more races to go. But still, if she was number one in this race, then she stood a good chance of beating out a lot of the people in the other races.

" . . . another seizure," the person carrying the stretcher remarked as he passed her. "None of these people have medical histories of seizures. What's happening?"

Eden stared after the stretcher as she absorbed the words. Then, she looked back at the screen. She was still number one.

Eden found a place to sit near the track as the runners for the second race lined up. She had to watch the races now, now that she wasn't immediately knocked out of the running. Her time had been good, even faster than she had ever run at home. Now, she just had to hope that everyone else wouldn't be on top of their games.

Tweet!

The alert for the start of the second race sounded, and Eden leaned forward as she studied the runners, her eyes flicking back and forth between them and the clock counting up. She silently begged for them to slow down, to not do as well as she had. She didn't have to get first, of course not. She just had to win something.

Their feet slapped the track in a strange tune of desperation.

Then, the first person crossed the finish line, clearing Eden's final time by a good twenty seconds. Her stomach sank as the second, third, fourth, and fifth people crossed the finish line and beat her time.

The screen adjusted itself, showing her in sixth place now. Sixth place wasn't bad. It was medal-worthy. But if five people beat her time in each of the remaining races, then she was doomed.

A girl who was happily prancing off the field after having achieved third place suddenly leaned over and wretched on the track, spilling out her breakfast.

Even from far away, Eden could see that her arm muscles were spasming. Clearly, something was wrong. Eden glanced around, but most people were watching the runners on the field, not her.

"Eden," Xander said, suddenly right behind her. "We need to talk."

Eden turned around, a smile on her face right away. "Did you see? I won first in my race! I'm not first anymore, but I'm pretty sure I can get a medal. I-"

Xander's face was grim. He grabbed her arm and pulled her away from the track. He meant business.

Chapter 18

Thirty Minutes Earlier

Xander hurried to Eden's room. He wasn't sure how much time he had. The officials in the dining hall had looked serious, and he knew that they were suspicious of foul play.

Xander looked down the hallway on the second floor, but most of the girls were probably out by the track. He should be safe.

He sped down the hall to Eden's room and pushed the key into the lock. It wiggled but didn't turn.

"Come on," he muttered, looking over his shoulder again. He took the key out and shoved it in again. It still wouldn't turn. "What's the problem?" he asked himself.

Oh, it was the key to his room. He exchanged that key for the one to Eden's room. They looked identical, but he didn't have time for silly mistakes.

Once inside, Xander looked around the room until he saw the jacket she had been wearing at breakfast that morning. He tiptoed over to it and examined the sleeves and pockets. There was telltale white powder on one of the sleeves for sure, and as he leaned over to sniff the pocket, he thought he inhaled something. He sneezed twice as he picked up the jacket by the neck.

He had to clear away the evidence, but it wasn't like he could just wash it in the bathroom. If the girls' hall was set up like his own, then there would be a bathroom every few rooms. Someone could be in there, and if his sneaking into a girl's room wasn't suspicious, sneaking into the girls' bathroom would be.

Xander looped the jacket over his arm and casually strode out of Eden's room and to the stairway. A girl was just entering the second floor, and she gave him a strange look before brushing past him.

Once on the stairs, Xander was in safe territory. He had to hope that girl wouldn't think to report him. Luckily, the cameras were only in public areas where they were allowed to congregate.

He made it to the third floor.

Down the hall and to the bathroom.

Once in the bathroom, Xander stepped into one of the empty shower stalls and turned the water on. It came cascading down in a warm flow, and Xander stood to the side as it ran into the drain, the tips of his shoes getting splashed.

Finding the offending parts of the jacket, Xander thoroughly washed them of the powder, turning the pockets inside out. The plastic bag with remnants of the white powder was still in the pocket too.

Xander ran his fingers through it until it was thoroughly cleaned. Still, he was worried that it might attract attention if they went through the trash. Would any of their sensors be able to detect whatever the drug was that used to be in the bag?

Xander shoved his sleeves up with his wet hands and stuck a couple of his fingers in the drain. He pulled and pulled, but it wouldn't come up. He picked at the screws, but they were doing their job.

He sighed. The back of his head was wet now, so he shook it, water droplets flying across the shower stall. There had to be another way.

Xander eyed the plastic bag for a new idea. Then, he began ripping it into tiny shreds, the plastic resisting him at first, and stuffing them into the drain one by one.

A couple of deep voices came into the bathroom just as Xander was finishing. He whipped off his half-wet shirt and leaned partway out of the shower.

"Hey, can you hand me a towel?" he asked one of the guys.

The guy grabbed one from the stack of clean ones and tossed it to Xander. He must have caught a glimpse of the ribbon connected to Xander's medal, because he laughed. "You even wear your medal in the shower? Dork."

"Won it in wrestling," Xander threw back as he dried his hair and upper body from behind the curtain.

The other guy's friends laughed at him. "Better be careful what you say, Chris. He'll beat you up."

Xander put on his shirt, pushed the wet sleeves up to his elbow, and stepped out of the shower, the damp towel around his neck.

"Ooh, look at him. He's coming to wring your neck," another guy teased the first.

Xander laughed with them, hoping the wet jacket didn't look too wet or too girly in his arms and hurried to his room. He would leave Eden's jacket there for now and worry about getting it into her room later.

Now, he needed to get back to the track with Eden's key and see how she had done.

He wove his way among the members of the crowd around the racetrack, searching for her familiar brown hair. Unfortunately, brown hair wasn't the most unique color, which didn't make finding her easy.

Then, he saw her, bouncing back and forth on her feet and staring at the screen that displayed the scores.

"Eden," Xander said, trying to get her attention without shouting.

She didn't even look around. Xander finally reached her and grabbed her shoulder. "Eden, we need to talk."

He could see the excitement on her face. She must have done well in her race. She started blabbering about the race and giving him a moment-by-moment replay. He would be all too glad to hear about it under normal circumstances, but this was anything but normal.

Xander tugged Eden behind him, trying to find a private place for them to talk. She hadn't seen the officials conferring and mentioning rewatching camera footage. Everything he had just done might have been for nothing, but he couldn't be sure. Eden continued to chatter about the race, and a small part of Xander was proud of her. Still, there were more important things happening at the moment.

Instead of going into the hotel, he yanked her off the path through some bushes.

"What are you doing?" Eden asked, upset at him.

Xander rounded on her once they were behind the bushes and presented her with the key to her room. "This is yours," he said.

"Yeah, why did you want it?" Eden asked. "I could have just put it in one of the lockers. It's not like I have anything worth stealing."

"They're looking into the seizures," Xander told her. "I was listening to the medics talk, and there have been more than six grand mal seizures this morning. A couple of other people have complained of cramps, and they think that something strange is going on."

Eden finally took the key he was holding out, running her finger along the edge of it. Xander watched her handle the key before driving his point home.

"They're rewatching the camera footage," he told her.

Eden's eyebrows rose. "They think . . . someone poisoned them?"

"They have to look into the possibility with so many people randomly getting sick before the races. Two girls couldn't even compete, giving up their chance at medals. I've been eavesdropping on the officials while they were investigating the dining hall, and they're sprinkling all the dishes with a chemical that's supposed to reveal any harmful substances."

Xander watched the news sink home on Eden's face. Her brow furrowed, and the corners of her mouth fell as she dug the edge of the key into the palm of her hand. "Do you think they'll figure it out?"

"I don't know," Xander told her truthfully. He wanted to tell her that everything would be all right, but he wasn't sure. He couldn't be sure until everything had settled. Until then, he would be on edge the whole time. He had helped Eden. Would he lose his medal for helping her even though it didn't affect his competition?

"What should we do?" Eden clutched her key even harder.

Xander reached back and peeled her fingers away from the metal, studying the imprint she had made on her hand. He mouthed his next words to her. "I washed the jacket you were wearing this morning. There was powder residue there. It's hanging up to dry, but if they have high tech tools, then I don't know if it'll work."

"You think they'll search my room?"

"Maybe," Xander shrugged.

Eden started pressing the key into her hand again as Xander tried to think of something comforting to say. "We should go back to the race," he said.

"Okay, I'm in sixth place," Eden told him.

"I hope it lasts." He didn't realize how pessimistic his statement sounded until it was already out of his mouth.

Xander walked ahead of her back to the racetrack where the third race was in progress. He glanced at the board, noted that Eden was indeed number six out of forty competitors so far, and tried to find a place to sit. He felt Eden trailing after him. She wasn't very good at hiding her feelings, and Xander hoped she wouldn't give anything away.

"You mind if I sit here?" Xander asked kindly to a guy sitting at the edge of a bench.

"Should be some room," the guy said. Xander felt the guy checking out the medal he was wearing.

"You won in wrestling?" the guy asked while pointing to his medal. Xander must not look like a logical person.

"Yeah," Xander sat on the now vacant seat. Eden stood beside him staring at the constantly changing screen.

"You're a lucky man. I'm not into physical competitions. I'm more likely to win in math or science, which isn't until the end."

"Good luck," Xander told him genuinely. He studied the group of runners as they came around the last bend. Several of them were going to easily beat Eden's time, pushing her down even more.

He watched as they crossed the finish line one by one.

"Nooooo," Eden moaned softly beside him. She had now fallen to fourteenth place, still in the running for a medal, but not nearly as safe as she had been before.

Xander didn't say anything, because no matter how he reacted, it wouldn't change the fact that Eden had run her race and given it her best. Now, they had to wait and see what would happen.

Two more races finished, and Eden dropped seven more places. She was currently twenty-first out of one hundred. That wasn't the top ten percent, but there were still more races to go. She stood a chance at winning.

"Do you want to sit down?" Xander asked, rising.

"Okay." She took his place on the bench, then stood so she could see the competitors lining up for their next race. Xander shook his head.

"So. . . are you going to sit down or just stand in front of the bench so no one behind you can see?"

Eden turned around, apologizing to the people behind her. "Sorry, sorry. I wasn't paying attention."

She hopped off the bench and stood in front of the other people who were standing. She rocked back and forth, and Xander tried to think of something he could do to soothe her nerves. He could think of nothing. She could still easily win a medal, especially with people experiencing muscle strain and seizures all over the place. Xander scanned the crowd again.

Just as the sixth race was about to begin, an announcement was made over the speaker. "If you hear your name, please come to the dining hall immediately." Xander's jaw clenched as he listened to a list of eight names. Eden's was one of them.

She looked at him with wide eyes. "What do you think they want?"

A couple of people were watching them curiously, so Xander put a comforting hand on her shoulder. "It's probably just because we didn't put our dishes in the right place," Xander said. "I told you we had to put them through the window."

The other people turned around, uninterested.

Xander walked beside Eden. He could see her breaking down already, and he needed to stay by her side to keep her strong.

"They know," she whispered.

"If they knew, then why would they call so many people?" Xander slung his arm around her shoulders and pulled her closer so that he could speak in a whisper. "They won't know unless you confess. If they already watched the tapes and don't know, then they don't have proof. Don't confess. Think about the medal you're going to win."

Xander couldn't believe he was urging Eden to cover up her cheating, but he wasn't sure what would happen now if she were exposed. She would probably lose the chance to win a medal at all.

"I haven't won one yet," Eden responded, the tears clearly in her voice. They were just outside the hotel, and Xander grabbed both of her shoulders hard so that she was forced to look at him.

"Eden, don't admit to anything. You ate your breakfast, then went out to get ready for your race."

Eden nodded mournfully, and the two entered the lobby together. Xander led the way to the dining hall where several people were sitting around tables, waiting for lunch to be served.

An official approached them and asked their names.

"Ah, Eden Pearce," he said, making a note on his screen. "Could you come over here please?" He seemed polite enough, not like he was arresting her.

"What's. . ." Eden cleared her throat. "What's the reason I'm being called in here? I'm still in the running for a medal in the races, and I want to watch them."

"We just need to check on a few of you," he said without giving many details. He looked at Xander. "Were you called?"

"No," Xander shrugged nonchalantly. "I'm her friend, and I've already won a medal. Nothing better to do than follow her around."

The official smiled and clapped Xander on the shoulder. "Congratulations!"

Xander watched as Eden made her way to one of the chairs in the corner of the room. It seemed like that corner was being reserved for whatever the official was doing, but the chairs just to the side of it were unoccupied. Xander sat down in one, within listening distance, but not too close. He stared mindlessly at the TV that was showing the girls' races.

Another few people entered the dining hall, and the official herded them over to the corner with Eden. He began his speech, and Xander eavesdropped expertly, tuning out the narration from the TV.

"My colleague and I here are investigating the chance that someone may have maliciously attempted to sabotage the runners in today's races." The official made eye contact with each of the girls in the area.

Xander shifted slightly in his seat to try to catch the look on the man's face. Was he looking at anyone in particular? Xander couldn't see clearly though, so he turned back to stare directly at the TV.

"None of you were hurt, but you were in the dining hall at the time when the problems started. Does anyone have something they want to confess before we have to begin a full-fledged investigation?"

Xander balled his hand into a fist, silently willing Eden to keep her mouth shut. He counted off the seconds in his head, but no one spoke up.

"We'll begin by questioning you then. Separately. Marks, will you stay with these girls while I question them one at a time in the room over there?"

Xander flinched when Eden's name was called first. He listened to their footsteps pad across the room and disappear behind the thump of a door. His heart started beating double time. Eden wasn't good at lying, cheating, or anything that involved deceit. She just wasn't born to deceive other people.

Xander played with his medal, his thumb running over his name burnt into it, as he hoped and prayed that Eden wouldn't give anything away. He heard a few of the other girls under inspection begin to talk behind him.

"Can you believe that someone would actually try to, like, poison someone?" one of the girls asked. When no one answered, she continued having a conversation with herself. "I saw that girl twitching on the floor like a car ran over her or something. It was kind of disgusting."

"What's disgusting is your lack of empathy for anyone," another girl responded.

The first girl shot back something about her lack of style being disgusting. Xander tuned out the stupid talk, his eyes glancing to the door again and again. The man sure was taking his time talking to Eden.

"Please keep your mouth shut," Xander murmured to himself.

Chapter 19

Eden settled into the chair and faced the official in front of her, stuffing her hands under her legs so they wouldn't be a dead giveaway.

"Hi, Eden," he said in a friendly tone.

Eden responded warily. "Hey," she quickly said, giving a weird wave that she instantly regretted.

The official rubbed his shiny head as he looked at a screen in front of him. "Can you tell me what you ate for breakfast this morning?"

Eden was so surprised by the question that she blinked for several moments before she could remember how to answer. "I had . . ." She really struggled to remember. The oatmeal and her many trips to the buffet seemed to be all that her breakfast had consisted of. She had better come up with a good answer, though.

"I had some of those rolls, oatmeal, fruit, and hashbrowns. Am I not supposed to take that much?"

"That's not the problem," the man responded. He made a note on the screen. "It looks like you are in the competition for running. You already ran, correct?"

"Yes." Eden's face flushed. She wanted to see the television so she could check on her ranking.

"And you ate all of that food before your big race?"

"I didn't eat all of it. My friend ate some."

"You should only take what you're going to eat. No wasting."

"I know," Eden responded automatically. She stared at the white light reflecting off his shiny head.

"Did you see anyone hanging out by the food line too long?"

"Um, I wasn't really paying attention." It flashed through her mind that maybe she should have pointed her finger at someone, but that wasn't fair. If she *was* caught, then she deserved whatever punishment they would give, but no one else deserved to take the blame for her.

The man looked up and suddenly made direct eye contact with Eden. She stared at him, entranced as he read her eyes. What were her eyes saying about her?

"Why are you scared?" he asked her.

Eden bit her bottom lip. It was up. He knew what she had done. They wanted her to confess, but she wouldn't. She would hold on to what little hope she had until the end. "I, uh, won first in my race this morning, but now, I'm dropping down the rankings. This is my best shot at winning a medal."

The man continued to stare into her eyes for a moment, then his face softened. "I remember when I was going through my Olympics. It's very stressful."

Eden looked more closely at the man. He was completely bald, which made him look old, but maybe he wasn't that old. He could be mid-thirties. She shuffled her feet, unsure what she was supposed to say in response.

"Good luck to you," the official said.

Eden glanced over her shoulder at the door. "Does that mean I can go?" she asked.

"Not quite," the man leaned forward and smiled at her. "I just need to know. Were you desperate enough this morning to put something in the food, something that would knock out your competitors?"

Chills broke out on Eden's body as she tried to stare back at him, keeping the filter over her eyes so he couldn't see what she was thinking. "I wouldn't do something like that," she responded.

"That wasn't my question." The man set his screen down and folded his hands in front of him. "The circumstances here aren't hypothetical. *Did* you do it?"

Sucking in oxygen like it was a precious commodity, Eden responded. "I didn't." She spoke the two words as confidently as possible.

The bald man shook his head and picked up his screen again. "You can go check on your stats now," he said.

Eden paused for a second to make sure she was really dismissed before she darted out of the room. As soon as she was outside the room, she whipped her eyes around to the nearest TV.

There was one on the far side of the buffet line. She saw her stats and took a deep breath. The sixth and seventh races had finished, and she was hanging on to her little bit of cushion. She could still win a medal. . .maybe. Eden took a deep breath. She needed to stop freaking out and just wait.

Xander waved at her, and she went over to join him at his table, sending a backward glance at the official standing with the other girls waiting for questioning. "I don't know if I'm allowed to really leave yet," she said.

Xander pointed to the TV. "You're still in the running," he announced excitedly.

"I'm done running for the day," Eden attempted a joke. "Let's just hope it was enough."

Eden wanted to approach the track and heckle the runners, just to get them to mess up, but no. There had been enough foul play. She couldn't risk something so obvious.

The questioning of the other girls took at least thirty minutes. Each minute that ticked by brought the eighth race to an end.

Eden took a few shaky breaths, purposely looking away from the television. The official who had been guarding the girls for questioning motioned for her to rejoin the group. Eden stood behind the seated girls, clasping her hands behind her.

"Thank you for taking the time to talk with us," the official said. "You may now go."

Eden's eyebrows shot up. They were just going to let them go like that? Good, she didn't need the stress of someone finding out what she had done weighing on her. They must not suspect her. Xander had taken things too far when he thought he had to clear out her room of any evidence. Still, she was grateful that he cared.

Eden rounded the table and sat across from Xander, staring at him mournfully. With everyone else leaving, the table was relatively private. "They let me go. Should we go out to the track and watch the last three races?"

"What did they ask you?" Xander said conversationally, like they were discussing something else.

Eden stared at him. Why did he want to know? "They just asked me questions about what I ate for breakfast and if I did something. It's like they know that someone sabotaged the food, but not who or even what food. I don't know. I'm not even sure why they wanted to question me."

"Maybe you just looked suspicious," Xander responded in a low voice, glancing at the TV behind her.

"Is it bad?" Eden asked, refusing to look for herself. "Is the ninth race over yet?"

"No, not over yet."

She couldn't tell anything from his voice.

Eden could see one of the officials moving closer to them, so she tried to keep the conversation on light topics. "Do you remember what you ate this morning? I was asked, and I was so busy thinking about the ongoing races that I had trouble remembering."

Keeping his tone light, Xander said, "I don't even know if I remember what I ate this morning. That would be a hard question."

Eden tried to fake a laugh, but she failed. "Is the race over yet?" she asked again.

"No. Just turn around instead of asking me," Xander suggested, his eyes still stuck to the screen.

Eden slowly turned around and watched the runners of the ninth race cross the finish line. Her eyes went to their times. Several of them, no, most of them, were better than her, but it was like in that moment, she forgot how to calculate. What place was she in after the eighth race? What had her time been? How many more spots could she lose before she was displaced from winning a medal?

She watched each runner's number flash up on the screen with a time, then disappear. Her nails bit into the back of the chair as she stared at the screen. Finally, the last runner's time, 10.40, was announced, and the TV showed the current race results.

Eden squinted as the results began scrolling.

No.

She hadn't.

There her name was in fiftieth place. She had dropped too far. Even if she beat everyone in the last two races, she wouldn't win a medal. Defeat settled on her like a whale, making it hard to breathe. Her eyes clouded over, and Eden opened her mouth to protest.

Xander placed his hand on her shoulder, but that didn't make it any better. How could he comfort her when he had no idea how she felt? Running had been her best shot at winning a medal. Even with her powder, she hadn't been able to secure one.

She had lost.

"Hey, it's okay," Xander told her. "There are still a lot more competitions."

"No," Eden choked out.

"You'll do well in one of them. I know you will." Xander's words were meaningless.

Everything was meaningless. She had given it everything she had, and it wasn't enough.

Eden stood up, and her chair clattered to the ground. A few people turned to look at her, but Eden couldn't process them. It was hard enough just to walk to her room. She had to get to her room. She took one slow step.

Before she could take another, Xander was there. He put his arm around her. "Are you going to your room?" he asked. "I can help you get there." His words sounded like they were coming from the other end of a long tunnel.

Eden started to push him away, but her hand bumped into something cold and metallic, something that wasn't normally in the middle of Xander's chest. Eden turned her head slowly to figure out what it was, what was shaking her out of her head.

"Why are you wearing your medal?" Eden asked angrily. It was like he was teasing her with it, waving it in her face, and showing her that he had earned adulthood while she was still struggling.

"Well, I know they have my fingerprint in the system and name and everything, but what if someone stole it? I just want to keep it on me." Xander touched the medal like it was his best friend.

Eden pushed him away. "Leave me alone. I want to be by myself."

"Hey," Xander didn't take the hint, and he hurried to catch up with her. "Do you want me to train with you? Endurance is tomorrow, and I can help you-"

"It doesn't matter. I'm going to lose. I deserve to be eliminated anyway."

"Hey, don't talk like that," Xander told her. "No one deserves to be eliminated."

What had she been thinking? That she would manage to make just the right people sick so that she could get a medal? There were a lot of competitors, a lot who were faster than her. She didn't want to think anymore. She didn't want to be around Xander and his stupid medal.

Eden stumbled toward the stairs, desperate to be by herself.

Chapter 20

Xander watched Eden disappear toward the stairs, battling within himself. Should he let her be alone? That was what she said she wanted, but Xander could tell that she was crushed.

He craned his neck up to see the screen as the names started rolling by again. Eden's name was definitely too low, and there were still two more races to go. She had lost her chance for a medal.

Xander shook his head. She was gone, probably to her room, which meant that Xander was left with free time on his hands for the first time in a long time. His first thought was that he should be training, but the real question was- for what?

He touched the cool circle of metal around his neck. He had already won the medal. Why else would he need to train?

Still, it didn't feel right just to stop caring about his physical condition. He headed toward the sixth floor where he would have an overview of the track below from the window for the continued races throughout the day.

When Xander had just settled onto an exercise bike, a speaker under the TV blared out an annoying tone. Xander winced. If it was going to keep making noises like that, then he wouldn't be able to exercise without losing his hearing.

"Xander Coxon!" the speaker blared out.

Xander whipped his head around. Only a few people were in the exercise room, and most of them just continued doing whatever they were doing. Xander stared at the speaker closely. Was he going crazy?

"Xander Coxon. Come to the lobby immediately."

Xander stood obediently as his heart started racing. It had to do with the poison. They must have found out what he had done with Eden's jacket.

Maybe they had cameras on all of the floors, and they had seen him going into her room.

Xander touched his medal and hoped they wouldn't take it away from him. He would beg them for mercy if that was his only option. He wasn't above anything.

As he jogged down the stairs, his feet landed on each one with a quick thump. When he reached the lobby, he whipped his head around, looking for the reason he had been called. A young adult sat behind the desk in the lobby, and she saw him looking lost.

"Are you Xander Coxon?" she asked, referring to a screen in front of her.

"Yes," Xander said. She shoved a screen in his direction and asked him to confirm his identity. "What's going on?"

"You have a phone call," she said, pointing to the tiny office behind her. Xander hadn't even known the office existed.

Xander tentatively stepped forward and looked around the office space. An old-style telephone was connected to the wall. The receiver had been placed face-up on the table, and Xander approached it like it was a dangerous animal.

"Hello?" he spoke loudly as the plastic pressed into his ear.

"Xander," his father said harshly. How could his father be upset when Xander had won a medal? Hadn't he been watching the competitions? Xander was just about to fill him in when his father spoke again. "Your mother went to the hospital."

"Why did she do that?" Xander's stomach dropped. His mother had promised she wouldn't. They all knew that it wouldn't be good if anyone found out how much her cancer had progressed.

"She didn't go on her own. She had to go into the office. They were having this meeting, and they *refused* to let her do it from home." His father sighed, but Xander couldn't focus on the details. All he knew was that this was bad. His mother was at the hospital. Xander's legs lost their strength, and he started to fall forward.

He braced himself on the desk as he dropped the receiver. It banged against the table loudly.

His mother was at the hospital.

"Xander! Xander!" his father must be yelling into the phone, but it sounded like a cartoonish voice on the other end as Xander missed the chair several times before pulling it under himself. He tried to steady himself with a few breaths. His father continued to yell into the phone.

"Xander! Are you listening to me?"

"I'm here," Xander finally answered, pressing the phone against his ear once more.

"They know how bad it's gotten."

"How bad *has* it gotten?"

"To be honest, they said that they don't know how she's still working and walking around."

Xander nodded. His mother was strong-willed, but even she couldn't beat an incurable disease. "Did they. . . did they mention anything about her job or. . ." Xander didn't know how to finish the question.

"They said that as long as she is still able to complete the duties required by her job that they will allow her to continue living, but if. . ." His father's voice broke. Xander had never heard his father cry, but he knew immediately that's what the raspy sounds were.

"How did Mom take the news?" Xander asked. His mother spent hours on the couch every day. She had stopped cooking regularly months ago, because moving around caused her to run out of breath too easily. Xander didn't think she would have long. "Can I talk to her?"

"No," his father answered, sniffing into the phone. "She didn't want me to tell you while you're competing, but it's important for you to know."

"I've already won!" Xander shouted into the phone. "It doesn't matter. I just have to wait for the other competitions to finish, then I can come home."

Xander didn't want to think about Sisimiut and what home would really feel like if his mother weren't there. He might have earned adulthood, but as he gripped the telephone tighter, he realized that adulthood didn't mean he could control everything around him.

"You won?" his father echoed faintly. "I haven't been watching the competitions. Your mother had to stay in the hospital overnight, and I stayed with her. I haven't turned it on."

"That's okay," Xander told his father. Suddenly, he couldn't think of anything else to say. His mother was sick. They knew that, but now, the hospital and everyone working there knew too. Her job knew, and the moment she was no longer able to do her work, then she would lose her ration coupons. His heart physically hurt as he tried to process what it all meant.

"I'll tell your mother that you've won. She's resting right now, and I didn't even know if they would let my call go through. You know how strict they are about no communication."

"Yeah," Xander was drained of words.

"Bye, Son."

"Bye."

Xander listened to the phone line go dead before a steady beep began emitting from the speaker. Xander carefully lowered the phone onto its cradle and sat staring at the desk.

He couldn't tell how much time passed before the lady from the lobby came in and tapped him on the shoulder. "You've spent enough time talking on the phone."

"I'm done," Xander said, pointing to the phone. "Thank you."

"You're welcome, and . . . I'm sorry." The woman made a sad face.

Xander didn't want anyone's sympathy. He just wanted to understand how this world could be so cruel. He had won a medal, but his family would never be the same.

He slowly stood, taking each step like he was carrying a huge burden. He steadily made his way to the stairs and noticed a camera right away on the wall directly in front of him, taking shots of his face as he climbed the stairs. More security. That was fast.

The white dust from the fresh installation of the camera sprinkled the carpet in front of him.

Xander rounded the landing and continued upward until he reached two men working on installing another new camera. He forgot how conversation was usually politely and meaninglessly exchanged as he stared at them before scooting around and up another set of stairs. On the third floor, he trudged to his room and collapsed onto his bed, willing the sheets to swallow him. He couldn't deal with losing one more person.

Chapter 21

Eden had been in her room for several hours, but she still didn't want to emerge and face the world of failure. She wondered who back home had seen her great run in the morning. Had there really ever been hope for her at all?

Eden's stomach grumbled. She hadn't eaten lunch, but she didn't want to see her sweaty competitors. The medal ceremony would take place soon, but she could watch it just as well from her room.

Trying to get comfortable, she rolled over once more. Something sharp jabbed her in the back, and she shouted louder than necessary. It was her science book.

"Ugh, why are you guilting me into studying?" she asked. She still had the endurance, math, science, and communication tests- four more opportunities. But were they really opportunities if she didn't stand a chance in any of them? As guilty as she felt about yesterday, Eden swallowed. She would have to find a way to cheat again. . . and more successfully.

"Oookay," she huffed. "I'll study. But only because I literally have nothing else to do."

She grabbed her book, and just as she was about to start blankly staring at pages and hoping she would be able to absorb the information, the television played a trumpet noise.

Eden squinted and saw a shot of the gathering room. Perspiring girls were settling into the front few rows. She should be there, but she already knew she hadn't won a medal. What was the point?

Still, she listened as the Lory person made a speech and then started handing out medals. Eden saw two girls that she kind of knew from school win medals, and she felt at least a little bit happy that they would be going home to their families. Even though she knew it wouldn't happen, she kind of half-wished that Lory would call her name. Eden would have to rush down the stairs and into the gathering room, dashing up to the stage to take the medal.

But no. It didn't happen.

Eden switched the TV off and stared at her book more closely. The periodic table danced before her eyes. Feeling guilty, she flipped to the dangerous materials section and learned all about the ingredients needed to build a bomb. That was very helpful except that she had exactly none of them and doubted that they would be building a bomb in the science competition. But still, who knew?

A knock sounded on Eden's door, and her heart leaped into her throat. Had there been a mistake? Maybe she had won a medal after all.

When she didn't answer, the doorknob started wiggling, and Eden froze on her bed, flipping the book closed from the bombs section just before two officials came striding in. She stared at them, and at least one of them appeared embarrassed to have entered her room.

"Do you *need* something?" Eden asked, more bravely than she normally did.

"We are conducting searches of-"

The second official interrupted the first. "We need to search your room. You didn't answer the door, so we assumed you weren't in here."

"Oh, I just didn't know who was knocking on my door, so I . . . didn't say anything."

"Would you mind standing by the door please while we search?"

"Uh, is this normal?" Eden climbed slowly to her feet, grabbing the science book because it gave her hands something to do.

"You were called in for questioning earlier, and we want to make sure that the inquisition has been completed," one of the officials explained as he began patting down the bed. Eden hugged the science book to herself as she watched. Her eyes went to where she had left the jacket, but no, Xander had taken care of that.

One official began picking through the clothes in her luggage, and Eden's cheeks warmed as he stumbled upon her underwear. She pretended to be busy smoothing down the bent corner on her book.

Her mattress was flipped over and thoroughly searched. They even moved the bed frame and looked under the bed posts. They thought of lots of hiding places that Eden would have never even considered.

"What are you looking for?" Eden ventured. She knew, of course, that they wanted a plastic bag with some white powder or residue inside, but she couldn't act like she knew that.

"Evidence that you are lying."

Eden's heart beat faster, and her face must have shown her terror. She had never been very good at hiding her emotions. "Lying?" She barely choked out the word.

"We're not saying that you are lying, but we have to make sure."

She tried to slow her heart down and act like normal. What was normal? It was like she had forgotten everything she knew about how to interact with people. "Oh, so you really think someone tried to . . . hurt other contestants?"

"We know that happened. It's always something every year. We try to stop it before it happens, but . . ." The official shrugged as he ran his hands along the TV stand.

Eden's eyebrows rose. Someone cheated every year? How could they do that?

"Do you . . . catch them?" Eden asked, trying to keep her voice steady.

The official eyed her. "Always."

Finally, they both made eye contact and stood. One of them nodded to the other one. "Thank you for letting us search your room. You can go back to your studying."

Eden nodded and shuffled awkwardly past them in the small space.

"You're into science, huh?" one of the officials asked quietly as he passed by her.

"Best hope of a medal," Eden answered shakily.

Then, the door to her room shut heavily, and she was left on her own. Her heart wouldn't slow down. She paced back and forth in the small open space. They knew. They totally knew! They might not have evidence, but they knew it was her. Eden's whole body shuddered as she realized what that meant. Would they arrest her? Take her to jail?

The thoughts whirled frantically through her mind. She had to do something, but what could she do? She had already cheated, and there was no taking that back. The cameras had probably caught everything. They just wanted to convince her to confess. Should she?

As Eden paced back and forth, she heard a raucous cheer outside. A race for the guys must have just finished. She had to find Xander. She had to talk to him. He wouldn't want her to confess. She already knew that, but she couldn't just do *nothing*.

Eden rushed out of her room, forgetting to lock the door behind her as she clambered down the stairs speedily. No one was in the lobby, and the dining hall was sparsely dotted with a few late lunchers. No Xander.

"Come on," Eden muttered under her breath, hurrying out the door to the track. Then she remembered something. There were cameras everywhere. She tried not to make eye contact with any of them as she slowed her speed. If anyone looked suspicious, it was her, running around like crazy right after her room was searched.

Xander wasn't on the walkway. He wasn't in the crowd watching the races either.

Eden walked calmly back to the hotel and up to the exercise room. She should have checked there first. No Xander.

That meant only one thing. He was in his room. She couldn't go on the third floor without drawing attention to herself, and that was the last thing she needed to do. As she scooped out the remains of the canned vegetables for her lunch, she wondered if these vegetables had been sabotaged by someone else.

A couple of hours later, Xander wandered into the dining hall looking lost. They were just beginning to set out food for dinner, and it didn't seem like he even saw her. Eden waved a hand at him, but he just stared at the food options mindlessly.

Eden approached him from behind and poked him. He jumped around, dropping the empty plastic plate on the floor. It clattered loudly, and everyone in the room looked at them.

"I was just saying, 'Hey,'" Eden told him. "Wasn't trying to scare you."

"Okay." Xander retrieved his plate and began scooping rice and beans onto it. Eden wasn't hungry after eating lunch so late, but she followed him down the line and back to the table, only grabbing something small for herself.

She leaned forward once they were seated, mentally eyeing the camera that was viewing them. She leaned on her hand so that it covered her mouth and spoke as quietly as she could.

"They searched my room."

Xander stopped chewing for a second, then nodded. "I thought they might. They say anything about what they were looking for?"

"No, but I think they know. I was looking at my science book, and the official said something about it. And who else but someone interested in science would do the sort of thing I'm accused of doing?"

"Don't worry about it," Xander said through a mouthful of food. "If they knew who did it, then they would have already taken care of that person. They don't know, so they're just stabbing in the dark."

"But what if they only searched my room?"

"We can't know that."

"Xander, I can't cheat anymore. If they catch me . . ."

"They won't, and if you don't try, then you'll die. I mean . . .be eliminated."

But the word had already been spoken, and it shoved through Eden like a knife. Die. She didn't want to die, or be eliminated, or whatever it was that happened to those who didn't win medals.

"Look, what I'm saying is that you only have a few more tests. You'll be eliminated anyway if you don't make an effort to, uh, fix the odds. So, do what you have to do."

Eden didn't know what she had to do. All she knew was that she had to get through the Olympics and have a medal with her name on it. Her eyes gaped hungrily at the medal hanging around Xander's neck. She wanted it so badly that she could feel it with her whole body.

But at the same time, she was scared. She kept seeing the official looking directly into her eyes and remembering the way he looked at the book she was holding. He *knew*. There was no way he didn't, but Xander was right. No one had come for her.

"How?" she asked quietly.

"I don't know! Why do I have to figure everything out for you? I got my own medal. You get *your* own!"

Eden's mouth dropped open. Who was sitting in front of her right now? His words hit her harder than a punch, and she felt tears building up behind her eyes. She may have cried in front of him many times before, but *now* was not going to be one of those times. She stood up, her chair screeching loudly against the floor.

A couple of people looked their way.

"Eden, wait," Xander said. He closed his eyes and bowed his head. Eden could see him struggling with something, but she didn't care. He knew that the Olympics would be a lot harder for her than they were for him, and here he was saying he basically didn't care if she were eliminated.

Eden started to walk away. It hurt whether she stayed or walked away, and she wasn't going to continue providing entertainment for the people around them.

Xander followed her and laid a heavy hand on her shoulder. "Eden, I have to tell you something."

Eden reluctantly turned around, her jaw set, and those pathetic tears barely under control. "What?"

"I . . . my mom was taken to the hospital. They know how much the cancer has progressed, and . . . she won't have long."

Eden's jaw worked up and down as she processed what he was saying. He didn't talk about his mom a lot with her. All Eden knew was that she was sick, it was serious, and she shouldn't tell anyone about it. "How long?" was the only thing she could think to ask.

"I don't know. Nobody knows. But . . . they said that she has to keep working. If she stops, then she's going to die. Because she has . . . cancer, they're not going to waste resources to treat something she probably can't beat anyway." Xander's voice broke, and he lowered his face.

Eden had never seen him as anything but the strong friend who always held her up. She processed what he must be feeling. Even though he had won a medal, his family would never be the same again. Were thoughts of Matt bothering Xander too? Eden never mentioned him, but Xander probably needed some extra understanding right then.

She threw her arms around his neck, standing on her toes so that she could reach him and pulled him into a hug. The circle of gold pressed into her collarbone as she hugged him. He slowly put his arms around her as well and embraced her back. Eden didn't want to pull away until she had something to say to him, but as much as her brain raced, she couldn't think of anything.

Finally, Xander pulled away and swiped at his face. Eden pretended that she didn't see it.

"Well, you're almost home," she finally said. It was so pathetic. He might get home, but it wouldn't stop his mom's sickness.

"I couldn't talk to her when my dad called. He said that she was sleeping, and it was the middle of the day. If she was sleeping, that means she wasn't working. And if she wasn't working, then they're going to come for her."

"It's okay. Um, maybe you can call back? You can talk to your mom and dad. I mean, if they let a call get through from home for you, then they would probably let you call them again, right?"

"I don't know," Xander said.

They stood there for a second, the anger melting away from Eden. Xander was under a lot of stress, and she knew he cared about her winning a medal deep down. She shouldn't rely on him so much. She had to do this on her own.

"Do you want to . . . finish eating?" Eden asked.

Xander nodded slowly, and Eden wondered if she sounded insensitive.

They went back to their table together, and Eden frowned. Her brain was telling her that something was off. Eden's eyes darted around the table. "Xander," she started to say.

"Uh?" Xander replied, his mouth full of food.

"Am I crazy or did I..." Eden shook her head. She thought she had left her fork on her plate, but it wasn't there now. It was beside the plate. But how would she remember? Xander was stuffing in another mouthful of food, his appetite clearly not affected.

Eden slowly grabbed her fork and took a bite of her food. She knew immediately that it was different. She looked around the dining hall, her heart speeding up. Someone must have known that she was responsible for poisoning the oatmeal. They were trying to get revenge.

Panic crowded around the edges of her vision as she pushed the plate of food away, mechanically swallowing what she was already chewing.

"You don't want it?" Xander asked. "You know we're not allowed to throw away food. I'll take it."

"It's. . . it doesn't taste right," Eden said, taking a few deep breaths. She looked around at the faces again, but the dining hall was filling up. She had no way of knowing who had done it.

Xander took a large bite from her plate even as Eden reached to stop him.

"Right?" she confirmed. "Something tastes weird."

Xander shook his head and took another bite. "No, you're weird. It tastes great. I should have gotten some of it."

"Xander, *stop* eating it," Eden insisted. "You're going to . . . something bad will happen."

He shook his head at her. "It's good. I want to eat it. Don't be paranoid."

"Xander-" Eden said, then she stopped herself. He was going through a lot of stuff, but so was she. She couldn't deal with him criticizing everything she said. He would see that she was right. She just hoped that whatever it was wouldn't kill him.

Chapter 22

Once Xander finished eating, he stared at the dirty plates in front of him. He probably shouldn't have been so flippant toward Eden, but he couldn't seem to understand himself lately. His mind kept going back to his mom, then he would try to think about something else, but his mom would pop up again.

He had to call her before he could try doing anything else.

Xander approached the woman behind the front desk. She wasn't the same woman who had passed the phone to him earlier that day.

"Hi," Xander said.

The woman looked up from her screen. "Can I help you?" she asked in a bored voice.

"Yes, I need to call my parents." Xander leaned on the no-nonsense metal counter.

"No." The woman looked back to her screen without letting him explain.

"Hold on," he said. "I talked to them earlier, and I need to call them back because-"

"No communication from home is allowed during the Olympics. That's one of the first and most basic rules. If you don't know that, then it's not my fault."

Xander sucked in his cheeks and searched for patience deep within himself. If he blew up at this woman, then she wouldn't let him do anything. That was for sure. Part of him said he could just come back tomorrow morning when someone else would be tending the front desk. But he didn't want to; he felt fired up about the whole thing.

"I *need* to talk to my parents. I've already won a medal, so you don't have to worry about me sneaking messages to anyone. My mother is sick, and I don't know how much longer she'll have." Xander hated playing the sympathy card, but it was all he really had.

"Your mother is sick?" The woman looked like she didn't believe him.

"You can ask whoever was working the desk earlier. My dad called, and my name was announced and everything. I need to call them back, because my dad didn't give a whole lot of details. I want the chance to say. . .to talk to my mom."

The woman glanced at the lobby behind him. There were a few people straggling into the gathering room for the upcoming medal ceremony for the boys' races, but it was mostly empty.

"Fine, but I'm going to listen in to your conversation, and if you're lying, then it will be a mark against your social score."

Xander hadn't thought about his social score very much yet. Now that he had a medal, he would officially become an adult, but his social score had always seemed like something he wouldn't worry about until after the Olympics. It didn't matter anyway, because he wasn't lying. The whole world might as well know that his mother was dying.

Xander followed the woman into the office and stood at the phone, dialing it with loud clicks after each number. He pressed the phone to his ear and took a few deep breaths, steeling himself for whatever his father might say.

The phone rang and rang. No one answered. Xander felt a sense of doubt settling into his stomach, or maybe it was eating too much food that was making him feel so sick.

Finally, it stopped ringing. All he heard was coughing, and his whole body flinched with each cough. At last, the noises calmed, and his mother was able to speak. "Xander, is that you?"

"Mom!" Xander exclaimed upon hearing her familiar voice. She was okay. She was still coughing and sick. That wouldn't go away, but she was at home, able to answer the phone, and . . .

"Your father told me he called you. I wasn't happy with him at first, but then he told me you had won a medal."

"Yeah, I. . . I did. It wasn't as hard as I thought it would be. It's-" Xander received a serious look from the woman and realized that he had promised his mother was sick, and here he was talking about his medal. "Um, Dad didn't tell me a lot about the hospital visit. He just said there was one."

His mother sighed, and Xander heard the familiar gruff snort that indicated she was trying to cover up a cough. He waited.

"We did. I had to take oxygen while they did a scan on me. As soon as they found out that the cancer had spread like it had, they stopped the treatment. They told me to go home."

"They don't care about you. You've worked hard for years and maintained an excellent social score. You just need some time to get better, and they don't even care." Xander turned away so that his face was toward the wall. He shouldn't be saying these things in front of the woman. He could be reported for treason.

"Son, I wish I could wave a magic wand and get better. I wish that the world had enough medicine and scientific brains to focus on researching cancer, but I don't have a magic wand, and they don't. This is the way it is, but I won't give up until you come home."

Xander froze. "You think it . . . could be that soon?"

"I don't know, but the fatigue I feel is overwhelming. I've never felt so exhausted before, and I'm worried that I'm at the end. I will keep working and completing my tasks for my job until you get home. I promise that."

Xander swallowed, counting the days until the end of the Olympics. There weren't very many. "Okay, Mom," he said. He wanted to say so much more than "okay," but he had never really been good at expressing his emotions. Just that day when he had wanted to tell Eden about what was happening, he had yelled at her.

The woman tapped the screen that showed the time, and Xander understood the hint.

"Well, I have to go," he said. "I'll talk to you later, okay, Mom?"

"Okay, honey. I love you so much, and I want you to know that I'm so proud of you."

"Thanks." Xander placed the phone back into its cradle gently.

As he left the office, his stomach wouldn't leave him alone. He wanted to go into the gathering room and watch the medal ceremony- see if Connor had been able to win a medal in running. Connor had never been the fastest kid, but he wasn't the slowest either. Unfortunately, Xander's stomach demanded he go to the bathroom.

Xander hurried up to the third floor to address his stomach.

The next morning, Xander had nowhere in particular to be, which was good, because he had spent at least half of the night before in the bathroom. He still wasn't sure his stomach was ever going to let him eat again. Eden's words drifted back to him about the food being contaminated. He hadn't believed her, because it seemed too outlandish. But could she be right?

Xander reached for his phone to text Eden. It wasn't beside his bed, so he looked on the floor underneath it. It took him a full three minutes of searching to remember that his phone had been confiscated before he boarded the plane. How dumb could he be?

He slowly got to his feet. Eden would begin her endurance test in a few hours. He would never say it to her face, but he highly doubted she would be able to earn a medal from endurance unless all the right people had already won medals before her.

Skipping breakfast, Xander stepped outside the hotel and followed the path to the gym. It was unusually hot outside, and he wondered why it was so hot in May. The experts said that even though everyone was using green energy now, the typical temperatures were unsustainable. Still, Xander wondered if it was just a hot day or a hot day that signified something more.

As Xander entered the gym, he scanned for Eden's familiar brown hair and freckled face. She wasn't in the stands. Then he saw her, and his heart stopped. Her face had fear written all over it in the way she was frowning. The corners of her eyes turned down as her bottom lip trembled slightly.

Why was she so afraid? These were just the endurance challenges.

Xander turned his attention from the group of contestants waiting to the challenge itself. That was when he realized that this test had changed quite a bit from last year.

A tank of water the size of the bathroom in the hotel was taking up one side of the floor. Someone was in the tank, but Xander couldn't really see what the person was doing.

He edged over to where Eden was standing. He wasn't technically supposed to stand with the contestants, but he didn't care about rules at the moment.

"You doing okay?" he asked.

She pressed a hand to her stomach. "Not really," she said. "I didn't feel well last night, like I was going to vomit or something, but I never did. I barely slept at all."

"Yeah, I spent most of the night in the bathroom too," Xander admitted.

Eden raised her eyebrows at him. "You did? Do you think I was right? There was some sort of poison in the food?"

Xander shrugged. "I don't know. If there was, it would mean someone targeted you while you and I were gone from the table."

"Me? Why not us?"

"Because I already have a medal. I'm not competing anymore. Plus, it was only your food that you think was affected."

Eden hung her head and began massaging her neck gently. She squinted as she worked at her muscles. Whether it was due to stress or the physical challenge of the competition, Xander could tell that her muscles were tight. He looked away.

Xander had never been a dreamer other than dreaming about winning the Olympics. But he flashed forward a week, two weeks, with both of them winning medals. What would their lives be like?

What jobs would they get? He wanted one that would allow him to have the same schedule as Eden, and he knew that he wanted to be with her. The only thing that had stood between them before was the fact that they hadn't won medals yet. But they were halfway there.

The line moved forward, and Eden cracked her neck as she examined the tank of water. "I don't know if I can do this," she said, watching one of the contestants submerge herself in water.

Xander evaluated the tank of water. "Seeing how long you can hold your breath?"

"I mean, I've never really been a swimmer, and you have to submerge your whole body underwater. I think I'm going to freak out before I really get a good time."

"All you can do is try. Besides, you still have science, and that's your best shot. You don't lose anything trying."

Someone laid a heavy hand on Xander's shoulder. "You're not supposed to be back here," an official told him.

"Sorry, I hadn't had a chance to wish my girlfriend good luck." Xander nodded to the man before realizing what he had said. He didn't look at Eden as he walked away, wondering if his red face looked like a believable sunburn or something else. That's what he got for thinking about the future. He said stupid stuff.

Xander found a place to sit and turned to look back at those in line. He couldn't see Eden anymore except as a distorted shadow behind the tank of water. Only a few more minutes, and it would be her turn.

Connor settled next to Xander on the stands. Xander checked quickly but saw that Connor wasn't wearing a medal. "Where have you been?" Connor asked Xander. "It's like you won a medal and disappeared off the face of the planet."

"I've been with Eden," he explained. "She hasn't won a medal yet, so. . ."

"I haven't either." Connor pointed to his medal-less chest. "Who thought I would get to day four of the Olympics without a medal?" He shook his head.

"How did you do in the endurance competition?"

"I've only done part one, the breath-holding challenge. I got seventy-two seconds. It was okay. I might be able to win a medal if I can hold up during the other two parts."

Xander patted Connor's shoulder. "I'll be here for you, man. When are you competing?"

"They're doing part two once they finish the girls." Connor nodded toward the tank of water.

Xander's eyes were trained on the water, and he saw Eden climbing the ladder. She looked so frail at the top. She glanced into the crowd for just a second, but she didn't catch his eyes before she jumped in.

Xander found himself holding his breath as he counted the seconds in his head, willing her to stay down just a little longer. *You're doing this for a medal. You're doing this for your future,* Xander egged her on in his head.

He had counted to fifty in his head when she rose to the top, gasping for air, her arms flapping around like a fish on land. He checked the official timer and saw that it said forty-eight.

"She got forty-eight seconds," Xander announced as she climbed shivering out of the water. "What are the winners in the girls' category getting right now?"

Connor squinted across the room. "Looks like place one has eighty-one seconds. But that's six seconds above place two. Wow, if I were a girl, I would be in third place right now."

Xander stood up and waved to Eden. She had a towel wrapped around her shoulders, but she was still shivering. She stood uncertainly before the bench, even though Xander patted the seat next to himself. "I should go change so I'm ready for the next challenge," she said.

"You did pretty well," Xander encouraged. "You must naturally have bigger lungs."

Eden coughed and coughed again, and Xander squeezed his eyes shut, transported back to home where the only thing his mother ever did was cough. Finally, Eden stopped, wiping her face on the towel. "I'm glad that's over," she said.

She looked white, well, whiter than normal. "Did you push yourself too hard?" Xander asked.

"I almost passed out," she said. "All I could think about was winning a medal. Do you think anyone has ever died from the endurance tests?"

"They have a medical team over there," Connor said, pointing to the far corner.

Eden smiled courteously, then excused herself to go change.

Xander kept watching person after person climb into the tank and come up sputtering more or less a minute later. His eyes flickered back and forth to the scoreboard. Eden was lower than medal status right now, but she might be able to pass some of the others in the second or third tests. He just hoped she would be able to triumph mind over body.

Connor smacked Xander on the back, shaking him from his thoughts. "I've got to go," he said. "Time for the second test."

Xander watched as Connor joined the other contestants on the floor. The tanks of water were being transported out of the gym by truck, leaving it much more open.

"Hey," Eden said, suddenly beside him.

"Oh hey, I think they're starting the second test. You should probably hurry."

"Just for boys," she said. "Ours doesn't start yet." Eden's voice sounded different, more cheerful than it should be considering the fact that she didn't have a medal or do very well on that test.

"Sooooo," she said, dragging out the word. "Why did you call me your girlfriend?"

Xander made eye contact with Eden and saw that she was smiling a little shyly.

He laughed. "Slip of the tongue."

"Slip of the tongue?" she asked, narrowing her eyes in disbelief. "A slip of the tongue is calling someone you just met Karen instead of Cara. Not a friend, a girlfriend."

"Well, you *are* a girl, and you *are* my friend. I mean, I'm assuming. I haven't checked up on that recently."

"Hmm, you're trying to get out of it easy, huh?" she asked, leaning closer to Xander. "You called me your girlfriend, and I don't think it was a slip of the tongue."

"It *was*," Xander protested. "I promise." He laughed. "You know that until you have a medal and everything, I don't really want to . . . think about all that."

Eden's face immediately fell. What had Xander said that was wrong? That was *always* what they had agreed. Still, he could tell that he had disappointed her somehow. He pretended that watching Connor compete was the most important thing to do right then.

All of the boys were placed in front of backpacks. On three, they had to pick up the backpacks and hold them as long as they could. Xander wondered how heavy they were. This looked more like a strength challenge than an endurance one. He felt Eden's eyes on him.

"You ready for that?" he asked.

Her eyes followed his to the group of guys holding the heavy bags. "No."

Xander's stomach sank. He didn't think there was any way she stood a chance either, but giving up wasn't an option. "You can do it," he encouraged as one of the boys in the competition fell over. A whistle beeped, and his time was calculated.

Eden pressed a hand over her heart. "Yeah, I can do it. I'm just not sure how well."

Xander reached over and squeezed Eden's shoulder, mentally flipping back and forth between hope that she would be able to win and a sinking doubt that it wasn't possible. He kept his doubt to himself as they watched the competition in silence. One by one, the boys dropped their bags and stumbled to the sidelines. Connor was still in it, his face strained and red. It looked like the vein on his forehead was going to pop.

Finally, he dropped his bag, quickly followed by two others, and Xander watched as his first and second times were evaluated. He had moved up to medal territory. Xander didn't want Connor to be eliminated. He might make stupid choices sometimes, but he would be an excellent addition to society. He would work hard and not complain. Xander hoped that he would be able to push through and make it.

Someone spoke fuzzily over the loudspeaker. "Girls for the second part of the endurance challenge. Please come to the gym floor."

Eden stood, stretching her arms behind her head, before she made eye contact with Xander. "Wish me luck."

"Luck!" Xander told her in his normal way.

She pushed past him and climbed down to the gym floor, where she selected one of the bags. Xander watched as she tested its weight uncertainly.

"Don't pick it up yet," Xander muttered under his breath. "Save your strength." She didn't hear him, of course, and started lifting the pack off the ground before the other girls were even in place. She looked around, noticed what was happening, and set it down, puffing.

Xander wanted to bury his face in his hands until it was over, but he couldn't. He had to be the one strong face in the crowd. He had to be the one she could count on when she was struggling.

"Go!" A voice shouted as a whistle beeped. Eden struggled to pick up the bag again. Xander wondered how much it weighed. Twenty pounds? Thirty?

He watched Eden's face straining, her freckles becoming more prominent as she adjusted her grip on the bag. Xander's eyes flitted over the other contestants just as three contestants dropped their bags. One of them started crying, and Xander momentarily flirted with the idea that he could force others to drop their bags. Maybe he should keep his eyes off Eden and focus on her opponents. It was stupid, but Eden needed any help she could get.

Three minutes passed, and eight more girls dropped out, one after the other. Eden wasn't close to the top ten percent, and she would need to get higher than that to balance out her breathing underwater position.

Five more girls dropped out.

Eden stayed steady. Well, maybe not steady, but she was still in the competition.

Then, she started swaying. She wouldn't let go of the bag, and Xander watched as she toppled to the ground with it. She lay there for a moment before finally getting to her feet. She was in almost exactly the same position as before. Too low.

She slowly climbed up to Xander. "Should I look?"

"You did great," he said.

She looked at the screen, and her face visibly fell. "I was literally just telling myself five more seconds. Then, five more seconds after that. But it doesn't even matter."

"Hey, you've still got one more test for endurance." This constant up and down was so hard for every one of the contestants, but Xander just wanted it to be over.

"Have they announced what it's going to be?" she asked, looking around the gym. The girls on the floor were still going strong.

"All the boys competing went outside." Xander motioned toward the door. "Maybe we should go out too. We can see what they're doing."

He and Eden plodded toward the doors. Xander was nervous for what they might see, though he knew Eden was probably even more worried. Once they were outside, they saw strange platforms scattered across the track. There were hundreds.

Xander's eyes darted across them as he tried to figure out what everyone would be doing.

"Boys, please sign in at one of the screens here," someone shouted through one of those annoyingly loud megaphones. "You are assigned a number. Find the platform with that number and wait in front of the platform. Do *not* climb on yet."

Xander squeezed Eden's shoulder. "We can watch the boys go, and maybe you can pick up a few tips."

They both found seats on the edge of the track. He could see most of the platforms which couldn't be more than a foot square. They all had a tall, skinny pole sticking out of the back of the platform. It had to be taller than six feet, but he wasn't sure what they were supposed to do. Pick it up?

Some others nearby were chattering excitedly. "There's no way that guy will make it longer than two minutes," one of them said.

"Look at those arms."

"It's not about strength. It's about mind over body," someone else said.

Xander recognized the boy with glasses from the airplane standing in front of one of the platforms in the third row. He still didn't have a medal. He was definitely more the intellectual type, but that didn't stop him from competing, even after he had probably broken down and calculated his odds.

Once all of the guys were in position by the platforms, someone with a megaphone explained the directions. Other officials repeated them so that there was a terrible echo.

Xander tried to focus on the first speaker.

"When I shout go, everyone will climb on the platform and grab the pole behind their heads. You must grab the pole above the knot. You will stay on the platform as long as you can. If at any point one of your feet slips off or your arms fall, or if you let go in any way, then you will be out, and your time will be noted. Does everyone understand?"

There was a mixed response of nods and "yeses".

"This doesn't look too hard," Eden whispered.

Someone fell off the platform almost immediately, and Eden frowned.

"Okay, maybe it's harder than I first thought."

"You can do it," Xander encouraged without tearing his eyes away from the competitors. He wasn't sure if watching the competition gave Eden an idea of what she could do or if it was making her more nervous. Either way, they had a while to go. Only a few guys had stepped off their platforms already.

"Do you want something to eat before you start this part of the competition?" Xander asked. "It looks like it will take a while before they're ready for the girls."

Eden shrugged. "I'll watch."

Xander remained quiet as person after person fell off their crosses. Colt joined those who had given up, and Xander was fairly certain that he hadn't stayed long enough to win a medal. Still, his main concern right now was Eden.

Finally, the boys had completed their competition, and the last competitor stepped off his platform, sinking to the ground.

"Good luck," Xander told Eden.

"Thanks." Eden glanced nervously at the platforms, then back at the screens as she got in line to sign in. Xander watched her from his place on the benches, wishing he could somehow influence the competition.

After the officials had repeated the same instructions they gave earlier, Xander clenched his hands together and stared at the group of girls on the left.

"Go!"

The girls climbed in unison onto their individual platforms. Eden grabbed the pole, twisted around so that her back was to it, and stared determinedly in front of her. Xander wasn't close to the platform, but he could see now that it was small. It wasn't big enough for someone's whole foot, so they had to stand on their toes or heels or try to turn their feet sideways.

Xander watched the challenge for a moment, his eyes darting from person to person. It didn't look very hard, but he knew that their muscles would begin cramping soon. He just hoped that Eden could keep herself on the pole as long as she needed. This had nothing to do with being fit. It had more to do with keeping her mind focused on how much she needed the medal.

One of the girls slipped and fell off the platform, banging her head as she went down. It distracted another girl into letting go as well. The medics attended to the fallen girl, and Xander started counting how many were in the competition. Eden had a long way to go, but she could do it.

He sent her silent vibes of encouragement, wishing he could stand right beside her and remind her why she was doing this.

There was a flurry of movement so far to the left that Xander couldn't see very well what happened, but when the officials moved, he saw that four more girls had abandoned their platforms. This wouldn't be too hard if girls were going to drop out that quickly.

Xander leaned forward on his knees, waiting for something to happen. But from that point forward, it was actually quite boring to watch. Nobody gave up for the next twenty minutes, even though he could hear groans, grunts, and other sounds of pain.

Then, eight girls dropped, one after the other. Eden stayed put. She was holding on steadily. Thirty more minutes passed before another couple of girls gave up. When Xander looked at the timer, he realized that they had been standing on those tiny platforms for over an hour.

"How can they stay up there so long?" someone else asked.

Xander looked at the person speaking, not to anyone in particular, but just marveling at their endurance.

"They're fighting for a medal," Xander responded.

The guy nodded. "If I hadn't been such a good runner, I would be up there right now."

Xander didn't say anything. He had to keep all his concentration on Eden. Every time she looked at him, he wanted her to see him looking right back, encouraging her that she could do it. What if he turned away to look at someone else right when Eden needed strength from him?

Another few gave up, one of them falling to her knees and sobbing.

Eden stayed.

"You can do it," Xander muttered under his breath.

Another hour passed, and less than twenty percent of those standing up there remained. Eden was one of them.

"Keep holding on," Xander told her.

He saw her grimacing and shifting, trying to find a comfortable position. There was no comfort after so long. She swung to the side, and Xander thought she was coming off, but she was just leaning on one of her arms.

"That's right. Keep going," he muttered.

A few more girls dropped out. "You're closer," Xander told her. "Closer every moment."

Eden suddenly fell off the tiny platform onto the ground, her arms wriggling in front of her as she tried to stop her fall. She hit the ground hard and didn't move.

Xander stood up. He wasn't allowed on the track, but he had to get down there. He pounded across the ground and leaned against the gate between the track and the seats.

"Is she okay?" he asked.

A couple of people looked up at him, but he didn't care. A medic bent over Eden and rolled her onto her back.

"Can I come out there?" Xander asked, one leg already over the fence.

"Stay back," the official warned.

A couple of other girls fell off their perches, walking on trembling legs out of the area. Xander leaned out further so he could still see Eden.

She slowly got to her feet, her legs shaking as the medic walked with her to the side of the track. Her eyes bounced over Xander.

"Are you okay?" he asked her.

"Uh huh," she said. "I think I passed out. Everything started feeling fuzzy, and I knew I was going to pass out. I couldn't move."

"We're going to check a few things," the medic said, sitting her in a chair directly beside the fence. "Then, we'll let you go. Excellent time, by the way."

Xander looked up. Only a few girls were still on their platforms. Eden had made it far. But was it far enough?

"How do you feel?" Xander asked, leaning over the fence, desperate to get a good answer.

"I'm okay," Eden responded.

The medic shoved a bottle of water in her face, and she drank slowly as he wrapped something around her arm and began pumping.

"I'm fine," Eden told him. "I'm fine now. Can I just . . . go?"

"If you start feeling dizzy again, please go to the infirmary." The medic opened the gate for Eden, and she slipped through, walking slowly and steadily as she sipped on her water. Xander kept himself moving at a turtle's pace to match her.

"Do you think it was enough?" Eden asked. "I could have stayed up there longer. I know I could have, but my head kept falling forward. It was like my body was shutting down."

"You did your best, and you were in the top twenty of this competition. I guess they'll weigh it with the other two competitions. I hope it's enough."

Once they were inside the hotel where the air-conditioning was blowing, Eden closed her eyes. Xander watched as she soaked up the cool air and seemed to become stronger with every minute.

He glanced at the screen in the lobby and saw that the girls' award ceremony would begin in twenty minutes. That meant that the last person must have dropped off the platform.

"Let's go into the gathering room," he suggested, leading Eden inside. A few rows were already full, and Xander took a seat halfway up. "I think all the competitors are supposed to sit in the first four rows," he said. This was only the second award ceremony they had attended, the first one where Eden might win a medal.

"I don't know," she said, sipping at her water. "I don't think I actually won a medal. I don't think it's possible."

"Of course it's possible," Xander told her. "You did really well in the last competition. I'm not sure if all competitions are given equal weight, but you were up there almost two hours. That has to matter more than strength."

Eden started gnawing at her lower lip, something she always did when she was nervous.

"Go on," Xander encouraged. "It doesn't hurt to sit up there."

"I just don't know if I should have hope or not."

"We'll know in eight minutes."

Eden slowly turned and trudged up to the first few rows. A few sweaty girls were already sitting there. Most of them weren't talking.

Xander crossed his fingers, literally trying to send Eden any extra luck she might need. When Lory Chambers took the stage, everyone quieted without her having to say anything.

"I want to welcome everyone to the award ceremony for the female endurance competition. If you watched that whole last test, then I applaud you. Can you believe that we had some contestants stay up there as long as two hours? Mind over body is such an important quality."

She smiled into one of the cameras. "However, all three tests have been weighed into today's results. The names I call are those who did the best over the span of the three tests. You can see the exact results online if you are interested in looking."

She adjusted the screen in front of her, flicking onto a new page. Then, she began calling the names one after the other without pausing. "Berta Vaughn, Priscilla Avery, Gracie Fitz, Natalie Cutting. . ."

Xander concentrated hard, but he lost count of how many names had been called. Then, Lory's voice stopped. No more names were called.

When Xander looked up at the stage, he saw it filled with medal winners. Eden wasn't one of them.

Chapter 23

Eden lay on her bed staring at her science book. It was her only hope of salvation, but she couldn't focus on the words on its page. All she could think about was the officials searching her room, looking for clues that connected her to the white powder in the oatmeal, if they even knew there had been white powder in the oatmeal. Everyone had recovered from that, at least as far as she could tell.

Still, this thing seemed more serious. Eden stared at the information in the book, given for anyone and everyone who opened the science book to know about something dangerous- prussic acid. In other words, hydrogen cyanide. According to the book, if created correctly, it had a faint almond taste.

Eden licked her lips, everything from the past three days of failures running through her mind. She had to cheat or she wouldn't win. If she cheated and was caught, then she would be eliminated for sure. But if she wasn't caught, then she stood a chance. That was where she was balancing- on the slim hope that if she cheated, she wouldn't be caught.

Eden read the short section about the acid again. It was something she had probably been assigned to read in school, but she had skimmed through it or never even opened the book. The Olympics had been years away. She had not felt the need to worry about them. Now, all of her procrastination was catching up to her.

"Prussic acid," Eden muttered. Apparently, it was something used to poison animals. The problem was that if it killed rodents, couldn't it kill humans too? If she created this mixture, then wouldn't she run the chance of actually killing another person? Was she so desperate to win that she would murder in cold blood?

Eden had to take a walk. She couldn't stay in her room confusing herself with these thoughts of moral decisions.

Eden stepped outside her room. It was ten p.m., but the halls were still bustling with activity. Lots of teens with medals around their necks and not a worry in the world were having some sort of dance party in the lobby. Eden entered the lobby and stared at the screen announcing the list of competitions. She entered her name and thumbprint and was taken to her account.

There she was, with her name in red beside each of the three competitions she had competed in so far. The number beside her name was final. There would be no changing it. Three more tests to go. She stared at the last three competitions, all mental ones. She wasn't really a "smart" kid, but she wasn't dumb either. She had to hope she could pass them.

Wondering if Xander was still awake, she meandered over to the screening room beside the lobby that the winners had started taking over. She heard one of the cameras mechanically turning and following her stride. Was someone controlling them and watching her right now?

The door was closed, and it wasn't usually. Eden paused in front of it. He probably wasn't there, but Connor had been pretty bummed after losing the endurance challenge. Maybe he and Xander were hanging out.

Eden knocked hesitantly when she heard a weird, coughing noise behind the door. She slowly eased the door open, wondering why it was so quiet. Maybe everyone who had been in here before had gone to bed.

"Hello?" she asked, freezing when she saw what greeted her on the floor. There was a person lying head toward Eden. The girl's body was twitching, but she wasn't the only unconscious person in the room.

Her eyes flitted from face to face, anxiously searching for Xander as she realized that none of these people were moving. Were they alive?

One person slumped over in a chair in the corner looked like he was just sleeping, but another gave a strange, gurgling cough, his medal slapping against his chest as he leaned into the personal screen in front of him. Eden's eyes ate the horror in front of her as she felt her dinner rebelling.

"H-help!" she finally got out, stumbling into the hallway. The hall was strangely vacant now as she rushed to the reception desk. Someone was always sitting there, and a woman playing a game on a screen barely glanced up in her direction.

"Something's happened!" Eden shouted at her. "The people in there! I think they're dead! They're not moving!"

That got the woman's attention. She snapped the screen back into place on the desk and hurried after Eden. Eden wasn't sure if she was that eager to see a dead person or if she just didn't believe her.

Eden almost ran up her heels when she stopped in the doorway. "I wondered. . ." the woman muttered. She turned around, stepping on Eden's toes as she ran back to her desk, and pressed the emergency call button prominently on top.

Glancing fearfully at the room, Eden pressed herself into the lobby's wall as she waited for an explanation. Meanwhile, fear was flying through her. She hadn't seen any blood or injuries. Had they been strangled? Poisoned? Who had hurt so many people, and would they be coming for her next?

An official and a medic rushed down the hall toward the lobby, and Eden pressed herself further into the wall, thinking she might be able to disappear like a chameleon.

The medic began muttering words that Eden couldn't catch, but she inched forward. If someone were poisoning the other competitors, she needed to know the cause behind the fallout. The weird thing was that only people in that room seemed to be affected. A pair of girls wandered down the hall, peering at the commotion with interest.

They began whispering. Finally, one of them approached her. "What's going on?" she asked.

Eden shrugged. "I don't know, but there are a lot of people not moving in that room."

"Dead?"

"I don't know."

The medic pulled one of the bodies out of the room, settling the girl on her back on the floor of the lobby and arranging a machine next to her head. He then placed a mask over her face, and the machine began humming.

He reached for a walkie-talkie. "I need backup. Carbon monoxide poisoning. At least fifteen victims. We're pulling them out into the lobby right now."

Then, he placed an oxygen mask over his own face and began dragging out body after body until two other medics arrived. They worked together to place oxygen masks on the victims' faces.

The crowd around Eden grew, and they all talked about what was happening and why. "Carbon monoxide poisoning?" someone asked. "How is that possible? What could have created it?"

Eden didn't know the how, but she knew the why. Someone was trying to take out competitors. She wasn't a threat to really anyone, but she should still watch out. What if she had been in that room?

But as she saw person after person laid in the lobby, she saw that about half of them had medals. Would a medal be redistributed if the person who had won it died? Whoever had done it wouldn't have gained anything from poisoning them, unless they were one or two places from winning a medal and that was *if* they could be reassigned. Still, there were enough people without medals that those with medals could have just been the collateral.

Eden took a few steps back from the scene, waiting for an announcement, for them to know exactly who did what so she wouldn't have to worry about them coming after her.

Someone emerged from a back room and spoke in low tones with the woman at the desk. Eden used her peripheral vision to pick up the security camera feed. So, they were checking into the room and who had been in there. Would they think Eden had done something? She really didn't need them examining her any more closely.

Eden crept backward toward the stairs, but the person behind the desk seemed to sense her movement. She looked up and made eye contact with Eden. She motioned Eden over. "We need to talk to you for a minute," she said, pointing to the official and herself. It was the bald official who had questioned her the day before about the poisoning.

"Oh, hi, what about?" Eden asked, focusing on the woman.

The official took over the line of questioning, though. "Can you tell us exactly what you saw when you entered the room?"

"Oh, well, I saw lots of people not moving." Eden motioned to the stills of the security tapes. "I'm sure they can show you better what was there."

Her mind felt fuzzy, and the details were starting to fade, all except that one girl's face as she lay on the floor. She clearly knew something was wrong, but hadn't been able to reach the door before it got her too.

"We didn't ask for your input on how we should go about this investigation," the bald man snapped. "Tell us what you saw!"

Eden bit her bottom lip as she felt people in the lobby start to look in their direction. "Um, I was just going into the room to see if my friend was there-"

"Which friend?"

"His name is Xander."

"Last name and country?"

"Xander Coxon, and we're both from Greenland."

The bald man put information into the screen, and Eden waited. He had a lot shorter of a temper than he had had before. Maybe he was getting frustrated with so many people targeting others. Still, this wasn't her fault.

"So, was he in there?"

"No, but other people were. They looked like they were sleeping at first, except one of them was coughing."

"How long did you look at them?"

Eden continued to chew at her bottom lip. What was the point of these questions? They had the video. "I think maybe fifteen seconds. I'm not really sure."

"Why did you think they were like that?"

Eden continued to chew on her lip. If she said that she thought they had been poisoned, then it might give away her connection to the poison from two days before.

"Well?"

"I knew they weren't sleeping. I knew something was wrong, but I wasn't sure what. I'm not very good at sciency stuff."

"Huh."

The noise sounded like he didn't believe her, and Eden remembered the officials searching her room and seeing her holding the science book.

Xander suddenly appeared behind Eden, placing a hand on her shoulder. When Eden turned to speak to him, she realized that the lobby was packed with onlookers as the few medics worked on their many patients, darting back and forth between them as they lay on the floor.

"What's going on?" Xander asked.

"Is this the friend- Xander?" the bald man asked.

"Yes, this is him."

"Let me ask you a couple of questions," the official said, fixing his eyes on Xander.

"Me?" Xander asked, surprised.

"Yes, you. Where were you just now?"

Xander smoothed the medal down to his chest in a motion that was starting to become familiar. Eden gazed at the golden circle hanging from his neck. Did he realize how annoying he was when he kept touching it? It wasn't really his fault, but he kept reminding her that she didn't have one.

"I was in my room, but I wasn't tired yet, so I decided to come down here. Saw something going on and stayed to see what."

"Did you and Eden have plans to meet up?" the bald man asked.

"No," Xander looked to Eden like he was asking her, but she just shook her head.

The bald man started muttering to himself, walking away without really dismissing them. Xander looked at Eden closely. "Is everything . . . alright?" he mouthed, nodding toward the people on the floor.

Eden shook her head, aware of the cameras scanning the current crowd. "I was looking for you, and when I opened the door, these people were all there not moving." She finally allowed herself to look at the faces of those on the floor. Some of them had fluttered their eyes open. One of them was sitting up and removing his oxygen mask, but at least seven individuals weren't responding at all to the oxygen. Could they really be . . . dead?

Eden pointed to a couple of people who weren't moving. "Those four have medals. Why would someone want to hurt them if they've already won?"

Xander shook his head. At first, Eden thought he meant that he didn't know, but then, she realized he didn't want to talk to her about this. Not here, anyway.

She watched, unsure of what she could do, if anything, when the medics began sitting down next to the people who were awake. They started asking them questions and helping some of them to their feet. They removed the oxygen masks and evaluated them one by one. The ones on the floor who weren't moving had their oxygen masks removed too, but Eden realized that it wasn't because they didn't need the oxygen anymore. They were dead. Eight contestants had been successfully killed.

"Amanda P. from Greenland," one of the medics called out after pressing the girl's thumb to a screen. Someone across the room began tapping away at another screen.

"Geoff H. from Greenland."

"Anya R. from Russia."

Eden couldn't watch anymore. She turned to leave.

Chapter 24

Xander woke up the next morning after another bad night of sleep like all of the nights at this hotel had been. It constantly felt like something was going wrong. He thought through the scene from the night before, bodies spread across the lobby floor. Some of them had started moving again. Others hadn't. He hadn't heard what the method of murder was, but he had a feeling that none of them had seen it coming or they would have tried to get out of the room.

Xander's body protested as he got out of bed. Today would be the math test, and even though he didn't think Eden stood a chance of winning a medal in this competition, he had to support her.

When Xander reached the dining hall to grab a quick bite, he saw that the buffet of food was empty. Only a couple groups of people were sitting around the dining hall eating. They had to have gotten the food from somewhere, but . . . where?

"Excuse me, where did you get your food?" he asked someone who was stuffing scrambled eggs into her mouth.

"Go through that door," she said.

Xander approached the nondescript door cautiously. It was cracked open, so he pushed it further open and saw the off-limits kitchen. Two cooks were working furiously over a stove while a third person ran back and forth, handing them ingredients and moving dishes.

The third person approached Xander. "What do you want?" he asked.

"Oh, I'm just looking for breakfast. The buffet is empty."

The person sighed. "If I have to explain this one more time," he muttered.

"Sorry, but there's no sign or anything. Am I too late or something?"

"You now have to order a plate of food to eat. No one is allowed to have contact with anyone else's food."

"Oh, okay," Xander said. "Can I get some eggs, sausage, oatmeal, and hashbrowns? Anything you're serving, I'll take some of that."

The person went to the pots and began scooping out portions much smaller than what Xander would have served himself. He took his plate with a grateful nod and began eating before finding a place to sit down. The only reason they would do this would be because they were afraid of someone poisoning the food again.

Xander had to give them credit. It was much safer, but he hoped he would be allowed to get some more food. He munched quickly, looking around for any sign of Eden. All of the tests had begun by eight or nine in the morning, and it was nearing nine now.

Just as Xander was taking his last bite, Eden strolled casually into the dining hall.

Xander waved his hand at her, and she smiled at him, pointing at the empty buffet area. Xander stood up to meet her. "They're serving directly out of the kitchen now so that no one has the chance to . . . alter others' food." He was aware of the cameras watching him.

"Oh, okay."

"What time does your competition start? Shouldn't you have already eaten? You don't want to be late."

"The math competition is after lunch," Eden informed him casually. "I guess since the guys and girls are competing together, they thought they would give us the morning off. How kind, right?" Her voice sounded sarcastic.

Xander relaxed when he realized that Eden wasn't going to miss a competition. "Okay, come eat with me, then. I'm almost done, but I don't have anything else to do." Xander returned to the table to wait for Eden to bring over her plate of food. She joined him a couple of minutes later.

"Last night was. . . weird," she said. "I watched news coverage of it once I went up to my room. And the cameras just panned the bodies, and then, there was me, in the back corner, watching it all. I looked so. . . scared."

"You were. I'm sure it wasn't easy to be the person to find the bodies," Xander assured her.

"It's weird, because I remember walking into the room. I saw the girl on the floor." Eden swallowed her food and stared at the table.

"What did you do when you saw her on the floor?"

"I just remember seeing her and the way she looked like she was reaching for the door. Something bad was happening, but she didn't know what. She wanted to get out of there, but she couldn't. What. . . happened?"

Xander had his theories. They started with the fact that half of those affected already had medals. It didn't make any sense to attack someone with a medal unless it could be reassigned. Once the adulthood ceremony took place at the end of the Olympics, medals couldn't be reassigned. But before? He had no idea.

"Someone wasn't happy that they had won," Xander said. He glanced toward the little black globes that hid the cameras along with the more obvious cameras mounted on the walls.

"But I just don't remember it." Eden looked worried. "Is that normal?"

"You mean, you blacked it out?"

"I guess, but I just want to remember what happened. I don't know. I'm worried that I could be a target. I don't have a medal yet."

"And some of them did. A medal doesn't protect you from whatever is going on here," Xander told her.

Instead of comforting her, Eden's eyes went to his medal. "So even *you* are not safe," she whispered. Maybe she was just summing up the situation, but her words crawled up his spine in a way he didn't like.

"I guess not," he said. Xander tried to think of a topic of conversation to distract Eden from her worries. "So, what are you going to do with all of your free time?"

"I. . ." Eden glanced down at her plate, then blocked her mouth from the nearest camera's view and started mouthing words. Xander wasn't sure if he understood them all. He *thought* she said,

"I'm going to study lying."

Xander frowned. "You're going to what?" he asked.

"Study sighing," Eden mouthed.

Xander shook his head. If she was just studying, why did she need to be so secretive about it? He wasn't going to ask again.

"Okay," he said, glancing toward the doorway. "I'm going to the screening room, if it's not still blocked off."

Eden peered at him curiously. "You want to watch the old Olympics?"

Xander shrugged. "If I'm not watching you compete, I might as well. Watching you study doesn't sound exciting."

"Can you walk me to my room, or at least my floor?" Eden asked. She had only gotten a scoop of eggs and a sausage, and she had already finished them.

"Sure, I can. Wouldn't want you to get lost."

They stood and started walking evenly toward the dining hall doors. They walked down the hall and to the doorway that led to the stairs.

Eden grabbed Xander's hand once they reached the stairs and pulled him toward the door and part way underneath the stairs.

"What are you doing?" Xander asked.

She pressed her back against the door and glanced at the wall on the first landing. "The camera can't see us here," she said.

Xander's eyebrows rose, and he motioned for her to lower her voice. He wasn't sure how good the microphones were.

"I found out about prussic acid," she said.

Xander didn't know what prussic meant, but he knew acid well enough. Some sort of poison. She was going to try again. He was really close to her, and he saw the fear in her brown eyes.

"I'm going to try to make it, but. . . it can kill someone if they take too much."

Xander nodded slowly. He saw immediately what was happening. She wanted him to talk her out of it, or into it, whichever way she wasn't leaning.

"How are you going to get someone to ingest it with the dining hall serving food like it is now?"

"I don't know. I don't know. I- no, I don't know."

Xander put a hand on her shoulder. "Okay, I'll think."

"I might. . . kill someone," Eden mouthed.

Xander shook his head as he remembered the bodies strewn across the lobby, some of them never to move again. "People will be eliminated anyway," he finally told her. "It might as well be someone else, not you."

"But eliminated doesn't necessarily mean dead," Eden protested quietly. "I mean, we don't know. Maybe they'll still have a chance of living, but if I use this, then. . . they won't."

"You should do it," Xander told her. What if this one thing, this acid, was what stood between Eden and a medal? He had to talk her into it.

"I'm scared."

Her freckles seemed to tremble along with the rest of her.

"Me too," Xander admitted. "I'm scared about what will happen if you don't get a medal, and I go home, and my mom isn't there."

Eden threw her arms around Xander's middle and hugged him. He hugged her back. As he wrapped his arms around her, she seemed so small and frail. He wanted to do everything he could to protect her.

She pulled back and looked up at him. She started to say something, but Xander didn't want her to voice her fears. He didn't want to think about dealing with his own problems. He just wanted to be there with her, so he kissed her. For the second time in their lives, he pressed into her lips.

He pulled back and studied her face, but she quickly smiled. "Well, I'm still scared," she said. "But, uh, thanks."

Xander took a step back, then one more. He felt so awkward, which wasn't usually something he experienced. "I think you can find your room from here," he said. "I'm going to the screening room." He had already told her that. Why was he telling her again?

"See you later," she said, the worry jumping across her face again. Xander stood back and watched her bounce up the stairs to the second floor.

Finally, he remembered what he was supposedly going to do, and he found his way to the screening room.

There were several screens with headphones connected to them. Xander's hands itched for a connection to the internet, but there would be no checking social media now. These computers did one thing and one thing only- give you access to the past Olympics.

Just as Xander was sitting down, he realized who was sitting in the chair next to him- Colt. Xander debated whether he should say something or not as he grabbed the headphones. Colt looked up and recognized Xander.

"Hello," he said, pausing his screen and taking off his headphones.

"Hey," Xander answered. He clicked on his own screen.

"You received a medal. Congratulations."

Xander touched the medal. It felt familiar around his neck now. "Yeah, wrestling." His eyes went to the empty spot on Colt's chest. "I saw you in the endurance challenge yesterday. You did really well."

"Not well enough," Colt responded.

He turned his screen to show Xander what he was looking at- the stats for various competitions over the past few days. "After running the results of these competitions, I'm not sure what happened. I didn't expect all of my calculations to be correct, but some people who had over a 95% chance of winning a medal, didn't even place in the top fifty."

"Well, I guess that 5% really mattered." Xander saw the names Colt was pointing to, but he didn't recognize them.

"Sure, it is a chance, but that chance was really only there in the case something unexpected happened. Unexpected circumstances withstanding, they should have all placed. They didn't."

Xander's eyes flicked to his own screen. He wanted to spend some time with his brother, not talk with this nerd. But at the same time, he felt bad for the guy, even if he didn't understand everything he said.

"Yeah, I guess it's hard to predict how the pressure will affect everyone."

"I already added that into my calculations." Colt frowned and pressed a few more buttons. "Let's look at the girls' race, for example. Six out of the predicted top twenty finished at least ten places lower than the lowest I calculated for them. Something interfered with their performance."

Xander knew exactly what that was, but he wasn't about to unconfuse Colt. "I guess it goes to show that nobody can tell the future," he said.

"It doesn't make sense." Colt reached for his headphones and began clicking on the screen again. "It makes me wonder if I've calculated my own odds too high. I don't know if I can possibly win."

"I thought you weren't going to calculate your own odds."

"I broke down," Colt admitted. "Besides, with different competitors out of the competition, I thought it would be encouraging. The math test is later today. I don't know if I'll do well enough."

Xander nodded. "If everything you've told me about calculating odds is any sort of clue, then I think you'll do fine." What else was he supposed to say to someone who was contemplating his potential elimination?

Finally, Colt immersed himself in his own screen, and Xander pulled up the Olympics from three years ago. The best shot was in the endurance competition. That was where he got the close-ups of his brother's face.

Xander clicked on the video and fast-forwarded until it was down to the last fifty competitors or so. The screen flicked to his brother's face, and he saw Matt straining against the weight. Xander paused the video and stared at Matt, trying to take in every feature on his face. His brown hair looked exactly like Xander's. He had always complained that Xander shouldn't be allowed to copy his hairstyle, but it was the one thing that made them look so much alike.

He had a birthmark on his left cheek, just below his eye. He had been teased about it for a little while until he punched the person who led the teasing. That was Matt. The gentle kid until you went too far. Except he wasn't a kid anymore. He wasn't anything, except eliminated.

Xander squinted at the screen, his hand hovering over the mouse. He wanted to keep moving. He should watch the rest of the competition . . . or do something else, but he couldn't move away.

Matt Coxon. His brother.

Their family was shrinking, and soon, it would be even smaller. He couldn't go back without Eden. She *had* to win a competition. He would do whatever he had to do.

Xander backed out of the endurance challenge video and went to the math competition. He watched the video with new eyes. He had seen bits and pieces of the competition years ago, but he hadn't been paying attention. His brother didn't compete in math, and Xander wouldn't either. Now, he looked at everything, pausing the tape every few seconds to study what he could see of the contestants writing down their answers.

Calculators.

They weren't allowed to use them for all questions, but they could use them for some. Xander went back to the beginning of the video and checked out the scene. Where were the math competitions done? Where were those calculators kept?

Finally, Xander had a plan. If everyone trusted the calculators, he would just have to make them a little less trustworthy.

Chapter 25

Eden frowned at her meal of tasteless oatmeal. Nothing to give her protein for the afternoon's competition- math. Not that she really needed protein to be able to answer some numerical equations.

Eden forked the food into her mouth as she stared at the table in front of her. She hadn't seen much of Xander that morning, but if he wanted to spend time in the screening room watching old tapes, then he deserved that time alone. She wouldn't keep bothering him.

A couple of girls were talking at the table behind her. At first, Eden didn't listen. Then, she couldn't help it. She heard "Sisimiut," and at the name of her hometown, her ears perked up.

". . . . the only one with real competition," one of the girls was saying.

Eden turned sideways and got a quick glance at both of them. One of them she recognized as the square-faced girl who had competed at the same time she had for the logic and problem solving medal. Eden couldn't see the other girl very well. She didn't think she recognized her.

"It'll be impossible for any of the Greenlanders to win the math competition," the girl said.

Eden rolled her eyes. She never understood this "national pride" thing. They were all part of one earth. Who cared if you lived in Greenland, Alaska, or Russia? None of it mattered if you didn't win a medal.

"They couldn't win in endurance. They can't win in math. They just can't win."

"Good thing *we* know how to win."

Eden's heart sped up. If she didn't know better, she would think the girl was hinting at some kind of cheating. She would be dumb to do it right here, though, where everyone could hear her.

Eden couldn't finish the tasteless oatmeal, so she carefully dumped it without being seen before returning her utensils to the cleaning area. The math test would start in half an hour, and she wanted to see the room where it was taking place. The gym had been transformed according to rumors, and Eden wanted to get comfortable with the location before the test began.

Xander ran into her as she was leaving the dining hall.

"Don't use the calculator," he muttered to her without really stopping or looking her in the eye.

That was definitely weird. He left her standing in the hall by herself thinking about what he had said. She swallowed. Had he cheated on her behalf?

She didn't have time to chase after him and ask, but she had to take the math test without a calculator.

Eden walked through the warm morning sun to the gym which had twenty or thirty of the other competitors milling around. Some had already claimed desks while others talked to each other. A few tapped their legs nervously.

Eden approached one of the desks and saw the screen placed on top of it. Beside the screen was a calculator. The 0 showed that it was ready for her to input numbers. Nothing looked wrong with it, but Xander wouldn't lie to her.

She approached another desk, one toward the back, and took her seat, signing in at the screen. It approved her sign in, then told her to wait. A counter of the time left until the test would begin popped up on the screen.

Eden settled into her chair and watched as the seats around the edge of the gym filled with people. She had eighteen minutes until her fate in regards to a medal in math would be decided.

Fourteen minutes.

Xander walked into the gym, wiping his mouth free from food crumbles.

Eleven minutes.

Xander finally found her with his eyes and smiled in her direction. She waved to him. Most of the seats were filled.

Eight minutes.

The officials took their places around the room and in between the rows of desks. Lory Chambers took her place by the microphone.

Four minutes.

All of the seats were filled, and Eden felt a camera panning over the group of competitors. She tried to look less nervous than she actually was.

Lory Chambers stood and tapped on the microphone. The room became silent. She spoke more to the camera than to the eighteen-year-olds shifting in their seats.

"We are now beginning the math competition for our girls and guys."

A camera panned over the seated individuals, and Eden shifted uncomfortably. The screen in front of her flashed red as the clock reached zero.

"I'm going to explain the rules, even though I'm sure you have heard these each year already." She smiled, but no one thought her attempt at humor, if that's what it was, was anything worth laughing at. "Everyone will receive the same questions at the same time. Depending on the difficulty of the question, the contestants will have a timer. Most of the easier questions will have a limit of five seconds. Time will not begin until I am done asking the question. Questions will not be repeated.

"As they become more complicated, calculators will be permitted, but no using your calculator until your screen tells you it's time. At no time will anyone be knocked out of the competition, but points will be added up at the end to see who has the most correct answers, more points going for the more complicated answers. Are we ready?"

Only a few of her competitors nodded enthusiastically.

"There will be *no* talking during this competition, including from the audience." Lory Chambers gave the audience a glare. "If someone shouts out an answer, then you'll be immediately removed from the crowd, and the question will not count."

Eden made eye contact with Xander again. Her whole mouth felt dry, like she had stuffed it with socks before the test, and she could barely breathe now.

"Please remember to write your answer on the screen legibly," Lory Chambers enunciated the direction carefully, and Eden nodded, poising her finger above the screen as it flashed. It turned into a whiteboard, and Lory Chambers began reading the first question as it flashed up on a screen in front of them.

"Eighteen plus twenty-three."

Eden wiggled her toes as she added it in her head. Forty-one. She scribbled the answer out and pressed the submit button. Her screen turned black just before the timer rang.

"The correct answer will now be revealed," Lory Chambers announced.

Eden glanced at one of the large screens mounted along the wall, and she saw the number forty-one flash up. A correct answer was a comforting way to start, but it was discomforting that everyone else might find this test easy.

"Remember that they're going to get harder," Lory Chambers told them.

Eden's screen flashed white again, and she readied her finger. She didn't have time to see what Xander thought of her right answer before she focused on the next question.

"You have a large pie. Gary is given one third of the pie, and John is given one fourth. Who has the larger slice?"

This was easier than the last one. Eden scrawled out Gary's name, hoped it was legible, and pressed submit just before her screen blackened.

Correct again.

Hope started to build within her.

Two more questions.

Two more correct answers, from her at least.

Then, the questions began to slowly get more difficult.

"What is the perimeter of a rectangular room with sides that are both seven feet and twelve feet long?"

Was the perimeter around or the middle? Did she have to figure out how long the middle was? No, that was in a circle. Maybe the area? Perimeter.

The timer on her screen flashed to two seconds, so she scribbled twelve, knowing it was wrong before the screen went black.

She saw the correct answer on the board. Thirty-eight.

Most people had answered correctly if their celebratory movements were any indication.

Eden felt a shiver of terror work through her body. She had to keep doing it. She had to answer them right. A camera panned by her, and Eden kept her eyes on the screen as the next question came. It was an algebra question, and they were given a full minute to do it. Eden hated not having the question right in front of her, but she tried to copy it down from the large screen as quickly as she could.

"You may use your calculators for this one," Lory Chambers announced.

Eden started to reach for her calculator, then remembered what Xander had said. She drew her hand back, then reached for it again. She had to look like she was using it or that would be suspicious.

She kept it close to her, bent her head over the screen, and started dividing numbers by each other. She thought she had a decent answer, but she still wasn't sure. Another thirty seconds would have been great, but the timer turned red just as she was submitting her answer. Her screen went black, and all the heads bent over desks looked up at the screen on the wall, waiting for the correct answer.

More than a third of the students had gotten their answers wrong, but Eden wasn't one of them. She pumped her fist in the air as a smile started to creep across her face.

"What?"

"How?"

Some girls were outraged that their answers had counted as wrong. No time to really celebrate. Lory Chambers began asking the next question. Eden read along.

"Riley puts $80 in a bank account that gains 20% interest per year. If she makes no withdrawals, how much money will she have at the end of the year?"

Eden jotted down the numbers- 80% and $20. No, that was wrong. $80 and 20%. Did it make 20% each month of the year, or only once in the year? What was 20% of $80? Eden clutched the calculator. She knew that if she did $80 x .2, she would have the number. Then, she would only need to add it to $80. But she couldn't risk it. She didn't know what had happened to the calculators.

Eden had fifteen seconds remaining.

She began muttering to herself. "$2 is 20% of $10. So. . . . $2 + $2 + $2. . . ."

Eden scribbled her answer- $16 -and sat back as the timer went off. Her adrenaline was pumping faster in this competition than it had in any of the physical ones.

The correct answer was revealed on the board, but hers was wrong. "Wrong? But . . ." Oh, she had forgotten to add the interest to the $80.

"It's okay. It's okay." She wasn't the only one who had gotten the answer wrong. Someone on her left slammed the calculator onto the desk, and a piece popped off it. She was upset, but she was clearly pegging the calculator as the culprit. Now, it would be a real math competition. If the calculators weren't involved, the people who were used to relying on them would have to use their brains.

Eden stared at the screen as she listened to the next question.

"You will have two full minutes for the next question," Lory Chambers announced. She didn't say anything else, but a deformed shape popped up on Eden's screen. She had to find the area. Area was easy to find when things were shaped like normal objects in the world. Not when they were shaped like *that*.

Eden took a deep breath and began dividing the bigger shape into smaller shapes and wondering if she stood a chance even with Xander's help. His meddling might not win her a medal.

The timer blinked continuously in the corner as she rushed to solve it. Even if she were good at math, she would need more time than this to answer it. As she scribbled down a guess in the last two seconds, she wondered if she really stood a chance at all in the science competition or if she should just give up now and enjoy her last couple of days.

Her thoughts caused her to miss a few precious seconds on the next question, but Eden could already tell that the questions were getting too complicated for her. They were things that had put her to sleep last year in school. Some of the questions didn't sound like anything she had ever learned.

After five wrong answers in a row, she stopped looking up at the screen to see how she had done. She didn't stop trying, though, even if she thought the questions were impossible.

Eden was glad when they reached the last question. She wasn't sure her brain could take it anymore. No one should have to go through three hours of math questions. Her stomach grumbled as she scribbled her best guess down and closed her eyes. They burned from staring at the screen.

"The awards ceremony will take place in an hour in the gathering room," Lory Chambers announced.

Eden didn't move from her seat right away. She thought she could fall asleep right there, in the middle of the gym.

A hand on her shoulder made her jump. "Are you really going to nap here?" Xander asked. He was smiling. Why was he smiling? She hadn't won a medal.

Eden slowly stood, her limbs protesting the movement after sitting stiffly for so long. "I didn't win a medal," she said. "I don't want to go to the gathering room."

The gym had mostly emptied out except for a couple of people reliving different questions from the test.

"You might have," Xander told her. "You got a lot of ones at the beginning right, and I think . . ." he dropped his voice and looked around. "The calculators really made a difference."

Eden smiled just a little as she imagined someone pressing the buttons confidently but still getting the wrong answer.

"Not enough," Eden said. She bent her head close to Xander's as they left the camera-filled gym and walked along the pathway that wasn't as monitored. "What did you do to them, anyway?"

"Switched the buttons on some of them," Xander said. "They thought they were pressing multiply or something, but it was really adding the numbers. You might figure it out quickly when there were just two numbers. But when you put in multiple numbers, it's harder to realize."

"Too bad the boys had to be affected too," Eden commented.

"Oh, shoot!" Xander's eyes widened. "I forgot about that. He probably didn't need one anyway."

"Who?"

"Some guy I met on the plane. He's a math genius, and I think he's hoping he'll win his medal today."

"I think I just need some sleep. I want to go up to my room."

"At least come to the ceremony first."

Eden reluctantly took her seat on one of the front rows, slouching down as far as possible. At the beginning, there had been five rows reserved for competitors, but with each competition, there were fewer people competing. There were now only three rows.

As Eden looked around, she realized that with so few competitions left, the majority of the people sitting here would be eliminated. She wasn't sure why she felt so alone in being eliminated when there were obviously others too. The girl next to her looked like she had just been crying. Eden tried not to stare at her too obviously.

Lory Chambers climbed on to the stage with a smile, despite calling questions for the last few hours. "Is everyone ready to see who has won medals in our math competition? We will give out medals for the girls first, then the guys."

A couple of people cheered, but most of the girls in the first few rows shifted awkwardly. Eden's stomach felt like a perpetual ball of knots. She bent forward, her head against her knees, her ears cocked for her name.

The names began.

She heard cheers as different girls were called, but then, Lory Chambers's voice grew silent. It had happened again. Eden hadn't won a medal. How many times would this have to happen for her to give up hope? Why was she always fooled into thinking she might have a chance?

Chapter 26

Xander sat up from the thin mattress, his eyes fixing on the wall across from him. His heart was beating a hundred miles a minute, but his hotel room was completely still. He turned his head slowly, taking in the shape of the silent TV and the sliver of window.

Why was he awake?

Had he been dreaming?

Xander tried to recall what had been going on in his mind, but all he could think about was Eden. She only had two more chances to win a medal.

The numbers on the clock read 1:12.

He lay back down on the mattress and tried to shut his eyes, but his heart was still racing. There was no set curfew in the hotel, per se, and there was no way he would be able to stay in bed another hour while he waited to feel sleepy again. He might as well walk around the hotel and maybe up to the exercise room.

Xander yawned and pulled on a shirt. Stretching, he exited his room and headed toward the stairway. Just as he set foot on the first stair, he heard a screech below him, quickly cut off. He froze, listening.

There was the distinct sound of several pairs of footsteps. He couldn't tell if they were going up or down the stairs, but they were definitely on the second landing. He ducked around the landing he was on and climbed a couple of stairs up toward the fourth floor, listening to the sounds and trying to figure out what was happening.

"-ey," a female voice said.

Someone else whispered, but he couldn't hear what was said.

Another few footsteps, then a couple of faster ones, like someone had tripped and was trying to gain their footing. That was when Xander realized the sounds were coming toward him. He shrank back further into the shadows of the steps to the fourth floor. The group didn't turn to look at him as they walked by, two girls with their arms around a third girl in the middle. Her head was hanging forward a little like she had had too much to drink.

Weirdly, they didn't try to keep going. They entered the third floor, which was full of boys' rooms, but there was something about the girl in the middle. Her brown hair looked too familiar. Could it be Eden? It couldn't. She wasn't buddy-buddy with any girls like that.

Xander slowly stood and crept to the doorway. He peered down the hall and saw them stumbling down the hall to one of the rooms on the right. One of the girls knocked, and the door opened quickly.

The three disappeared inside, and the door shut soundly.

It wasn't Eden, right?

Xander walked casually down the hallway, angling for the bathroom, and noted that they had gone into Room 311.

There were no cameras in the hallway leading to the dorm rooms, but there were cameras on the stairs. Xander didn't know if anyone would be actively manning them at this time, but they were probably recorded.

As he entered the bathroom, the light automatically came on, but he pressed the button to turn it off again, his back against the wall. If he stayed where he was, he could see the door to 311 whenever it opened.

Xander took a couple of deep breaths and thought through his options. He could alert someone at the front desk, because the girls were breaking the rules being on his floor anyway. He wasn't sure what sort of consequences there were for that, but a part of him couldn't let go of the fact that the back of that girl's head had looked like Eden's.

She had spent the rest of the evening in her room, probably moping over not winning a medal in math, and Xander hadn't seen her since the awards ceremony. But what if . . .

Xander's thoughts were interrupted as someone else came down the hall. This hotel sure was busy for one in the morning.

It was two more girls with a third girl between them. One of the girls had that square jaw. He recognized her from his eavesdropping behind the sofa. They knocked on the door to 311. That room *had* to be getting full now. What was happening?

This time when the door opened, two of the girls came back out. Neither one of them had Eden's brown, curlyish hair. The middle girl was gone.

Xander's stomach sank. Something was wrong. Something was definitely wrong.

Once the hallway was clear, Xander crept toward the door, ready for action with every part of his body. When he got closer, he could hear someone laughing inside. The laugh calmed him right away. If they were just having some late night fun, then it was really none of his business.

He stopped right in front of the door and held his breath, trying to catch some words, something to soothe his nerves so he could go on his way to the treadmill without a feeling of trepidation following him around.

Instead of another laugh or a comment, he heard a whimper. It cut through him like ice. Something was going on in there, something that wasn't right.

Xander pounded on the door, and the voices behind it died immediately. A scuffling sound was followed by footsteps. Someone was coming to answer the door. Xander hadn't won a medal in wrestling for nothing. He took a stance, ready for whatever might happen.

A guy's voice called through the door. "Who is it?"

Well, Xander wasn't ready for that. Should he act like himself or like an official investigating the noise?

"I . . . heard there was a party going on in here and want in."

"You're wrong, dude. No party." The guy yawned loudly, and Xander could tell it was 100% fake. "Can't believe you woke me up for that."

Xander didn't move, and he didn't hear the guy walk away either. Clearly, he didn't want to open the door, not to Xander anyway. He wasn't going back to bed though.

Finally, Xander decided he would wait to find out. There was no way he would be able to go back to sleep or even up to the exercise room knowing that something shady was happening. Xander walked away, back to his hideout in the bathroom, snapped the automatic light back off, and waited.

He waited nearly ten minutes before he saw three girls coming down the hall. It was the same as before, the girl in the middle was being balanced by the others.

Xander emerged from the bathroom, trying to fake a middle of the night run, and the girls completely ignored him.

"Hey, what are you doing on this floor?" Xander asked.

One of them gave him a hard look. "We're visiting a friend. You don't have a problem with that, do you?"

Xander held up his hands as his eyes darted over the girl in the middle. "I don't care, but it looks like your friend isn't feeling very well."

"She isn't," the girl agreed, continuing to stare at Xander. His eyes fell to her chest where her medal glinted. The girl on the far side didn't have one and neither did the one in the middle.

"Excuse us." She brushed past Xander and led the other girl the rest of the way down the hallway to the stairs on the far side. Xander frowned. He had thought they were going to Room 311, but they had kept going. He didn't trust them, so he went to the stairs and climbed them, pausing on the fourth floor to listen.

Nothing on the fourth floor.

Taking off his shoes, Xander crept back down to the third floor and peeked around the frame. The girls were just going into Room 311.

Thinking he was probably an idiot, Xander ran down the hallway, shouting "Hey!" just before the door closed.

He slammed his body into the door and heard the thump as the door hit a body and bounced off. Xander didn't stop to think. He pushed through, stumbling over something in the doorway.

He fell, curling his body instinctively so nothing important would take the brunt of it, but he didn't hit the floor.

His body landed on something soft. It was the square-faced girl.

"Uh, get off me!" she shouted. "Idiot!"

Xander stood and raised his hands in the air. He wasn't trying to hurt anyone, but something weird was definitely going on here. His eyes scanned the room, and then, they stopped. There was Eden on the far side of the room. She looked dazed and confused. She squinted at him like she wasn't sure if she recognized him or not.

"Eden?"

Someone punched Xander from behind, and something snapped as he stumbled forward again. Despite the number of people in the room, Xander tried to gain his footing and face his attacker.

"You just won't stop nosing around," the guy said, his fists up. He also had a medal around his neck, and Xander recognized him as the one who had stood beside him when they were receiving their medals for wrestling. As Xander tried to assess the situation, the guy dove at him.

Xander dodged, stepping on something as he did so. "Sorry, sorry," Xander apologized, and the guy took the opportunity to grab Xander's legs, toppling him.

Xander fell on someone else. "Sorry," he apologized as he rolled over and tried to protect himself.

The guy jumped on Xander, but Xander dodged the blows, falling into a familiar rhythm. One, two, three.

He got in an offensive punch on the guy's jaw, snapping the guy's head back.

Xander scrambled to his feet, taking a quick turn to see if anyone else was going to attack him. The guy didn't get up from the floor.

"Oh my god," the girl said. "You killed him! Oh my god! That's a crime, you know!"

"And what you're doing isn't?" Xander kept one eye on the people by the door as he stepped over other girls to get to Eden. She was sitting under the window ledge.

"Xander," she said quietly, reaching for him.

"Are you okay?" he asked her.

"Where are we?"

"We're in some guy's room." She reached for him like she was going to hug him, but Xander checked her over for bruises. She had one forming on the back of her neck.

The guy he had punched was already getting to his feet and approaching Xander, so he didn't have the chance to finish seeing if Eden was okay.

"Dude, what are you doing? Did you drug these girls? That's sick."

The guy laughed. "Not for what you're thinking, though you never know what might happen."

"No," Xander said. "You're done. I don't know what you think you were doing, but you're done now. They're leaving."

The guy laughed and crossed his arms despite the fact that he was moving his jaw like it hurt. "You stood a chance when you were on the other side of the door, but now, you're not leaving. You can just take a spot on the floor with all of them."

Xander shook his head as the square-faced girl got to her feet and dusted herself off. "Derry," she said to the guy. "What are we going to do? We're going to get in trouble now."

"Shut up," he said. "Go sit with the others."

"I'm not going to-"

"You're going to!" he shouted at her.

Xander laughed. "Yeah, keep shouting. Wake up all your neighbors."

Xander went to the wall on the left and began pounding on it with a closed fist.

The guy didn't look worried at all.

"They're in on it too," he said, shrugging. "You can stop."

Xander didn't hear anything coming from the room, so he went to the other side and started pounding. Nobody seemed to hear him, and the girls sitting around the room were still dazed. He wasn't getting any help from them. This was a true test of his survival skills, not the stupid Olympic contests that everyone was so focused on winning.

One of the girls on the floor was stirring. They were waking up from their drugged state, but Xander couldn't be sure when they would be ready to act. He made eye contact with Eden again, but she was gazing up at the ceiling like it was the most beautiful thing she had ever seen.

As Xander turned back to the guy, he was met with a fist in his face. Xander reeled, tripped over someone behind him, and hit the ground hard. The guy attacked Xander again, and all he could do was protect himself. He wasn't focused enough to make his own offensive move.

Still, he wouldn't give up. He had to do something.

The guy landed a good blow on Xander's back, and he felt the pain start to take over his brain. Xander forced himself to relax all his muscles, not tense up. He wasn't passing out, but he could pretend he was. He just had to hope the guy wouldn't take the opportunity to actually kill him.

Bam.

Bam.

Bam.

After three more punches, the guy stopped. Xander tried to relax his breathing. He had seen his fair share of people passed out in wrestling practice, and he hoped he was imitating it well enough.

"He's gone," the guy, Derry, said.

"Oh my god. Will we have to kill him or something?" his co-conspirator asked.

"Shut up. I didn't tell you to speak."

She muttered something but didn't comment.

Not only was this guy doing something illegal in here, he wasn't even a kind human being. Shouldn't they have to pass some sort of basic humanity test before being given a medal?

Xander didn't move as the guy paced around the room. Xander heard something metallic in the corner. "I think this is enough," the guy said. "I'll get started. You can go back to your room."

"I want to stay with you," the girl whined. "That's why we're doing this. To be together, right?"

"Yeah, that's why," the guy said. "Fine, you can stay."

Xander almost lost control of his eyelids when he heard Eden say something. "Where am I?" she asked. "I don't remember this place."

She was closer than Xander had thought. He willed her to keep her mouth shut. She didn't need to draw attention to herself for whatever this guy was planning. If Xander was putting the pieces together correctly, it sounded like this guy had won a medal and the girl hadn't. They were trying to help her win a medal. Xander understood the struggle, but this was too much.

"Shut up," the guy told Eden.

Xander couldn't move. He couldn't do anything to comfort Eden or tell her to be quiet. He just had to hope. This was not a good situation for hope to be his only weapon.

Xander heard a sound in the hall. It could be a girl coming back with more, but he thought that they weren't expecting anyone else. He wasn't the type to ask for help. Besides, he couldn't run out and get someone while leaving these girls here.

Xander leaped to his feet and yelled as loudly as he could, the scream tearing through his throat.

The sudden movement made him dizzy, his stomach groaning with pain.

Derry whipped around, a knife in his hands. He jabbed at Xander, and Xander stumbled backward. He almost fell when a hand grabbed him. Eden.

Her eyes were scared, panicked, but she was on her feet. She took a deep breath and screamed, staring into his eyes, asking if that was the right thing to do. Xander nodded and started screaming again. He stepped forward again, ducking the knife. He wasn't an expert in combat that included weapons.

Derry slashed at him again, cutting his arm. Eden continued screaming like a maniac in the background. Her screams seemed to wake some of the other girls from their stupors, and one of them started whimpering, tears streaming down her face.

Xander glanced at Derry, then the door.

He dodged the knife again, stepping to the side. He winced as he stepped on someone's arm. One of the girls tried to grab him from behind, but he knocked her away.

Another dodge.

Another step.

He was even with the door now.

All he had to do was . . . .

Run

To

The

Door.

The door opened easily under his grasp, and Xander slammed it into the wall.

"Eden, out now!" he shouted. Then, he screamed as loudly as he could even as his throat burned.

Heads began peeking out of doorways all up and down the hall. The head next to Room 311 looked angry. He came toward Xander with his fists balled, and Xander remembered what Derry had said.

"Get the officials!" Xander shouted, making eye contact with one of the heads further down the hallway.

Xander fell forward as Derry landed a punch on his back. This pain was different. Instead of the slow, steady ache, the pain twisted inside him.

Two of the guys who had come out of their rooms ran toward the stairs.

As Xander tried to rise, the pain in his back thudded through him. Why wasn't Derry attacking him again?

A cry.

A thud.

Xander stood on his feet again. He reached toward his back where pain was echoing through him, and his fingers brushed something metallic.

A knife.

The knife.

If it was here, then it couldn't be used against Eden, but that didn't mean Derry didn't have other weapons.

Xander gripped the handle, then shook his head. He wouldn't take it out right now. But as he moved, the knife cut through him harder. He felt dizzy and gripped the door frame.

He saw some officials pound around the corner of the stairwell and toward him.

Xander pointed helpfully at the room as he tried to keep from passing out.

Chapter 27

Eden blinked up at the official from the office by the lobby. He was speaking to her. She knew that much, but she wasn't sure what he was saying.

"Can you . . . repeat that?" she asked.

"Look at me," the official told her. "I know the drugs are still filtering out of your system, but I need you to answer a couple of questions right now."

"I forgot the question," Eden told the official. He had really long hair. Eden wondered if it was soft. She reached out to touch his hair before she realized that probably wasn't appropriate. She giggled.

"The question is . . . how did you get in Room 311?"

"I don't remember," Eden giggled.

"The tape shows you walking to the room with some other girls. Are they your friends?"

"Xander is my friend."

"Xander Coxon?"

Eden laughed. "He's really handsome too. I love his brown hair." She laughed. "I think he rescued me, right?"

"He did. Okay, he's your friend. What about friends that are girls?"

"Well, I always wanted to be friends with one girl, but she's got, like, 1000 friends. So, it's kind of me and Xander."

"Do any of these girls look familiar?"

Eden tried to focus on the pictures in front of her. She ran her hands over them, her fingers pausing over one. She knew she had seen *that* girl before. "Did she kidnap me or something?" Eden asked.

"Perhaps. What do you remember about being in the room? Did they do anything to you?"

"I was just sleeping, then I woke up." Eden stumbled over her own tongue. She knew that there were more details, but sleep seemed more important at that moment. "I liked sleeping. I want to sleep right now."

"Me too. It's three in the morning."

Eden giggled. "I need to be ready for the test tomorrow."

"We're going to have someone walk you back to your room. Sleep if you can and good luck in the science competition in a few hours."

Eden watched him stand up and walk toward the door. It took her a couple of seconds to figure out that he was trying to kick her out of the room. Eden stood up. She felt drowsy, unsteady, and ready to sleep right there. Even the floor looked comfortable.

"Where's Xander?" she asked.

"He's in the infirmary. One of the medics is caring for him."

"He's hurt?" Eden tried to remember what had happened to him, but she just remembered him hugging her, then disappearing. There had been a lot of noise, but sleep had seemed more appealing than paying attention to what was happening.

"Yes, you can visit him in the morning. Do you need someone to wake you up for the science competition?"

"I can put an alarm." Eden giggled as a woman official offered her arm to Eden.

"Don't you think she should be in the infirmary too?"

"She just needs to sleep it off," the other official said.

"Sleepy, sleepy, peep." Eden laughed at her joke. Even the official laughed. They took the stairs slowly up to the second floor.

"Which room is yours?" she asked Eden.

"I think 205."

"Okay, let's try your key."

Eden patted her pocket. "I think my key is in there." She patted the door. She was outside her room, and the key was inside. What if she were inside the room and the key was outside?

"Okay, let's get you a replacement."

Once Eden was settled into her bed, she asked the woman if she could check on Xander. "He's hurt, but I have to sleep. Tell him I'm going to see him when I wake up."

Eden yawned and rolled over. Sleep came easily.

Beep. Beep. Beep. Beep.

The annoying sound dragged Eden out of dreamland. She looked at the clock. It was 7:00 a.m. The science competition began at eight thirty, but everything on Eden hurt. She slowly rose from bed, thinking about a weird dream she had had where Xander had rescued her from some crazy people.

Eden stretched, and her neck and back ached.

"Ouch, what's wrong with me this morning?"

Eden lifted up her shirt and looked at her back in the mirror. There were red marks all up and down her back.

"What?" Eden gently probed at one of them, then winced. "That didn't really happen. Did that really happen?"

She quickly dressed, flinching as she bumped one of her bruises. She had to see Xander ASAP.

Eden jogged down the stairs and out into the lobby. There were a lot of officials milling around. "No running!" one of them shouted at her.

Eden pulled a face but slowed down, still aiming for the infirmary. When she reached the area, the door was locked. She knocked once, then more insistently. She could hear some movement inside, but nobody was answering the door.

"Xander?" she asked, her mind jumping to terrible conclusions.

A medic finally answered the door. "No visitors allowed in here," he said. "This isn't a social club."

"I need to see Xander. Is he in there? What happened to him?"

"Are you one of the girls who was . . ." The medic looked down the hall. "Come in, quickly."

Eden slipped through the door and saw Xander lying on his side on one of the beds. There were two other people on beds too. One had a leg up in a cast. Another was sleeping.

"Xander!" Eden said, rushing over to him and bending beside him. Xander smiled at her, but he didn't move. "What's wrong with you? Who hurt you?"

"Don't be late for the science competition," Xander told her.

"What? I'm not. It's early. What happened to you?"

"I'm going to have to ask you to keep your voice down," the medic said. "Do you mind if I take a look at you since you're here? I can't believe they didn't bring all of you in here last night." He shook his head.

"I'm fine," Eden told him. "I have some bruises, but I don't need an examination." She pulled over the medic's stool and sat so that she could look directly at Xander.

"Why are you on your side? Did you break something?"

"Got stabbed in the back. I had to get some stitches, and even with the bandage, any pressure on it hurts. I can lay on my stomach, but they made me wear one of these dumb hospital gowns, so . . . yeah."

Eden smiled along with Xander. "Okay, so you're going to be fine, right?"

"Yeah." They just looked at each other, and Eden hoped Xander was telling the truth, not just lying to her so that she would be able to concentrate on her test. "How did you get in that room? Do you remember anything?"

"No, not really. I just remember pieces. I remember you arriving and hugging me."

Xander shook his head. "They only took that one boy. I know at least one of the girls was involved, but I think there were more. I don't know how many."

Eden glanced over her shoulder where the medic was definitely eavesdropping on their conversation. "What are they going to do about it?"

"They're trying to hide the whole thing. I'm not sure the reason, but that guy is definitely going to be eliminated. I saw the official take his medal."

Eden shivered. "What do you think they were planning to do?"

"None of the girls in the room had medals. It was clear that they were trying to fix the competition today. They should reschedule the competition. It's not fair to you and the other girls. Even though you got away and are able to compete, you didn't get a full night's sleep. You won't be your best, and . . ."

"I can still do it." Eden tried to sound confident. "I have to do it."

"You're right. You can do it. Eden, I can't watch today. I'm supposed to stay here until the numbing around the stitches wears off. You're going to be okay?"

"Yeah, I'm fine."

Eden sat there a couple more minutes, trying to understand what had happened the night before. But there really were no words to describe it. "Okay, I'm going to eat, then take the test. I'll come here when I'm done."

"You got it," Xander said. He closed his eyes, and Eden stood, leaving the infirmary as quietly as possible to hide the fact that the medic had let in a visitor.

Eden picked at the small plate of food she had taken from the kitchen, her eyes flitting around the other girls eating. She wondered if any of them had been with her last night. It was hard to remember details, but she noticed a bruise on a girl's arm and thought she might have been one of them.

The girl stopped when she saw Eden, staring at her for a minute before she moved on. Eden should have said something, but she didn't know what. Anyway, she needed to stop thinking about it and prepare herself mentally for the next competition- science, her strength if Claire was anyone to go by. Eden wondered if Claire was watching her in the Olympics. Did she wince at how badly Eden had done? Did she still have hope for Eden?

Eden thought through the cheats she had been considering the evening before. She didn't have the ingredients for prussic acid, so that was out. There were several things she could do, but as Eden considered how to do them without getting caught, she realized something.

Last night, someone had been cheating, to rig the competition so that they could win in science. It would have been impossible for them to kidnap and drug every girl who was taking the science test, so the girls must have been chosen carefully. Why was Eden selected? She wasn't a threat to anyone.

Eden almost choked on her food as she hurried out of the dining hall to the nearest interactive screen. She checked the standings for girl scientists, not considering everyone who had already won a medal. She was number twenty-two.

Eden clicked on her face and looked at the picture more carefully to make sure it was really herself. Yes, there she was. She was almost in medal-winning range now that other competitors had already won medals in other competitions.

She was close, but she wasn't sure if she was close enough. Yes, she had to do something to make sure she won.

Eden went back to her plate in the dining hall and looked for anything she could use. The salt shaker. She didn't think it would be enough, but she only had so many resources at the moment.

She collected a small amount of salt in her pocket and steeled herself for the science test.

Eden entered the gym, which looked the same as it had the day before for the math competition. There were fewer desks, though, and Eden breathed a sigh of relief. Anything that gave her a better chance was appreciated.

Eden perused the containers of materials at the front of the room. They were all sealed, so she couldn't tamper with them. She could at least see what they would be required to do.

Then, she went to the back of the room and selected a desk with no one behind her. This was her last chance to win a medal. There was another competition tomorrow, but it was communication. She didn't think she stood a chance in that one.

Science.

Eden breathed in and out.

This would be her day.

When Lory Chambers announced that they would be starting in five minutes, Eden couldn't sit still any longer. She stood up and began walking around her desk, shifting her weight back and forth on her legs. She wouldn't have the chance to move around for a few more hours.

"Everyone be seated please," Lory Chambers said.

Eden scooted back into her seat, then turned to find Lory Chambers looking directly at her. Eden shrank down a little further. She didn't want to draw attention to herself. As Lory Chambers looked away and began going through the same, basic instructions, Eden's mind was at war.

Should she cheat?

She might be able to win without cheating.

But probably not.

But what if she could win without cheating and then she was caught?

She wouldn't be caught.

She would be really careful.

Her eyes darted to the cameras on either side. There was no more time to plan, Lory Chambers was announcing the first question. Eden tuned in carefully.

The first five were easy questions about biology. She could predict the probability that a child of certain genes would possess certain qualities all day long.

Between each question, she glanced up at the seats, scanning for Xander. She knew he wouldn't be there, but on the off chance that he might be, she wanted to make sure he saw her. Fifteen questions later, Eden was still doing pretty well. She wasn't sure of her exact position, but she had to be high.

Eden eyed the girls around her. The three girls in front of her were tapping their legs and fingers and acting all kinds of nervous, but the girl beside Eden was calm, staring confidently at her screen. She looked too happy about the questions, and Eden had to do something about it.

"You will be asked to make several compounds," Lory Chambers announced. Eden's head snapped up to face the front. "Please come to the front of the room and select three bottles."

For the first time since Lory Chambers had started giving directions, no one immediately moved to follow them. A hand in the front row cautiously rose above the sea of heads.

Lory Chambers looked unimpressed at the question, but after staring at the individual for a couple of moments, she finally nodded.

"How do we know which ingredients to gather if we don't know what we are going to make?" the faraway voice asked.

Eden thought it a perfectly valid question, but Lory Chambers still raised her eyebrows for a few minutes before finally shaking her head. "You should gather the ingredients you think are most important. Only three."

That sparked some panic, but Eden didn't immediately shove her way to the table. If she could only select three ingredients, then she had to make sure the ingredients she selected were useful in a lot of different things.

She finally rose and made her way slowly to the front, one of the few still going forward instead of backward. A girl next to her began opening the miniature bottles and sniffing them, which even Eden knew was a dumb thing to do. Still, she couldn't help it. This was her chance to really mess them up.

She slipped some salt into her hand, holding it carefully so that her hand looked natural. She could sprinkle the salt in a few bottles, mess up their compounds so that they wouldn't work correctly. But. . .no, she had to rely on her own strength. Maybe she could win without the salt. Taking a deep breath, Eden dropped the salt back into her pocket.

At the front of the room, Eden grabbed three bottles. There weren't many left, and her body shook as she realized how much of this competition relied on chance. What if being last in line meant that she didn't even have the opportunity to get good ingredients?

Great. They weren't even labeled. That was helpful. Lory Chambers looked at each competitor like she wanted to make sure they were paying attention. Why wouldn't they be? Their lives literally depended on it.

"The first thing you need to do is determine what elements you collected. You can do anything you like with the elements except consume them. You will have five minutes to determine their names and write them on your screen."

Eden took a deep breath. One of hers was easy to identify. It was copper. She opened the container and took a tentative sniff. The smell just confirmed her answer. Copper wasn't very useful unless she wanted to make brass or something, but at least she knew what it was.

She scribbled the answer on her screen and set the first jar aside after scanning it into her screen's camera.

Jar number two.

Inside was a silvery mass. The jar was warm, and the mass looked as though it had been melted. Now, it was hard, bright and hard. It had to be a natural element. What was that element that wasn't silver? It was mixed with copper to make brass. Eden pressed the jar into her forehead, hoping to somehow transfer the information, but she couldn't remember.

She set the jar aside and looked at the third one. There was a pale blue liquid inside it. This had to be a base element, so water wasn't an option. There were some gasses that could turn into liquids.

Eden scribbled down oxygen and looked at the shiny rock-thing.

She had no idea. The only element she could remember at the moment was hydrogen, and she knew it wasn't that. She left it blank.

The timer sounded, and she looked up at the screen. Two out of three!

"Set your elements aside, and click on the elements of the periodic table you need to make each of the following mixtures."

That was it with the bottles? It seemed like a lot of work for nothing, but at least she hadn't risked putting salt in someone else's bottle. It wouldn't have messed up their results.

Lory Chambers began naming different things, and Eden quickly tried to click the elements in the periodic table needed. Some of the things she had studied with Claire came back to her, but others, she guessed completely.

Once everyone's results were noted, Lory Chambers remained quiet, everyone looking up at her hopefully. "Your results will be tallied shortly. Medals will be awarded in the gathering room in one hour."

Eden swallowed. That was it. The competition was over, for her at least. There was nothing else she could do to change the results.

She took a deep breath as she stood, trying to find her balance and remember things like where she was and what she was supposed to do next.

She had an hour. That was enough time to visit Xander, so Eden hurried out of the gym, toward the hotel, then to the infirmary. She knocked on the door again, but this time, it was answered by a different medic.

"What is your medical emergency?" the medic asked.

"No emergency for me. I'm just here to check on Xander . . . Coxon. He was stabbed with a knife."

"He's already been checked out," the woman responded. "He said that he had something important to do, even though it was against the medical advice to leave. He is an adult, now that he has a medal, so he can make his own decisions."

"Oh, did he say where he was going?"

"No, but he wasn't moving very quickly." The medic shut the door in Eden's face, and she froze in indecision. She couldn't go to his room to check on him. Where else would he have gone? Was eating food considered very important?

Eden meandered back down the hallway to peer into the dining hall. She scanned every face, but Xander wasn't there. She had wasted thirty minutes, and even though she didn't want to acknowledge it, the medal ceremony was going to begin before long. She should probably go to the gathering room.

When she entered the gathering room, she saw Xander on the back row. He was lying on his side with his head sticking out into the aisle.

Eden laughed when she saw him. She rushed over. "What are you doing here?" she asked him, then noticed he was still wearing the dumb paper gown.

He smiled when he saw her. "I'm laced up on pain meds, so I'm here to see you win your medal."

"Did you watch the competition?" Eden asked.

His face fell. "No, I couldn't go, but I'm here for this. The medic didn't want me to leave, but I was doing nothing in the infirmary bed that I couldn't do here. See? I'm lying in the exact same position."

Eden patted his head. "Good job. I'm sure a doctor somewhere would be proud of you for following instructions." Her face fell. "The last part of the competition was impossible. I don't think I got a medal. I really don't think I did."

Eden closed her eyes and sank to her knees next to where Xander was stretched out. It was okay that she hadn't won a medal in the other competitions because she always had science to fall back on, but now, she didn't have a fall back. This would be her fate.

"Hey, you have a good chance at this one," Xander told her. "I didn't get stabbed in the back for nothing, so march up to those chairs and get ready to accept your medal."

He sounded so confident, but Eden didn't know how he could be. She was nothing but nerves.

Chapter 28

Xander shifted in his chair as Eden stood up beside him, turning his neck so that he could see her better. He wished he could have seen the science competition; then he would know better how likely she was to get a medal. Still, he couldn't think about the alternative.

She reached toward him, and he moved his hand to grab hers. He squeezed it, and the room hushed. They both turned toward the stage. Lory Chambers was climbing the steps. Eden's eyes widened, and she dropped his hand, hurrying down the aisle to take one of the last chairs in the two front rows.

Xander shifted on his bed of chairs to get more comfortable. He might not be able to feel his back, but he knew it was going to start hurting soon. Then, he would have to hobble back to the infirmary holding his paper gown closed in all the right places.

"And now, we will announce the names of those who have won medals in our female science competition. Please come up to the stage and accept your medal when you hear your name called."

Lory Chambers touched the screen in front of her and began calling the names in rapid fire as she always did. "Helen Tethers, Brianna Flores, Josie Spencer."

Xander craned his neck to see the back of Eden's head, but he couldn't see very much other than the people who were crowding the aisle as their names were called. This couldn't happen. Not again. She couldn't miss out this time.

"Vivian Waters, Penelope Brown, Eden Pearce, Johanna Gregory."

Xander blinked then sat up, leaning on his elbow. Had she just said Eden's name? Then, there she was. Eden was in the aisle, running up to the stage. She cleared the aisle and climbed the steps, forgetting to punch her thumb into the machine by the stairs.

Xander watched her familiar freckled face bend forward to allow the medal to pass over her head. Then, she was backing up with the others on the stage, and another girl was taking her place.

"Eden," Xander whispered. He sat up fully, reached behind himself, and pulled the paper gown closed. He slowly stood. Eden ran down the exit aisle after the last of the names were called. Her eyes were on him, and Xander held out one hand in welcome. She launched herself into his arms, almost tumbling him over.

Xander stumbled as she embraced him.

"Oh my gosh. I got it. I got a medal. I'm really going to be an adult. I won't be eliminated. Oh my gosh. Can you believe it?" Eden finally pulled back out of the hug, and Xander admired the medal around her neck. He turned it over and ran his fingers over her engraved name. It was still hot from where they had cut it.

"You really have a medal," he said. "Wow! That's . . . awesome!" He didn't want to let go of it. This was real.

Eden buried her face in the chest of his papery gown, and he felt it shift. He grabbed the back a little more securely and looked around. A few people were giving him strange looks.

"Can I maybe get dressed before we celebrate?" Xander asked.

"Oh, yeah, sure, uh, do you need me to help you? I mean, not help you get dressed, but maybe help you get the clothes?"

Eden brushed her brown hair behind her ear and avoided eye contact. Xander laughed. "I think I can take care of it myself. Wait outside the infirmary?"

"Okay," Eden agreed, matching his slower pace to the infirmary. Once inside, Xander sat on the side of the bed he had occupied earlier. The medic wanted to give him another look-over before letting him go, so he reluctantly released his grasp on the paper gown.

She examined the stitches, and Xander winced as she poked the skin. "I can feel that," he announced.

"You'll slowly have sensation coming back to your skin. You should be able to feel everything in a couple of hours." The medic came back around in front of him. "I'm going to give you enough pain medication for tonight and tomorrow morning. You need to come back for more before noon tomorrow. Do you understand?"

Xander nodded respectfully. He just wanted to get dressed and join Eden to celebrate her newly won medal. "Yes, I'll be back for it then. Two pills tonight, then two in the morning, about twelve hours apart." Xander nodded again, and the medic finally left him alone to get dressed.

When he was alone, he approached the mirror and examined his back as best as he could. The skin was red and angry, but he couldn't see much other than that around the white gauze padding. He would make sure that Eden didn't try to leave her room for any reason that night. He also had to make sure that neither of them consumed tainted food.

Even though Derry had been placed in solitary confinement until time for the elimination, Xander didn't put it past one of the girls to try something else.

Once he emerged from the room, Eden hugged him again, her face one big plastered grin. "I can't believe I actually have a medal," she said, one hand clasping the circle of life. "Sorry, should I be careful with your back?"

"Yeah, the numbness is wearing off. I think I'm going to really start feeling it soon."

After sharing a meal together, all he wanted to do was go somewhere private and have a real talk with Eden. The only place to do that would be in one of their rooms.

Xander checked the hallway. When he saw someone walking toward them, he ducked back into the stairwell and leaned casually against the wall, trying to make random conversation with Eden.

"So," he said. "What are you going to do first when you get home?"

"I can't even think about going home right now," she replied, touching her medal.

The person passed into the stairwell and went down the stairs. Xander peered into the hallway again. It was empty. He motioned Eden forward, leading the way to his room. He fumbled with the key, finally got it into the lock the right way, and pushed the door open.

Eden entered directly after him, and he closed the door. He stood there for a moment, listening for movement in the hallway. No one had seen them.

He didn't think it really mattered if they did. There wasn't much they could do to Xander and Eden now that they had won medals.

Eden fiddled with Xander's TV and turned it to a rerun of the day. "I want to see what I looked like when I got the medal," she said, settling onto Xander's bed, her back pushed up against the wall. Xander sat next to her, his legs extending to the end of the bed as he touched the skin gently on his back to see how it was progressing.

Xander reached over and grabbed Eden's medal, turning it over to make sure it really had her name on it. He had imagined her winning a medal so often that he had to make sure this was reality, not just something else he was imagining.

"I don't want to go to sleep," Eden said, staring at the TV. "I don't want to wake up and find my medal gone or someone coming into my room and . . ."

"Yeah," Xander cut her off. "Explain to me how that happened. How did you manage to get caught up with them?" He shifted as his back reminded him that he was still injured.

"Well, I couldn't sleep last night, so I went downstairs to see if there was something to do. I couldn't study anymore. And they were down there all eating some cake. And cake . . .my mouth started watering. They asked me if I wanted some. I said yes. I guess the cake was drugged, and everything is kind of fuzzy after that. I think I tried to go to my room, and this girl said she would walk with me. But I don't know if I went to my room or not. I don't remember."

"Do you remember who gave you the cake?"

"Yeah, I remember that well enough. It was the guy that they took away this morning and two other girls. One of them had dark hair, longer, and the other girl was kind of angry looking. Like, her face was just always angry."

"Did you tell this to someone?"

"They had asked me a bunch of questions early this morning, but I don't really remember what they asked me." Eden pointed at the television. "A replay of the awards ceremony is starting!"

Xander kept quiet as he heard Lory Chambers make the same annoying speech yet again. Finally, she began reading the names off rapid fire, and Xander caught Eden's name seconds after it was spoken, just like before.

Eden laughed as she saw her surprised face bending down to receive the medal. "Look, you can tell that I didn't think I would ever be called. Can you believe I actually got a medal? I mean, I know I . . ." she looked around. "I know I did things I wasn't supposed to do, but I was still good enough to win one. And . . . I feel like I can finally relax."

"You have a whole day to relax, then we fly back home."

"Yeah, there's the adulting ceremony before we leave," Eden reminded him.

"Okay, yeah, but once we get home, we'll have to pick a career, then no more leisurely training when we want to. We'll have real jobs." Xander wasn't trying to be negative, but he was trying to prepare himself for life, the life that was coming after this.

"Are you going to apply for one of the apartments?" Eden asked.

"I don't know." Xander didn't want to tell Eden that it really depended on how long his mom lived. He didn't feel right leaving her when she might not have that much longer, but he also didn't want to miss the application deadline and be forced to live with his dad and only his dad for a year.

Xander hung his head, which somehow made the wound in his back twinge gently. Reality was coming. He would see his mom in two days. Two days wasn't so long, but now that Eden had won a medal, all he wanted to do was go home.

"What's wrong?" Eden asked. She bent forward so that her face was even with his. "Is it your mom?"

"I haven't thought about anything else other than this competition in so long. I kept thinking if we both win medals, then it's like all the worry will disappear. We have medals. We're guaranteed jobs, apartments if we want them. We can do what we want now. But it's like, now my mom's cancer is kind of serious. The doctors won't help her, and I keep wondering if she'll still be there when I get home."

Xander wasn't the kind of person who cried when he was upset, but he felt a tight ball of sadness in his throat. It made it hard to swallow. He didn't want Eden to see him weak like this, but he couldn't pull himself together.

Life after the medal wasn't easy.

"Is there something I can do to help you?" Eden's question sounded hopeless. They both knew that there was no cure for cancer.

Xander tried to control the knot of uneasiness, but it was hard to see around it. "I guess I just keep pushing. I have to accept the fact that my mom isn't going to be around much longer."

It felt weird to say it out loud, this thing he had been turning over in his mind. But it was reality, especially now that the hospital knew about her condition. She wouldn't be allowed any medicine or extra resources as she was seen as a "lost cause." He didn't know how much longer she had or if his mom was okay even now.

"I'm sorry."

Xander clenched his jaw. Her words did nothing to make him feel better. They didn't change his mom's situation. What was the point of them? Two little words that affected nothing, like a plea for him to feel better.

"I . . . need a second," Xander said, standing up and striding out of the room. He didn't normally have to deal with these . . . emotions, but now, it seemed like everything was confronting him all at once. It wasn't Eden's fault. He shouldn't be mad at her, but at the same time, he had all these pent-up feelings and no way to release them.

He marched down the hallway and reached the stairway at the end. He had to keep moving, even though it was late at night. Most people were probably sleeping, except for the group of medalists in the lobby and screening room living it up.

He pounded into each step, taking them two at a time, as his back screamed at him to stop. This was his life. He had earned adulthood, but nothing could save his mother. Nothing he did, no matter how great, would bring his brother back. He had so little control over his life.

Once he reached the top floor, his breath was coming quickly. He studied himself in the mirror of the exercise room and saw how angry he looked. He almost looked frightening, unrecognizable.

Xander stepped closer to the mirror until he was a few inches away, ignoring the other people in the exercise room. He had a lot of things to be upset about, but he still had Eden. She was his friend, his closest friend, and he didn't want to lose that. He was already sinking underneath the waves of uncontrollable problems.

He took a few deep breaths and hurried back down the stairs and to the door of his room. Just as he was about to enter, he doubted himself. What was he thinking? They had just won their medals. They hadn't even complet-ed the adulting ceremony yet, and what he was about to do wouldn't fix any of his problems, not really.

Xander paced back down the hallway, reaching the stairs and building up his courage so that he could force himself to turn around. He turned around and walked back to the room purposefully, stopping himself just before he touched the door handle.

Why was he being such a baby about this?

"Xander, you have to do it now," he said. "She'll probably think you've died or something. You've taken way too long."

After coaching himself, Xander finally pulled open the door, the words ready.

When he peeked inside though, he realized that Eden had fallen asleep. She stirred as Xander entered the room further. Blinking her eyes, she sat up and yawned.

"What happened to you?" she asked.

"Just walked around for a while. Cleared my head."

Eden yawned again. "Sorry, didn't mean to fall asleep. Is everything . . . okay? Do you want to talk about it?"

Xander had already lost the words he had collected with his pacing. He sat on the edge of the bed and stared mindlessly at the television. Two news anchors were talking about the upcoming competition the next day. Who would win a medal and who would lose their last chance?

He tried to push out the words anyway. "We both have our medals now, so do you want to be my girlfriend?" Well, that didn't come out as smoothly as he had hoped it would.

Eden smiled at him, her freckles crinkling together. "Yes! Of course!" She laughed, and Xander chuckled along with her, relieved that it was done.

"So . . ." She yawned again, interrupting herself. "I guess it's official now."

"Official," Xander nodded. He settled himself onto the bed so that his back was against the wall. Surprisingly, he didn't feel that different. Eden was his girlfriend, but his mom was still sick. He couldn't get rid of the pit in his stomach.

"So. . .yeah," Eden concluded, clearly feeling awkward now that they had just decided things. "Speaking of official, do you think you'll be one, even if it's dangerous?"

Xander shrugged. "I don't have a lot of options. I don't want to be a wrangler, which is probably my only other option."

"You could coach wrestling," Eden suggested.

Xander nodded. He hadn't actually thought of that option before, probably because being a teacher didn't come naturally to him. "What about you? You have a medal in science. That pretty much means you're going to be a scientist, right?"

"Yeah, I guess so. I don't feel smart enough to be a scientist."

"They'll train you, so you get the chance to learn more before you start experimenting."

"What if I found the cure for cancer?" Eden said excitedly. "I mean, I would have to learn a lot before that, but you never know."

"It would be too late," Xander told her. Even though he was trying not to think about it, things kept circling back to his mom and how little time she had left.

Eden bit her bottom lip, and Xander regretted his comment. But it was true. If Eden thought she was helping him, she wasn't. Xander liked her a lot, but they still had so much to learn about each other. He couldn't wait until the adulting ceremony in two days. Then, he could go home.

Part 3- The Ceremony

Chapter 29

When Eden woke up the morning after winning her medal, it felt heavy around her neck. She liked the feel of it reminding her that she would go home again.

That wasn't the only thing that was making her smile. As she sat up and stretched, trying to decide if she should stay in bed longer or watch the communication competition, she thought over Xander's question from the night before. He had asked her to be his girlfriend. He had been kind of awkward about it too, but at least he had asked. Now that she had a medal, she could actually think about the future and what might happen.

Eden took her time getting ready that morning, not worrying about a competition for the first time in months. She brushed her hair to princess quality as she thought about how things would be when they got home. She would *definitely* apply for one of the unmarried apartments to rent. She hoped that she would get one in the same complex as Xander. Then, they would move into their new apartments and see each other every day. Now that they didn't have to worry about who would become adults, they could really . . . well, *like* each other.

Eden studied herself in the tiny mirror. She didn't think she looked particularly pretty with her boring wavy brown hair and freckles, but Xander saw something in her. That was what mattered.

Humming a song under her breath, Eden went down to breakfast and hoped Xander would find her soon. She wanted to spend the whole day with him.

As she entered the dining hall and approached the door where she could order what she wanted, an official came up to her. "Eden Pearce?" he asked.

"Yes?" Eden glanced behind him, wondering why he was approaching her. If he had more questions about the weird drugging incident, she really couldn't remember anything other than what she had already told him.

"Please come with me. I have a few questions for you."

Eden glanced longingly at the woman serving the food. "Can I get a plate of food first? I'm hungry."

"Fine."

Eden felt the man's eyes boring into the back of her as she ordered food and took her hot plate. She turned around, clutching the plate. "Okay, what did you want to ask me?"

"Let's come back here so that our conversation won't be interrupted," the man suggested, leading her to the office where she had been questioned a few days ago. As Eden followed him, she realized that she hadn't taken a fork from the table. Now she would have to eat with her hands. Great.

Eden settled into the seat across from the balding official as he tapped away on his screen. She looked longingly at her plate of food. "Is this going to take long?" she asked, trying to decide if she should wait or eat with her hands.

"Yes," he responded, unamused. Eden started with the danish, savoring each bite. It wasn't very sweet, not like that cake, but it was good. So good. She closed her eyes to fully enjoy its taste. Did food always taste this good?

"I need to ask you a few questions."

"Okay."

"We want to know more about your involvement with the boy who drugged you about thirty-six hours ago. Can you tell me what you knew about him?"

"I didn't know anything," Eden answered quickly. Why were they asking her questions about him again?

"Had you spoken to him before, even a conversation that might not seem very important?"

"No, at least, I don't think so. Not before they invited me to eat with them. I'm confused. You already have him in custody. He's going to be eliminated. Why are you asking me more questions about him?"

"Some things don't add up," the official responded. "Sometimes, people are involved in things like this, but they don't get their hands dirty. Anything you can tell us would be helpful. Why would he target you?"

Eden shrugged. "I don't know. I figured it was just to take me out of the science competition." This talk was making her feel uncomfortable. She took another bite of the pastry.

"We think the motive was revenge."

"Re-venge?" Eden asked the question slowly, because it didn't make sense. Why would someone she didn't even know be targeting her for revenge?

"Yes, it appears that you stopped his girlfriend from winning a medal in running."

Eden's heart started beating quickly, too quickly. Could he see through her? He couldn't be referring to . . . no. There was no way after all this time that they knew anything. She just had to play it cool.

"I didn't even place in that one," Eden finally spoke. "I think I got, like, in the 100s."

"You were in place 87," the official said with quiet assurance. The way he knew exactly where she had placed scared Eden.

"Yeah, that sounds right." Eden tried to sound normal, but her voice trembled a little bit.

The official leaned forward. "Why do we have the Olympics every year?"

Eden frowned, picking at the pastry but not able to eat anymore with her stomach doing flips. "Because the population is too high for the resources we have." It was a typical answer that she had learned growing up. It didn't matter. What mattered was that she had a medal, and she wasn't about to get into a long conversation with this official. "I'm not sure why you brought me in here."

"Eden, we have been reviewing the tapes. There are a lot of cameras in this hotel, so it took some time. But it seems as though you have cheated."

Eden's heart stopped.

"Do you want to tell me about it?"

Part of Eden wanted to break into tears and beg for mercy, while the other part of her told her that she had to hold onto her facade of innocence as long as possible. "You think I . . . cheated?" The word felt poisonous in her mouth as she tried to maintain eye contact with the official. She couldn't. Her eyes gave her away as the official leaned back in his chair and shook his head.

"We already know that you did it. There's no question of that. Now, you have the chance to tell us what happened and where you got the drug."

Eden's eyes darted around the room, looking for some sort of escape. "I . . . don't know." She stumbled over her words, and the official shook his head again.

Disapproval leaked from him. "Eden Pearce, tell the truth. We can proceed without the details, but giving us the details might help you."

Eden remembered how to breathe, and a little groan escaped from her. "I . . . don't know. I just, the only way to get a medal was if I was able to push myself to the top."

"Is that what you call this? Pushing yourself to the top? You could have messed up countless results. We have the Olympics so that those who don't have the skills to survive in a world that is nearing the end of its life don't take resources from those who can. How could you decide that the girls you poisoned don't deserve to win medals?"

The tears bubbled up, and Eden couldn't stop them. "I'm sorry," she mumbled. "I know I shouldn't have done it. I'm sorry. I don't know why, but I had to." She reached up and touched her medal gently.

"Where did you get the poison?"

"It wasn't poison. I don't know what it was. I just . . . found it." Eden couldn't tell them about Claire. Even though she was already an adult, her social score would be seriously affected for a crime such as altering Olympic results. Besides, she and Claire had only met once. Then, Eden's brain screamed at her. Why was she protecting Claire when she should be protecting herself?

"Where did you find it?"

"At home, before I came here."

"In your home? Where was it hidden?"

"No, not in my home, just near my home. Like, it was just there on the ground, so I . . ."

"You picked up something from the ground, an unknown substance, and you decided, 'Hmmm, let me mix this in with some food right before a big competition and see what happens'?" The sarcasm in the official's tone told her that he wasn't buying it.

"I don't know." Eden was breaking under the pressure. She hadn't prepared a cover story. She thought this was done and over after the first questioning. But now, he clearly knew everything. She buried her face in her hands and refused to come out.

"Eden, tell me where you got the drug."

Eden didn't respond. He already knew everything.

"Who were you trying to hurt?"

"I wasn't trying to hurt anyone," she mumbled through her fingers.

"How can you drug people and not be trying to hurt them? Do you think this is a game?"

What was going to happen to her? What about her medal? Eden didn't want to ask, but she was trembling inside. The tears escaped between her fingers and trailed down her face. Eden sniffed repeatedly, waiting for it to happen.

"If you won't help me, then I can't help you," the official said. He stood up. "Hand me your medal."

"No," Eden protested, clutching it tightly. "Please, I won the science competition fair and square." For a moment, she was grateful that she had resisted the temptation to cheat during that competition.

"We can't trust cheaters. You can't be given adulthood. Hand me your medal, or I will forcibly take it from you. I don't want to do that, but I will."

Eden slowly unglued her hands from the ribbon that held the medal and bent her head forward. She couldn't take it off herself. The official leaned closer, grabbed the medal, and yanked it off her neck. He ran his hand over her name on the back as he sat back in his chair.

"Am I . . . eliminated?" Eden asked, her lower lip trembling.

"Yes, you are going to be eliminated."

Eden couldn't control herself anymore. She started crying, ugly sobs wracking her whole body. "Please don't eliminate me. I'm going to be a good adult. I'll be a scientist, and I- I- I. . ?"

"I'm going to turn this in to those in charge." Then, the official seemed to feel something like sympathy for her. "You can make a call to your parents if you like. The phone is right there." He pointed to an old-school telephone connected to the wall. "Once you are done, you may leave this office. You are welcome to attend the adulting ceremony if you like, but then you will be taken with the others who will be eliminated."

Eden couldn't focus on what he was saying as she cried. The door thumped shut behind him, and her first urge was to run. But there was nowhere to run. Upertavik Island was an island. She couldn't just swim somewhere else. She had no survival skills. She couldn't do anything.

She had lost her medal.

She would never be an adult.

The thoughts hit Eden one after the other.

All she wanted was her mom to hug her, but she couldn't have that. She could only call her. Eden reached for the phone and slowly dialed her mom's number.

Her mom answered on the third ring. "Hello? Who is this?"

"It's me," Eden whimpered into the phone.

"Eden? What's wrong? Why do you sound like that? I saw you-"

"Mom, I'm going to be eliminated!" Eden started crying into the phone as her mother tried to pry more information out of her.

"What do you mean? I saw the medal ceremony yesterday, and they called your name. I'm already organizing a celebration for when you get home. You aren't being eliminated. What are you talking about?"

Eden tried to stop crying so that she could answer her mom, but each time she thought about never going home again, a new wave of tears hit her.

"Eden, talk to me. What's happening? Are you okay?"

"I- I cheated," Eden got out. "They caught me cheating."

"You cheated? How did you cheat? What did you do? They already gave you a medal. They can't take it away."

"They. . . they already did. I don't have a medal anymore. I'm going to be eliminated." Then, she thought of Xander. He wouldn't believe her. She couldn't tell him. The tears started coming again, until she didn't think it was possible for her to cry anymore.

"Oh, Eden," her mom said, all of the questions knocked out of her. "Oh, baby. I'm so sorry." Then, her mom started sobbing too. Eden didn't have any tears left, so she just pressed the phone against her ear and listened to her mother.

"I don't know how they found out," Eden finally murmured. "I'm sorry. I wish I could take it all back, but . . . I don't think I would have won a medal if I hadn't cheated. I thought it was the only way. And I was so close with running."

Her mother sniffed. "I'm so glad you got to call. Do you know . . . when it will happen?"

"I don't know," Eden's voice broke. "He said I could attend the adulting ceremony tomorrow, so I guess . . . after that." Her whole body was shaking, and Eden sank into the chair she had previously occupied, knocking into her plate of breakfast food. There was no way she would be able to eat it now.

"Eden, I wish I could be there to hug you right now. Eden, my Eden."

"Moooom," Eden moaned, more tears spilling over. "I'm going to die. I don't want to die. There has to be a way out. Please, help me."

"There's nothing I can do," her mom said. "Eden, I'm so sorry."

The official entered the office again, holding a screen. He stopped when he saw that Eden was still there. "You need to wrap up your call now," he said, standing in the door. He didn't look as sympathetic as he had before.

Eden swiped at her face, but it was still wet. "Mom, I have to go."

"Oh, Eden, I love you so much. I love you with all my heart. Please know that."

"Mmmhmm. I love you too," Eden responded. She didn't think she could say anything else without bursting into a fresh set of tears. She couldn't put the phone down, so she just listened to her mom's sobbing until the official came and placed the phone back on the receiver.

He stood looking at her for a minute, but Eden couldn't make eye contact. She just wanted to be miserable in her room alone, but she was scared of running into Xander on the way there.

"I'm sorry," the official told her, but he didn't look very sorry.

Eden rose to her feet, surprised that they still worked. It seemed impossible that everything else was so normal when her life had fallen completely apart. She touched the place just above her stomach where her medal had hung, but it was gone before she had even gotten used to its weight.

A few deep breaths later, and Eden pushed open the office door. She hung her head and hurried through the dining hall, avoiding eye contact. Up the stairs. Down her hall. Through the door. Mission complete, Eden looked around the tiny space.

This was it. She was guaranteed one more night, maybe two. "Why am I such an idiot?" she whispered to herself. She curled into a tiny ball on her bed and covered herself with the soft blanket. This was where she would stay until they came to get her. She couldn't say goodbye to Xander.

Chapter 30

Xander wandered around the hotel, but Eden had either turned invisible or gone to her room. He didn't understand why she would want to hang out in her room. She should be celebrating!

The last competition would finish in an hour or so; then the adulting ceremony would take place early tomorrow. This was their last chance to enjoy freedom before they returned home and waited to see whether their applications for apartments would be accepted and where they would live.

Xander revisited the dining hall. If he couldn't hang out with Eden, then the next best thing was to eat. He touched his stomach as he carried back a plate of food to a table. He hadn't kept up his regular exercise routine since winning a medal, but he hadn't thought it would affect him this quickly. Was he putting on some fat?

He began shoveling food into his mouth and evaluating what sort of exercise and dieting plan he would need to go on since he was going to have a real job instead of just preparing for the Olympics.

"Hello," someone said.

Xander looked up and recognized the thick glasses. "Colt, what's up?" Xander asked cheerfully, reaching out a hand to greet Colt.

Colt sat down across from Xander. "I'm going to sit here, since it doesn't look like you're sitting with anyone else."

"Uh, sure, go ahead." Xander motioned to the chair that Colt was already occupying. "So, how's-" Xander stopped himself. The competition must be over already if Colt wasn't competing. His eyes fell to Colt's chest, and there wasn't a medal there. He closed his mouth and awkwardly tried to maneuver around the topic.

"What are you eating today?" Xander asked. It was probably the dumbest thing he could have asked, but he didn't want to draw attention to the obvious- Colt was going to be eliminated.

"Beans," Colt said. "My favorite food. I should be able to eat something I like before I'm eliminated, right?"

Since he brought it up . . . "I thought you were going to win a medal in mathematics."

"I'm not good at taking tests. I just get nervous. I knew everything, but I got confused. I could have won a medal, but I just didn't." Colt shook his head and blinked several times. "It doesn't matter. I suppose we just have to trust the process, right? And I'm glad that you won a medal. You get to be an adult."

"Yeah," Xander nodded. He looked behind himself to see if Eden was going to come save him from this awkward conversation anytime soon.

"I just hope elimination is quick. I don't want it to be drawn out or painful. I hate pain."

"I don't think anyone really likes it," Xander replied, taking a big bite of food so he wouldn't have to say anything for a few moments.

"At least you'll never have to find out."

Xander chewed his bite of food slowly and carefully, trying to think of something to say to this strange individual.

"I wish they would let us talk to our families one last time. It feels like the airport was forever ago, and I've thought of a lot more things I should have said."

"Maybe they'll let you call your family if you ask," Xander suggested.

"They don't allow that. I've checked already." Colt wasn't crying. He was very matter of fact about being eliminated in twenty-four to forty-eight hours.

"Are you coming to the adulting ceremony?" Xander asked.

"Yes, I have nothing else to do, and I would like to cheer on some of my classmates."

Xander glanced over his shoulder again, but didn't see Eden. Where could she possibly be? Maybe he should just go knock on her door.

"I still wish I had a chance to be a scientist. I don't think anyone realizes how much math is required in science. I could be an excellent addition to a scientific team. I even presented a project I have created to try to convince them to give me a medal, but they explained that they couldn't break the rules for me or they would have to break them for everyone."

"What kind of project?"

"Mathematically, Mars could be liveable if a few adjustments to the atmosphere were made. We have the resources to do it right now, but I don't know how much longer they will be available. The human race could be eliminated completely if a solution to global warming isn't found, you know."

Xander didn't like being reminded of the permanence of the global warming problem. They were living in a place where people used to die of exposure to the cold. Now, freezing to death was some weird, historic phrase.

"Yes, I'm aware." Xander took another big bite of food as Colt chattered about his plan to save the human race.

"I left them all my plans and everything. If they want to experiment with it, well, who am I to stop them?"

Xander's eyebrows rose. If he were about to be eliminated, he didn't think he would care what happened to the people left. "Nice to talk with you, man," Xander said. "I'm going to go find my friend, Eden."

"Right, yes, go find Eden." Colt nodded.

Xander strode out of the dining hall, still thinking about how crazy Colt was. Part of him admired the guy, but the other part just felt sorry for him. Before trespassing on the girls' hallway, Xander decided to check all other places that Eden might be.

She wasn't in the gathering room, or in the gym, which was mostly empty. She wasn't outside or in the training room on the sixth floor. She had to be in her room.

Why was she hiding?

As Xander stood on the landing of the second floor, he decided he would leave her alone. Maybe she wasn't feeling well. She had to have a good reason for wanting to be in her room, and he shouldn't interrupt that. Even though she was officially his girlfriend now, that didn't mean he had all the answers about her.

He went up to his room and hoped that tomorrow would come quickly. He couldn't wait for the adulting ceremony.

The next morning, Xander hurried to the dining hall. He waited over an hour, but Eden didn't show up. Now, he was getting worried.

"Excuse me, sir," Xander said to one of the officials. "I'm worried about my friend. I haven't seen her in twenty-four hours, and she was one of the girls kidnapped. I'm probably being crazy, but can I go check on her?"

The official frowned at him and brought Xander over to his screen. "What's her name?"

"Eden Pearce," Xander said, peering at the man's screen without looking like he was trying to see what it said. The man typed in her name wrong. "Pearce is P-E-A-R-C-E."

"Here she is." He clicked on a button, and the screen began pulling up a list of stats.

"I don't see her on any of the cameras. She's probably in her room. You're not allowed in there."

"Well, the adulting ceremony is in two hours. I just want to make sure she's okay."

The man frowned. "Everyone deals with it differently. You shouldn't make her go if you're a true friend."

"What do you mean?" Xander asked. Was this official speaking English?

"Some people like to support their friends who become adults, but others don't. Let her figure things out herself."

"But she has to be there," Xander argued. "She won a medal. Just two days ago, in the science competition."

The official frowned. "No, she's slated for elimination."

"That's not right!" Xander yelled. "Your system has that wrong. She won a medal! I saw the ceremony myself. She got a medal in science. Check. Something's wrong."

"Lower your voice." The official narrowed his eyes, and Xander tried to keep his tone respectful.

"Sir, I don't understand why you're telling me she's going to be eliminated. She won a medal."

"Give me a moment," the official said, scrolling through the screen. "Okay, it looks like you're right. She did win a medal." The official turned the screen and played the footage of Eden receiving the medal in the science award ceremony.

"So, what's going on?" Xander asked.

The official frowned. "I'm not sure. She won a medal, but she's . . . oh, I see." The official clicked a few things on his screen and shook his head. "She didn't win her medal fairly. She cheated, so her medal was taken away. She'll be eliminated. Whoever was just below her will receive her medal."

"Uh," the tiny sound escaped Xander as he tried to process what he was hearing. "What?"

"You can talk to her about it if you like, but she's going to be eliminated. Now, I have other things to do. Congratulations on your medal." The official walked away, leaving Xander with his jaw hanging open.

As soon as his brain understood what the official had said, his legs moved into action. He jogged to the second floor and didn't hesitate on the landing. He knocked on Eden's door several times, then listened carefully.

He could hear her moving around inside. "Eden!" he called through the door. "It's me, Xander."

He heard shuffling as a girl peered down the hall at him with angry eyes. He ignored her as Eden opened the door. He stared at her chest. The medal was gone.

"Eden, what happened?" he asked.

She let go of the door and sank into a little pile on the floor. Xander stepped inside and closed the door behind him so no nosy onlookers could see inside. He bent down next to her on the floor.

"I'm going to be eliminated," Eden mumbled. "I'm going to die. Xander, I'm so sorry." She leaned her head on Xander's shoulder, and his throat closed up. *She* was apologizing to *him*?

"Eden, calm down. Tell me what happened."

"They knew. I don't know how. They knew I cheated, and they said I couldn't get a medal. They took it away."

"When?"

"Yesterday," she murmured, wiping at her face.

Xander wrapped an arm tightly around her shoulders, trying to figure a way out of this. "Did they know, really know? Maybe we can get you out of this."

"No, they knew already. There was nothing I could do. I tried to play dumb, but they knew everything except where I got that white powder from."

"Did you tell them? Maybe you can try to barter that information for a medal."

"No!" Eden almost shouted. "They aren't going to give me back my medal. I don't know when it's going to happen. Today, maybe, or tomorrow. I don't know, but I'm so scared."

"Okay, Eden. I'm here. It's okay." Xander's mind was churning through what had happened, trying to find some loophole, some way he could save Eden. But the rules were pretty clear. She had cheated. She wasn't worthy of adulthood.

The thing that no one seemed to know was that Xander had cheated too. He had messed up all the calculators. If Eden didn't deserve a medal, then neither did he. The difference was that no one had pinned the calculators on him.

"I already called my mom, and I told her. And I think it was worse than if I hadn't called her. She told me she had already started planning a party for when I returned- a celebration of my adulthood. But now . . .I'm never going to go home." Xander swiped at the tears on her face. He didn't know anything about being a boyfriend, but he knew what his friend needed right then. She just needed someone to listen.

"It's like I'm just not good enough. If I hadn't cheated, I. . .I could have still won. But I did cheat, I won, and I still lost my medal. I wish I had never cheated."

"Come here," Xander guided her to her feet and back over to the bed. He took the blanket and spread it across her shoulders as she hunched forward. It was stupid to think he could make her feel better with a blanket, but he didn't have a lot of options.

"What time is it? Is the adulting ceremony about to start?"

Xander glanced at the clock on the mumbling TV. "There's an hour and a half," he said.

"You have to go get ready," she said. "I think . . . I'm going to come, okay? I'm going to be there for you."

"Look, this isn't about me. I was so worried about you. You should have come and found me so I could know what had happened."

Eden's face crumpled, and Xander stopped his scolding.

As he searched his brain for something he could say, he realized there was nothing. What he had feared was happening. He had won a medal, and Eden hadn't. He rested his head on the wall behind him and tried to understand. His back twinged in a reminder of the stitches that were still healing.

"I just wish I could change everything. I thought it was a good idea, but cheating. . .it didn't help me."

"We can't change it," Xander stated. He squeezed Eden against himself. He wanted to kiss her or something. Their plane was supposed to leave mid-afternoon, once the adulting ceremony was over. But she wouldn't be on the plane. They only had a few more hours left together, and Xander couldn't miss the ceremony.

"I'm sorry. This is all my fault. I should have just trusted myself. I could have won science, and. . .running wouldn't matter." Eden wiped her tears away and pulled away from his hug so that she could look at him.

"It doesn't matter," he said, looking down. Xander reached for her, his mind racing. Because there was one more thing he could do. It was kind of crazy, but he wasn't above crazy. He didn't have a lot of time though.

"Can I . . . kiss you?" he asked.

She wiped at her eyes even though there weren't any more tears. "Why? I mean, I'm going to be eliminated. Don't you want to go get a real girlfriend?"

"No. What do you mean? I like you. You know that."

"Yeah, but I'm not going home. Did you miss that news bulletin?"

"No, I didn't miss it, but it doesn't mean my feelings changed."

Eden clenched the blanket tighter around her shoulders. "I mean, sure. I'm not going to stop you or anything."

Xander smiled just a little, not sure how he could even smile with this being the end of the Olympics. "Well, that's really romantic. Now, I definitely want to kiss you."

That got a tiny spark of a smile from Eden. "I mean, if I'm going to die, it's like who cares about rules right now? Part of me wants to race down to the dining hall and break a bunch of plates or something, just throw them against the wall. I've never been that person who causes trouble, but now, I really want to."

"You want to cause trouble?" Xander asked.

She shrugged. "Why not? There's nothing else they can do to me."

"But you know what will happen, right? They'll put you in a holding cell if you start causing trouble. You don't want to be Derry's cellmate."

Eden wrinkled her nose. "I have a few hours, maybe one more day. I don't really care what people think of me. Other than you. I'm really sorry and stuff. I tried."

"Stop apologizing. It's not your fault. You're really artsy. No one else is as creative as you are."

"Oh yeah, when you get home, tell my parents that they should look at my phone. The password is 0000. I tried to make it something easy, but I don't know if they would even think to look."

"Why?"

"I made something for them, for my mom." Eden's lower lip trembled. "And I want her to see it. But you can see it too."

"You made something on your phone?" Xander was really confused.

"A video, dumbo," Eden said, shoving him with her shoulder. "Welcome to the twenty-second century."

"Ohhhh, a video." Xander played dumb, but his mind was racing. The adulting ceremony was in just over an hour, and he had to get moving if he would be able to pull this off.

He squeezed Eden's hand. "I should probably go," he said, nodding toward the door.

"Yeah, you don't want to get in trouble for being in here, even though they probably have better things to do than worry about who is in whose room right now."

Xander stood in front of the bed, looking down at Eden. He wanted to tell her, but he couldn't promise it would work. He couldn't get her hopes up.

"I'll miss you," Eden told him. "I guess not for long or anything, but just know that I'll miss you when you're on the plane and I'm here, doing whatever happens to the eliminated. I don't know if we get a last meal or something." Her eyes widened. "What if they just make us starve to death- leave us on this island with no way to get off? I'd much rather have a bullet to my head. That would be fast. I don't want to become a cannibal."

"Eden, stop thinking about it," Xander advised. "It's not making things any easier."

"I'm going to the ceremony. I'm going to sit as far forward as I can, and I'm going to cheer for you. You deserve this."

She stood and hugged Xander tightly. He hugged her back, that annoying ball of tears in his throat again. He wasn't sure what love felt like, but he knew that his connection with Eden was the strongest he had ever had in his life. As he left her room, he knew he shouldn't have hope, but he did anyway.

Chapter 31

When Xander left her room, Eden tried to pull herself together, but she felt herself falling apart all over again. She only had an hour left. She had to at least wash her face and try to make it look like she hadn't been crying off and on for the last twenty-four hours. She would wear her one dress, the one she had packed way at the bottom of her suitcase just in case.

She wanted Xander to have a nice last memory of her, not with a snotty face and red eyes.

Eden dressed herself and washed her face. Other girls were in the bathroom around her, applying makeup and chattering about what sorts of parties they were going to have when they got home. She ignored them as she brushed her hair and checked her reflection in the mirror. Her eyes were still rimmed with sadness, but there wasn't much she could do to get rid of that.

"I bet my mom is going to be at the airport with, like, our whole garden in her arms or something," one girl laughed. "She's been growing these flowers for my adulting party, but I kept telling her she should wait until I actually got a medal before planning some celebration."

"Girl, why were you even worried? You've been in the top 10% since the beginning."

"You never know. You get a twisted ankle, and you're screwed."

"Oh my gosh, look at her. She doesn't have a medal."

"I can't believe she's in here getting ready. She's about to be eliminated."

"If I was her, I would be in the dining hall stuffing myself with food. I mean, who cares about carbs when you're about to be eliminated?"

"I can hear you," Eden said darkly, looking at them in the mirror.

They froze, then started laughing. "Come on. Let's finish getting ready in my room," one of the girls said. They laughed on their way out of the bathroom, and three other girls came in to apply last minute makeup.

Eden was ready. She looked nice, and for some reason, she hoped a shot of her going to the adulting ceremony would be shown on TV. She wanted her mom to see her and be proud. She was going to be eliminated, but she would be there for Xander.

The gathering room was already buzzing with talk as people waited for the ceremony. People had been claiming seats for hours, so Eden hovered in the back, trying to scan the space for Xander's head.

She didn't see him, so she started walking down the aisle slowly, checking each row for him. Where was he? The ceremony was going to start in twenty minutes, and as always, it looked like Xander would be late.

By the time she got to the front three rows, she could tell he wasn't in there, so she returned to the back and waited impatiently.

Finally, ten minutes before the ceremony, he came in. Eden grabbed his arm. "Where have you been?" she asked.

He had wet his hair and combed it down nicely even though he had been wearing it down in the front and shaggy the whole time they had been on Upertavik Island. He looked different, but definitely still cute.

"Getting ready," he said. "You look really nice."

Eden blushed, and for a second, just a second, the stress of being there at the Olympics faded away. Xander was telling her that she looked nice.

"We should sit down," she said. "There's two seats right there." Just as she pointed at them, she realized that they were beside the giggling girls from the bathroom. Her eyes bounced around for other seats, but she didn't see any options. Xander was already heading toward the two chairs without looking back. He plopped into one with a wince, then looked over his shoulder.

"Come on." He waved her forward.

Eden sat beside him, purposely ignoring the two girls on her left. She leaned forward and turned her head to him so it would be hard for anyone else to hear what she was saying. "You took longer to get ready today than you ever have in your life."

Xander nodded, his face grim. "Well, I . . . forgot to pack the clothes I was going to wear. So, I kind of had to put something together." He motioned to the dress pants and the sports shirt.

"You should have just gone all sports gear, rather than half-and-half."

"I wanted to be a fun coffee ingredient," he said.

Eden turned her head to face the front. Lory Chambers was taking the stage but not saying anything yet. Not only were the wall cameras on the move, but there were also several people with cameras on their shoulders like giant bugs watching the ceremony and the audience.

"A lot of people here," Eden commented.

"Nothing else to do right now," Xander replied.

Sudden fear gripped Eden's stomach. Xander was calm. Of course he was calm. He was going home in a couple of hours. He would get a job, be an adult, do everything he was supposed to do. But she had no idea what would happen to her when the adulting ceremony ended and the cameras shut off.

She felt like she was going to vomit, but she hadn't eaten anything in almost a day. She had been too busy hiding in her room. Her vision swam before clearing in front of her. She could do this. She just had to be strong for Xander another hour or so. Then, she could fall apart all she wanted.

Someone stepped up to the front of the stage, not Lory Chambers, and spoke into the microphone. "Did anyone forget to put their suitcases in the lobby? If so, please go do that now before the ceremony starts."

A few people exclaimed in surprise and ran out of the room to grab their suitcases. Eden shook her head. How could these people call themselves adults when they couldn't follow simple instructions?

"Welcome, everyone, to the official adulting ceremony of 2165," Lory Chambers said from up front. "We are pleased to announce that the Olympics have been completed for this year, and there has been a lot of great competition. You who have earned medals have earned jobs and a place in society as adults. We will also provide you all with a kit that will help you get started. This kit is updated every year, but should contain everything you need to get started in your new lives as adults. Congratulations!"

She paused, expecting everyone to cheer. Some joined in excitedly, but Eden couldn't even open her mouth. She just stared at the ground, willing the ceremony to be over, but at the same time, never wanting it to end.

"Now, we've had a long week and a half here on Upertavik Island, and I'm sure all of these adults, well, almost adults, are ready to get home. No long speeches from me! Let's begin the ceremony. When you hear your name called, come up these steps on your left, my right, to receive your adulting kit. You'll pause with me for a good picture, then exit there. Once you've received your kit, please don't go back to your seat. Sit in this area over here. As soon as the ceremony is over, we'll start sending you home on your planes."

Some people began chattering quietly, and Lory Chambers began announcing names.

Eden eyed the boxes that they were handing the new adults. Would she be able to look inside Xander's? Every year, they held different items, the most updated things that the heads had decided were necessary for successful adulthood.

"Are they going alphabetically?" Eden whispered to Xander. She had just heard the name Gianna Henderson.

"I don't know," Xander replied. "I haven't been paying attention."

"How can you not be paying attention?" Eden asked. "If you miss it when they call your name, you're going to look dumb."

Xander just shrugged. Eden noticed him touching his back through the fabric on his shirt. She hadn't seen his knife wound since the day before, but she hoped it would heal quickly. Whatever profession Xander was given, he would be active a lot.

Eden tuned back into the names being called, rotely clapping for everyone even if she didn't know who they were. She wished there was some sort of program that listed all of the names that would be called. Then, she would know when Xander was going to be called. She was sure now, though, that they weren't going in alphabetical order as a Mary Burch was called.

"Your parents are watching, right?" Eden whispered. "I bet your mom is watching right now."

"Yeah, she probably is." Xander looked sad, and Eden wished she hadn't brought up his mom. She hadn't really lost anyone in her life. She'd had no siblings go through the Olympics like Xander had, and her parents' siblings lived in Alaska, so she didn't really know them as family.

Eden touched Xander's arm gently, hoping that he understood she supported him. She listened to some more names, but none of them was Xander's. The area on the far side of the stage was filling up.

"Are they saving you for last or something?" Eden asked, but Xander just shrugged.

"Colt Gerbert!" Lory Chambers called. Eden didn't know who it was, but Xander started whistling and clapping his hands.

A boy a few rows ahead of them rose slowly, looked around, then made his way up onto the stage like he was moving through water. "Congratulations," Lory Chambers said, pausing and looking toward the camera. Colt looked at the camera too, but he looked more confused than anything else.

That was when Eden noticed that he wasn't wearing a medal around his neck.

"Xander, look! He doesn't have a medal! Do you think he's the one who got my place? That's not fair. They should have picked a girl. I thought they would pick someone that I knocked out or something."

Xander didn't pay attention to her as he kept up his raucous clapping. Finally, Colt went down the far side of the stage. Eden watched him until he disappeared into the rows with the other adults.

"What was that all about?" Eden asked. "Do you know him? I've never seen him before in my life."

"He sat beside me on the plane," Xander told her. "I guess we kind of know each other."

"Oh, okay." Eden settled back into her chair and looked up at the front of the room to see who would be called next. That was when she realized no other competitors were on the stage. Lory Chambers touched her screen.

"Let's give one big round of applause to our new adults of 2165." Those who were left in the audience were the eliminated, and the applause was half-hearted. A few officials stood by the cameras, though, and they clapped loudly.

Eden whipped her head back and forth to Xander then the stage. "Wait! They didn't call your name! They forgot you!" She half-stood, before Xander pulled her back down.

"They didn't forget me," Xander told her.

"What are you talking about? They were supposed to call you. Look! The adults are leaving the room."

Music sounded as the group of adults filed one by one out of the room to the lobby, where they would begin taking their flights back home. Xander wasn't among them, and he didn't appear surprised at all.

"Eden, I need to tell you something."

Eden's stomach knotted up in fear as Xander kept his hold on her arm.

"I don't have a lot to live for at this point. My mom doesn't have very long, and you won't be in Sisimiut. And just the thought of going to a job every day and coming home to my dad. I . . ." Xander took a deep breath. "I couldn't do it."

"So you *chose* to be eliminated? Xander, you can't be eliminated."

A couple of people in the rows around them turned to see what was going on. There was no way to hide her tears. "Xander, what are you doing? Are you an idiot? People fight for the chance at adulthood, and you're just giving it up?" She yanked her arm from him. She couldn't even believe what he was saying right now. He was such an idiot!

Lory Chambers was saying something at the front of the room about everyone left in the gathering room going to the dining hall to enjoy one last meal. She actually used those words: "one last meal."

Eden pushed through the crowd of the eliminated and into the bathroom off the lobby. She took a few deep breaths. Xander had given up his medal. For what? Nothing. He got absolutely nothing out of that. Even a life with sadness was better than none at all, right?

Chapter 32

Xander waited in the dining hall for Eden to rejoin him, but it took her awhile. What could she be doing in the bathroom? They only had a couple of hours left, and he didn't want to waste them by letting his last meal get cold. Most of the other people in the dining hall were silent, thinking about what would happen after the meal. Some people were shoveling food into their mouths so fast their hands blurred. Others were just staring at their plates in front of them.

Now that the excitement over pulling his plan off was fading, Xander realized what he had done. He wasn't going home to see his mother one last time. He was going to spend his last few hours here with Eden . . . that is, if she would ever come out of the bathroom.

Eden finally entered the dining hall and ran to the table where he was sitting. Her face was streaked, and Xander knew she had been crying.

"Are you eating already? Good. I don't think I can eat anything."

Xander could. He started into his plate, glancing at Eden between each bite.

"Just so you know, I think you're really dumb. No one has probably ever given up a medal in the whole history of the Olympics."

"Let's not spend this time talking about how dumb I am. Can we just agree to disagree on that and get on with life?"

Eden raised an eyebrow at the familiar saying. "You mean get on with death? Man, I'm so morose. I know I'm going to die, and I'm scared, so scared. But it's like, there's nothing I can do about it."

"Nope, nothing except enjoy our last little bit."

"I still kind of want to smash a plate," Eden said. "Just one." She was eyeing Xander's plate.

"Hey, this still has my food on it." He hovered a protective arm over it.

"Fine, I'll wait until you're done."

Xander glanced around the dining hall. The number of officials standing around was triple what it normally was. They clearly anticipated trouble. He didn't even get to finish his plate of food before Lory Chambers appeared on all the televisions around the room. Xander looked for where she was standing, but apparently, she didn't deign to be in the same room with them even though she was talking to them.

"I'm sorry to those of you being eliminated this year. You know why this must be done." She didn't sound sorry at all, and some of the kids in the dining hall started making noises and booing her. Xander wanted them to shut up so he could at least know what was going to happen.

"You will be eliminated in two different groups. You may choose your group. If you would like to be in group one, please go toward the side of the dining hall with the serving door. If you would like to be in group two, please go toward the side of the dining hall with the door to the lobby. You have five minutes to make your decision."

"They don't waste any time," Xander muttered. He looked at the plate of food in front of him, suddenly not so hungry. "If you want to break it, now's your chance."

But Eden was barely looking at him.

Her eyes glanced back and forth at the few people who were moving around. Most of them were frozen in their seats.

"She's so kind, huh? Letting us choose our elimination group. Whoo hoo! I can hardly wait." Xander fake cheered.

Eden didn't respond to his sarcasm. She just stared at the TV, but for the first time since they had arrived at the hotel, it was black. There were no reports of standings or a schedule of which competitions were when. The Olympics were over, and so was everything else.

Xander looked back at Eden, but she really wasn't responding. Had she gone into shock or something? Xander pulled together all of his strength and left his food on the table. He rounded it and took Eden's arm, helping her to her feet.

"Come on," he said, pulling her toward the serving door. He couldn't remember which group was which, but it didn't really matter anyway.

Xander wrapped his arms around Eden, and she buried her face in his chest. They stood there in silence until an official motioned for the group to follow him. This group was small, much smaller than the other group.

"Man, what are you doing here?" Connor asked, punching Xander in the shoulder. Xander disentangled himself from Eden and punched Connor back.

"Being eliminated." He didn't owe Connor an explanation, so he ignored his friend who had started protesting the unfairness of it all.

The group was led down a hallway and out of the hotel. They followed the path to the gym. Were they going to be eliminated there? That seemed messy. Maybe they were taking them far away from the hotel so not as much clean up would be necessary.

Eden grasped Xander's hand tightly, and when he looked over at her face, tears were leaking down it. He was glad right then that he had made the decision he had. He didn't want her to face this alone.

Officials surrounded them, but as they were rounding the gym, going to an area Xander had never seen before, one of the eliminated tried to break away. He pushed through the officials surrounding him and started running down the path, laughing maniacally. Two bullets in his back stopped him.

"Idiot," one of the officials muttered.

Xander didn't think he was stupid. What was the point? They were all going to die anyway. At least that kid had taken a chance. It could have ended well, maybe. Though what he would do if he got away was anyone's guess.

"Keep moving," another official told them. Xander knew they were on an island, but he hadn't realized how tiny the island was. They were already nearing a beach. He guessed that made sense. The officials could shoot them there and roll them into the water. Easy.

But when the trees stopped blocking his view, Xander saw a boat waiting for them. "Get on," an official commanded.

Xander was shocked. He stumbled as he tried to walk while taking in every inch of the boat. Why would they transport them somewhere before offing them? It didn't make any sense.

"What's going on?" Eden asked.

"I don't know. Let's get on the boat." Xander helped her up the ramp until they walked onto the rocking ship. "We can sit there," he said, pointing at a bench under a canopy.

"What's going to happen?" Eden whipped her head around. She wasn't the only one trying to figure out what was happening. Everyone looked bewildered. The last of the officials boarded with them. There was some scraping and slaps of water on the side of the boat, then one of the officials looked directly at them.

"You are being transported to the research facility. No one will answer any further questions. If you make a move toward one of us or the side of the boat, you will be shot. Does everyone understand?"

The boat pulled away from the shore.

"What about group two?" Eden asked under her breath.

Xander shrugged. He didn't have any answers. As the boat pulled away, though, he had a lot of questions. Why were they going to some research facility? Were they going to be killed there? Or would they be living science experiments?

After a few minutes of the boat rocking across the water, Eden laid her head on his chest. "Thanks for coming with me," she said like they were going on some bike ride together, not a boat ride to an unknown destination. Which was worse- this or death? Only time would tell.

About the Author

Laurel Solorzano has enjoyed writing since she was in middle school, exchanging manuscripts for years with her best friend. After traveling the globe for a time, Laurel set her goal to become a published author. As she works teaching English and Spanish, she writes stories in her free time. Laurel currently lives in Raleigh, North Carolina with her husband, Yader.

Read more at https://www.laurelsolorzano.com.